WILLIAM S RUSSELL

Shallow Water Predator 2

Newhouse Creative Group

This book is dictated to my wife, Margaret, who continues to inspire me in my writing. With her help and support, I could plow ahead with a story related to my many years working with and for the U.S. Navy and Northrop Grumman.

Acknowledgement

Thanks to Mike Dorman, (MMCM(SS) USN, a 26-year submarine force veteran. His knowledge of the operational aspects of the nuclear plant and the overall performance of the day-to-day shipboard activities has helped me smooth out the rough edges.

Thanks to Duane Moss for his technical insight into the day-to-day operation of *Buffalo*'s Torpedo Room and the general process of weapon loading and handling equipment. Duane Moss, a retired Submarine Senior Chief Torpedoman, served 24 years in the US Navy, four of those on the USS *Buffalo*. Duane currently works for the Naval Undersea Warfare Center in Newport, RI.

Special thanks to my good friend, a great and generous editor-in-chief, Mark Newhouse. Thanks to Keith Newhouse of the Newhouse Creative Group for his support and preparation and publication of the Shallow Water Predator 2.

About the Author

William Russell holds a Master of Business from Salve Regina University in Newport R.I. and has spent his career working in Naval programs. As a Program Manager, he supported the Surface Ship ASW Effectiveness Measuring Program (SHARM), developing tactical guidelines and publications to assist the surface community in localizing, tracking, and detecting threat submarines. Mr. Russell developed and participated in at-sea training programs for SURFLANT, and worked at the Naval War College, Naval Lessons Learned library. During the latter part of his career, he supported the DDG 1000 Integration Verification and Validation (IV&V) program as a Software Test Engineer responsible for developing test procedures and verifying software dealing with Surface Ship Combat Operations. Bill and his wife Margaret are enjoying their retirement in sunny Florida.

Principal Characters

Note: See this book's back for the complete characters list and assignments.

USS *Buffalo* SSN 715

Commander Joseph Leo Scott, Commanding Officer

Lieutenant Commander Thomas Varney, Executive Officer

Lieutenant Patricia Morton, Oceanographer

Dr. Janice Lace, Professor Oceanographic Department University of Hawaii

Master Chief Sonar Technician Submarines, (STSCM) Jack Norris

Presidents Security Council/ Advisors

Mr. John Washburn, President of the United States

Mr. Raymond Richard, Secretary of the Navy

Dr.Jack Ure, Director of the Central Intelligence Agency

U.S. Navy SEALs

Commander Mike Walsh, SEAL Team 6

Bandar 'Abbas Naval Station Iran

Admiral Al Jujair, Islamic Revolutionary Guards Corps Naval Commander

https://simple.wikipedia.org/wiki/Strait_of_Hormuz#/media/File:Strait_of_hor muz_full.jpg

iv

"One who knows the enemy and knows himself will not be endangered in a hundred engagements. One who does not know the enemy, but knows himself will sometimes be victorious, sometimes meet defeat. One who knows neither the enemy nor himself will invariably be defeated in every engagement."

"Every Battle is won Before it's Ever Fought."
                                                     –Sun Tzu, The Art of War

"The only way to do things is to take risks."
                                                     –Hymen Rickover

Chapter 1

Bandar-e-Abbas; Naval Base, Iran -

The Commander of the Islamic Republic of Iran Navy, Admiral Al Jajair, was furious he had received a no-confidence vote from the prime minister after the nuclear weapons facility at the Bandar-e-Abbas Naval Base was destroyed. He knew his career and life were at stake if he could not secure the Straits of Hormuz and the Persian Gulf from the American Navy, the Great Satan.

A graduate of the University of Tehran with a Science and Technology degree, Jajair continued his studies at the Imam Khomeine Naval University in Noshahr, Mazandaran. At 50, he was the youngest Admiral in the Iranian Navy. Nothing was going to stop him from destroying the American submarine operation in the Persian Gulf.

"Admiral Mokri," Jajair interrupted his junior officer's report, "Did you notify our Naval Bases? I want them to immediately secure their facilities against any further enemy actions."

Admiral Mokri rifled through his notes. "Sir, I briefed—"

"I'm waiting, Admiral," Jajair snapped. After the attack on the nuclear weapons facilities, he had become less tolerant of his subordinates.

"Sir, I ordered all fourteen Naval Bases locked down," Mokri said anxiously. He knew his life was on the line. Jajair did not tolerate failure.

"How do you intend to stop the American ships and submarines from infiltrating our waters?" Admiral Jajair demanded, frustrated at the lack of security resulting in the vital nuclear factory's destruction.

"Sir, I ordered mine layers to disperse surface mines between Larak Island

and the Musandam Peninsula," Mokri replied. "The exception being the commercial corridors, which we cannot mine for obvious reasons."

"What else," Jajair barked, leaning forward in his seat.

Mokri stood and moved to the front of the room. "Sir, please, direct your attention to the map of the Persian Gulf on the wall. There is a twenty-seven-mile gap between Larak Island and the Musandam Peninsula. I divided the area into two lines of contact mines moored to the seafloor. They will present formidable barriers—"

"How powerful are these mines?" Jajair interrupted.

"Each mine is packed with one hundred pounds of TNT, enough to blow a large hole in the hull of a ship or submarine."

"Is it enough to sink the fat American vessels?" Jajair demanded.

"Depends on the size and location of the explosion—"

"I want those ships destroyed! Do you hear me? Destroyed! Increase the amount of TNT to two hundred pounds. We will sink every American vessel crossing the barrier." Jujair glared at his officer.

"Yes, Sir. Allah be praised," Mokri responded.

"What is the distance between each mine?" Jajair asked, picking up a steaming cup of Persian tea.

"One-thousand yards."

"Is this sufficient to block all transit?" Jajair asked, not convinced Admiral Mokri had done enough to close the Straits of Hormuz from infiltration.

Mokri studied his notes before replying.

"I'm waiting," Jajair frowned. "I'm beginning to believe you are not the right officer to command the surface fleet."

Mokri shot his eyes up at the Admiral. "Sir, these mines will create a choke point, not allowing ships to enter or leave the Persian Gulf without our consent. Our Navy will control all traffic in and out of the commercial channels. Ships ignoring the blockade will be boarded, captured, or, if we wish, turned back."

"Good," Jajair said. "Remember, the Rules of Engagement remain in force. No Iranian ship is to attack any vessel unless fired upon. We don't want to instigate a war with the Americans."

Admiral Mokri remained standing. Not yet, he thought. His jacket concealed his sweat-soaked shirt. He understood if Jujair was not pleased, he could be removed and face a firing squad. He searched the Admiral's face for clues to his superior's mood.

Jajair looked back at the map and spoke. "Admiral Mokri, I want you to place our mines every five hundred yards in a sawtooth pattern." He slyly smiled. "It will be far more troublesome to our enemy than linear placement." He nodded, pleased with this idea. "Be sure to inform our ships and submarines of the location of the mines." He imagined the uproar if one of our ships struck a mine.

"Yes, Sir." Mokri breathed a sigh of relief. The Admiral was not replacing him. At least, not yet.

"What measures are you taking to stop the enemy minesweepers? We can't allow them to neutralize our weapons."

Mokri handed him a sheet of paper. "I ordered swarms of high-speed Boghammers and Bladerunners into the area. The enemy will steer clear of them."

"I don't want another incident like last month when one of your Bladerun-ner crewmen fired on an American Patrol Boat. It better not happen again. Understood?"

Mokri nodded.

"I repeat, you may harass the Americans, but we do not want war. Also, inform your commanders to look for the new American underwater drones. Some of their minesweepers are now deploying these new devices to search for subsurface mines."

"Yes, Sir," Mokri replied.

Jajair displayed a sinister smile. "Make every effort to capture one of their drones," he said, thinking what a coup that would be for Iran, specifically, for him.

"One of our top priorities," Mokri replied.

"Excellent." Jujair gave his subordinate a rare smile. "Mokri, I'm satisfied under your leadership the Persian Gulf will remain secure for our great nation."

"Thank you, Sir," Mokri responded, thankful the grueling questions were behind him.

A shadow appeared at the door. "Excuse me, Admiral Jajair."

Jajair turned to the familiar voice. "Yes, Mr. Khadem," he said, bristling at the interruption by the Intelligence officer, a man he neither liked nor trusted.

Khadem half-smiled entered the room and sat down without being invited. "I learned last week that you received a warning about a submarine lurking in our area. It was either the Americans or the Israelis who blew up our nuclear weapons facility." He paused, a puzzled look on his face. "You took no preventative action?"

Jajair stared at the Intelligence officer. "Mr. Khadem, are you aware I am still commanding all naval forces by order of our supreme leader?"

"Yes," Khadem answered in an icy tone.

Jajair thought I have dealt with your kind from the Ministry of Intelligence my entire career. I will not be intimidated. "Mr. Khadem, there is no conclusive evidence the submarine detected by our surface ships was American. The Americans decommissioned their last diesel submarine in 1990. Therefore, we may be looking for a German or Israeli submarine as the culprit."

Khadem's tone was menacing. "Perhaps. In any case, we suspect an informant made this attack possible. I have interrogated all but one person and I'm unable to find him—"

"Someone is missing?" Jajair interrupted.

Khadem sneered. "A nuclear physicist, Dr. Aslan Mehman. He was last seen on vacation with his grandmother on Larak Island; last week, she reported him missing. My divers have been searching around the Island now for a week without results."

Jujair knew an informant in his arena placed him in serious jeopardy. "The fact a scientist is missing does not necessarily mean he was an informant," he replied, fearing reprisal if his superiors learned of this breach in security.

Khadem stared hard at the Admiral. "Dr. Mehman was a known opponent of our nuclear weapons program—"

4

"What was he doing working in the plant?" Jajair wanted to deflect the blame on whoever approved Mehman for the facility.

"Threatened with prison, the doctor agreed to work at the weapons facility," Khadem said.

"Who gave him this choice?" Jajair asked.

"The Intelligence officer did not respond. We're checking the records now. We also want to know who allowed Mehman to work on our nuclear torpedoes," Khadem said, eyes like gun barrels on Jujair.

"And it happens he worked at the facility," Jajair said, shaking his head. "Mr. Khadem, your department is responsible for clearing all personnel stationed at the Naval Base. Correct?"

"That is irrelevant," Khadem replied, anger showing on his face.

"I don't think so. Suggest you review your records and personnel to see who, besides you, approved this scientist." Jajair enjoyed twisting the knife.

Khadem's face reddened.

Jajair continued, "And while discussing your role, you examined six bodies found in the rubble. Correct?"

Khadem nodded.

Jajair stared at the intelligence officer's face. "Tell me, who manufactured the bullets?"

Khadem pulled out the autopsy report. "Fiocchi Ammunition, Lecco, in Italy," he replied.

Jajair nodded. "Italian bullets? So, we don't know who was responsible for our men's death and the weapons facility's destruction. We also do not know who killed our two divers." He shook his head as if showing pity for the embattled intelligence officer. "I understand you believe these invaders were Mossad Israeli Special Forces?"

Khadem sighed. "We're still in the early stages of our investigation."

Jajair shrugged. "I suggest you leave and do your job. You are not going to learn anything sitting here."

Khadem remained seated, glaring at Admiral Jajair.

Jujair smiled benignly. "You have your orders, Mr. Khadem."

Khadem stood slowly. He picked up his case, glared at Jajair again, and said,

"You will bear full responsibility for any further action to our Naval Bases."

Jujair looked on silently as Khadem marched from the room. As soon as the door closed, he turned to his junior officer. "Admiral Mokri, you know what's at stake."

Only my life, Mokri thought.

"Alert all commanders to the possibility of a U.S. or Israeli submarine operating in the Persian Gulf," Jajair ordered. "Find that damn submarine and fast. We cannot afford another mistake. Do you understand?"

"Yes, Sir," Mokri responded, grabbing his briefcase and rushing from the room.

Once Mokri left, Jajair slammed his fist on the table. "Allah help those Americans if they cross my path again."

Chapter 2

USS *Buffalo*; Persian Gulf -

A knock at his door interrupted Captain Scott's thoughts of Janice held tightly in his arms.

Executive Officer Tom Varney entered. "Captain, the radio handed me the latest message traffic." He gave Scott the pages.

"Did we receive our orders to return home?"

"On the contrary, Washington has ordered us to remain in the Persian Gulf."

Scott pushed the thoughts of Janice out of his mind.

Scanning the messages, he looked up. "I expected Washington to order us back to Guam."

"Looks like that's not going to happen anytime soon. What concerns me is SEAL Team 6 is to remain aboard. A clear indication Washington has big plans for Commander Walsh and his men," Varney said. "Remember when you said *Buffalo* would be heading back into harm's way? The fact that Washington has ordered us to remain in the Gulf confirms my suspicion, and this intel report explains why." He handed another message to Scott.

Tom Varney was into his eighth month of a twenty-four-month executive officer tour of duty. Scott liked the African Americans, who, as they encountered enemy threats in their first mission together in the Persian Gulf had the uncanny ability to anticipate his thoughts. He gave Varney much of the credit for their success.

"Fifth Fleet confirms a dramatic increase in the number of high-speed surface craft operating around Iranian bases, and in the commercial channels," Scott read aloud. "There's nothing new in this message; this is the information we already know." He flipped through the satellite pictures. "Based on previous messages and this intel report, the Iranians have escalated their mine deployment. Now that we are ordered to remain in the Gulf, XO do you have any suggestions as to why they are doing this?"

"No, I do not, Captain. But recommend we move into deeper water and launch Hunter, our robotic minisub, to search for mines. There's no sense in taking chances at *Buffalo* being spotted by their surface craft in the shallows."

Scott nodded. "Good! Any word about the minesweepers we requested?"

"No, Sir. It looks like mapping and neutralizing the mines lies with us."

"The threat to *Buffalo* will be more serious the closer we move to Iran's bases, and it will be like playing dodgeball in school."

Varney would have laughed at the analogy but recognized how threatening the Persian Gulf had become, especially after Walsh and his team of SEALs destroyed the Iranian nuclear weapons factory. "Waiting for the Iranians to throw the first ball is nerve-racking," he said.

"Here's another twist," Scott said. "Intel reports the Islamic Republic of Iran informed Washington it will shut down all shipping in the Persian Gulf and the Straits of Hormuz if any other facilities come under attack."

"Someone must be pissed off at our little foray yesterday." Varney laughed.

Scott frowned. "Tom, imagine if Israel executes plans to destroy another of Iran's nuclear facilities?"

Varney nodded. "Hell, we could be right in the middle of a war if it came to Iran and Israel trading blows."

"Correct. Both sides have threatened each other many times. Thankfully, at this point, we've received no possible indications of an attack by either." He handed the message board back to Varney. "Let's place Hunter into the water and see what she can dig up." He saw Varney's expression change. "You have a question, Tom?"

"You ordered five runs over the past two weeks," Varney said. "We might be overdoing it."

Scott glanced at a photo of Hunter on its operations manual sitting on his desk. "Dr. Stone stated they wanted to work their vehicle under extreme conditions. I can't think of a better way. Can you, Tom?"

"No, Sir. Dr. Stone reported only seven-wire canisters that guide Hunter are left. We've got to be selective in how we use this asset."

"Okay. Check with the scientists and ask if leaving Hunter in the water for more than twenty-four hours will negatively impact their operations. We'll take up station at the Northern boundary, near Lark Island." He handed Varney his Situation Report. "Read this SITREP and forward it to Radio for transmission. We need to determine what type of mines the Iranians are deploying and, most importantly, if they threaten our vessels."

Varney understood Scott also meant a threat to the crew of *Buffalo.*

Scott was still in the wardroom evaluating the intelligence reports when Drs. Thomas and Stone arrived, followed by Lieutenant Jeff Obermeier.

"You wanted to see us, Captain?" Thomas asked, sitting down at the table.

"Captain," Lt. Obermeier said.

Scott looked up. "After our little party last night, Central Command ordered us to remain in the Gulf to monitor Iranian deployment of mines," he said. "You demonstrated Hunter's, our UUV, usefulness in general underwater surveillance, bottom mapping, and identifying insurgent points. Congratulations."

"Thank you, Sir," Thomas and Stone said.

Scott slid a notepad to Dr. Stone. "Your work isn't done. Please draft a message to your office and inform them your return date is unknown. Give it to the XO when complete."

"Yes, Sir," Stone replied, looking anxiously at his brother.

"Jeff, " Scott said, glancing at the navigator. "Will you fill them in on the details?"

The lieutenant uncovered the chart on the wall. "Based on our latest Intel and our observations, the Iranian navy has increased mine-laying operations in the area of Bandar-e-Abbas Naval Base." He pointed to a body of water north of the Straits. "*Buffalo* will remain here, at one hundred eighty feet, while your UUV sanitizes the Northern Gulf."

The ship's phone buzzed.

Scott removed the phone from under the table. "Captain?"

"Captain, intermittent contact on an unknown submarine designated Sierra seventy-four," Sorenson reported.

"Opening or closing?" Scott asked.

"Closing, Sir," Sorenson responded.

"Gentlemen, we will continue the briefing after I review the contact reported by Sonar. XO, please join me."

The two men walked quickly from the room, leaving the engineers puzzled at their abrupt departure.

Scott hurried to Control. "Sonar, give me an update on your contact," he ordered upon entering the room.

"Contact bearing three two zero° and opening," Sorenson replied.

"OOD, come left at twenty degrees, speed seven knots," Scott ordered.

"Twenty degrees, speed seven knots," aye Obermier repeated.

Scott saw the speed indicator increase.

Varney observed the fire control operators manipulate the bearing dots received from sonar and compress them into a vertical line. The XO announced, "Captain, target speed six knots, range three thousand yards."

"OOD, come left ten degrees," Scott ordered.

"Turn left ten degrees aye."

"XO, close within two thousand yards, and maintain track of the contact." He shot a glance at Varney. "Don't let anyone maneuver behind us. Remember, we're not here."

Chapter 3

USS Buffalo; Persian Gulf -

"Another Iranian diesel, Tom," Scott said. "Designate Sierra seventy-four as Master seventeen," he ordered. "Officer of the Deck, station the Fire Control Tracking Party (FCP)."

Men attached to the FCP hurried into the control room and sat on their bench seats. They started to manipulate the information displayed on their consoles.

"Lost contact," Sorenson reported, leaning closer to the spectrum analyzer, trying to differentiate the submarine trace from the background noise. "Come on. I know you're hiding."

Senior Chief Paul Richardson stood over Sorenson's shoulder. He thought, peering at the monitor, that the second pair of eyes wouldn't hurt.

"Yes!" Sorenson rolled the trackball to the dark streak emerging from the top of his scope. "Gotcha!"

"Price, sit here and operate the conformal array," Richardson shouted.

Second Class John Price sat down, adjusted his chair, removed the headset hanging on the hook, and placed the phones on his head. "Sorenson, give me a bearing," he said with a Kentucky drawl.

"Zero nine zero," Sorenson replied, keeping his eyes glued to the waterfall display.

"Contact confirmed." Price rolled the trackball to the dark smudge on his screen.

"What do you hear, Sorenson?" Scott asked, entering Sonar.

"Our K-901," Sorenson pointed to a dark line walking down the spectrum analyzer's screen.

"Are you sure?" Scott asked.

"Submarine Squadron Fifteen reported one of the Iranian subs, K-901, had a shaft rub. I matched the tonal in our acoustic library and correlated it with the broadband line Price holds on the conformal array."

Scott compared the two signatures on each analyzer.

Sorenson continued, "Our K-901, Captain. We recorded the correct tonal and frequency for the turn count several weeks ago. I'll bet the farm on this one."

Scott straightened up. "Okay! For my life, I can't figure out how you can match the narrowband line to the hull number."

"That's why the navy pays us the big bucks," Sorenson said, half-joking.

"We're overpaying you," Scott replied, smiling as he left for Control.

"Captain," the Officer of the Deck (OOD) announced, "Completed a ninety-degree baffle clear to port and starboard. Master seventeen is opening astern."

"Sonar, give me one more sweep around the bearings. I don't want to encounter those Iranian Jet Skis or Boghammers," Scott ordered. "All set, XO?" he asked.

Varney stood behind the Fire Control Operators. "Yes, Sir," he responded. "Should be relatively quiet this time of night."

"I'm counting on it," Scott replied, leaning against the rail circling the periscopes, waiting for sonar to complete their search cycle. He glanced over at the Dead Reckoning Table (DRT). Janice and Lt. Morton were speaking with the two Naval Undersea Warfare Center (NUWC) engineers and Navigator, Lt. Jeff Obermeier. "OOD, switch Control to red lights," he ordered.

Janice glanced at Scott with a slight smile. *Why was I so foolish to push him away last year? Pressuring him to leave the navy was what split us apart. They say love is blind. Well, I can attest to that, and I ignored the signs.*

Scott smiled back and returned to preparing to come to periscope depth. He wished they were anywhere else but on this sub.

Varney's voice broke into Scott's thoughts. "Conn, no close contacts; Master seventeen bears two eight three degrees two thousand five hundred yards and opening."

"OOD," Scott ordered, "Make your depth six-zero feet. Sonar, proceeding to periscope depth. Report all contacts."

"Coming to six zero feet," Lt. Obermier repeated.

Scott stepped up on the pedestal and faced the search periscope. He felt the deck tip upward as he turned the hydraulic lift ring above his head. He bent over and flipped down the handlebars. The noise from the hydraulic fluid raising the periscope hissed above him. Pressing his eyes against the rubber buffer surrounding the lens, he said, "No shapes or shadows," as the scope broke the surface. "Shit! Down scope!" Scott exclaimed, "Chief of the Boat (COB), take her down one hundred feet. Make turns for eight knots. Come left thirty degrees."

"Passing seventy-five feet, coming to one hundred, feet," COB reported.

Varney looked at the Skipper.

"Where the hell did the *Boghammers* come from, Tom," Scott muttered, looking at the monitor.

Tom Varney studied the screen. "There," he pointed to a string of blips stretched across the monitor as he increased magnification. "I see ten *Boghammers*."

"Looks like a full-court press," Scott remarked. "Let's open the area and take another picture. I'm starting to feel penned in with all this surface activity."

"I'm sure the worse will be over in the next few days," Varney said.

"Sonar, do you hold any noise, bearing three four zero degrees?" Scott asked.

"Negative, Captain, only the K-901 reported earlier," Senior Chief Richardson replied.

Scott and the XO continued scrutinizing the video taken through the digital imaging camera.

"We can't detect those surface craft without their engines idling," Varney said. "We could have placed our periscope right in the middle of them and not known it until it was too late."

"The only way around this is to staff the Automatic Plot Board 24/7," Scott said. "Have the plotter record all contacts and sudden noise losses. We can assume the surface craft are either Jet Skis, Boghammers, or Bladerunners," Scott replied. "Wait! Go back," he ordered. "Is that a number on that sail?"

Varney looked closer. "Yes, Sir. I read nine."

"Sorenson, the K-901 you reported had a nine on her sail. Right, call. Add it to your log," Scott said.

Sorenson was about to log it in when he exclaimed, "What the? K-901 is venting her ballast tanks. She is submerging."

"Range to K-901, XO?" Scott asked.

"Thirty-five hundred yards and opening," Varney replied.

"OOD, increase speed to seven knots," Scott ordered.

"Increasing speed to seven knots," The Chief of the Boat (COB) announced.

Scott saw the plainsmen bend over and place the new speed into the engine order telegraph.

"Mr. Powers set Ultra-Quiet conditions. Verify all nonessential personnel is in their racks." Scott felt the chilled air from the air conditioning stopped blowing, and the circulation fans shut down, customary when the ship went to ultra-quiet conditions. The temperature began to rise from the operating equipment. "Electronic Support Measures (ESM) operator, any radar contacts?" Scott asked after several tense minutes.

"We picked up electronic pulses, signal strength three. None deemed a threat," the ESM operator reported. "Wait! Belay my last. Computer analysis confirmed two Plessey AWA-1 air/surface search radars, bearing three three zero and zero two zero degrees."

"XO, range to K-901?" Scott asked.

"Twenty-two hundred yards and closing," Varney replied, checking the digital readout on the fire control console.

"XO, close to within one thousand yards," Scott said, glancing at the Automatic Plotting Board.

Sorenson's voice came through the overhead speaker, "Captain, hold two broadband contacts closing K-901. Sierra seventy-five and seventy-six, re-classifying, destroyers Master eighteen, and Master nineteen, respectively."

"Sonar, I'm willing to bet those are the two new Iranian destroyers," Scott said.

"Do you think we were detected?" Varney asked.

"I'm afraid we're about to find out," Scott replied, eyeing the bearing lines stacked on the tactical display.

"Control, Master eighteen and nineteen are slowing," Sorenson announced.

"Range to K-901, XO?" Scott demanded.

"Eighteen hundred yards, and opening," Varney replied.

Two sonic booms pounded against *Buffalo's* hull.

"Damn," Scott exclaimed, seeing the Signal-to-Noise level jump ten decibels.

"They're within detecting range of our submarine, Captain," Varney said.

"OOD, make turns for six knots," Scott ordered. "Let's back off and let the Iranians play their game." He glanced at Varney and said quietly, "On the other hand, if we close and remain in K-901's baffles, their surface ships may not suspect another submarine."

"It's worth a chance, Captain," Varney said, concentrating on the target information showing on the screen. "Unless K-901 changes course, in which case we will be placed directly in the path of the destroyers."

Sorensen announced, "Control, Master seventeen is changing course to port."

Scott smiled. "He must have heard you, XO. Too late for us to run. Diving Officer, bring your depth two-zero feet off the bottom. XO, range to Master seventeen?"

Scott watched as Buffalo started to descend toward the bottom.

"One thousand yards and closing," Varney answered.

"OOD come to 'All Stop'," Scott ordered. "Let's see if the destroyers follow K-901."

"Control, Sonar, Master eighteen has changed course. Master nineteen continues to close," Sorenson reported.

"XO, range to Master nineteen?" Scott asked.

"Three-thousand yards, speed twelve knots," Varney answered. "Captain, we are right in the middle of the two destroyers."

Scott eyed the depth gauge. He listened to the transmissions from Master nineteen pounding against *Buffalo's* outer hull. To minimize the effects of the active returns, he kept the submarine pointed at the destroyer's bow, twenty-two feet above the sea bottom.

"It's working," Varney whispered.

"Well done, diving officer," Scott said.

"Master seventeen continues to have a port-bearing drift," Varney reported. "Master eighteen has increased speed to fifteen knots and continues to close Master seventeen. Master nineteen has also increased its speed to fifteen knots and closing."

Scott shook his head. "It doesn't make sense why the destroyers eighteen and nineteen would increase speed and mask her hydrophones?"

The alternating pings from both destroyers continued to lash out against *Buffalo's* hull.

Varney muttered, "If Master Nineteen continues on her heading, she'll run down our port side."

Scott nodded. "OOD, increase speed to ten knots and remain on present heading. While he is blind, we'll try and get astern of him. We'll wait for the destroyers to fall astern of us before we alter course and open the area."

"Sonar, Control detected four splashes astern of K-901," Senior Chief Paul Richardson reported.

"All hands standby for underwater explosions," Scott announced over the 1MC. He held onto the railing around the periscopes as the percussion from the four bombs forced *Buffalo* to keel over forty degrees.

Scott waited for the boat to reach the centerline. "All departments report," Scott announced over the 1MC.

An alarm sounded behind him.

"Captain," the Chief of the Boat announced. "We have flooding in the Advanced SEAL Delivery Vehicle (*ASDV*)."

"XO, take the Conn and secure the damn alarm," Scott ordered, hurrying out of Control and down the passageway to the after-escape hatch. Without the submersible, I can't complete our mission, he thought.

Chapter 4

USS Buffalo; Persian Gulf –

Scott arrived at the ladder to the aft escape hatch, leading up to the *ASDV*. He saw Janice disappear through the hatch.

Master Chief Norris was waiting for Dr. Lace to enter the submersible.

"Master Chief, I want the engineers to go over the submersible with a fine-tooth comb?" Scott ordered. "I need the *ASDV* operational."

"Yes, Sir. The two engineers just arrived, and Dr. Lace is checking out the sonar and navigation systems."

"Secure the pressure and the escape hatch once you are inside," Scott ordered, water dripping on his face.

"I'll contact you on the intercom," Norris said as he hurried up the ladder. Scott headed for Control.

"Kelly, keep me informed on your progress," the Master Chief ordered, securing the watertight doors. Standing in ankle-deep sea water, he opened the high-pressure valve releasing air into the Lockout Chamber. The water trapped between the two sealed compartments drained into the ballast tank. He bled the air from the chamber and opened the door leading into the Control Room. Entering he sat down next to Dr. Lace and picked up the phone. "Mother this is Ground Hog. OVER."

"This is Mother," Scott replied.

"Captain, the engineers have found a ruptured saltwater valve."

"Can it be repaired?" Scott asked.

"I don't know," Norris replied. "I'll contact you once they contact me."

"Have you had time to confirm the electronics are operational?" Scott asked.

"Dr. Lace is getting ready to perform diagnostic now."

"Thanks, Master Chief. Keep me informed."

"Here goes, Master Chief," Janice said, pressing the power switch. A red light flashed on. "Looks like we have a problem," she said resetting the switch.

Norris stared at the light. "Try it again."

Janice pressed the power button. "No good, the light came on again. The explosions damaged the sonar system."

"We'll need Price to take a look," Norris said, reaching over and grabbing the phone. "Mother, this is Ground Hog, OVER."

"This is Mother, OVER," Scott replied.

Norris said, "There is a problem with the submersible's sonar. I need Second Class Price up here."

"Senior Chief Richardson send Price with his bag of tools to the *ASDV*. Have him take a look at the onboard sonar equipment," Scott ordered.

"Sending Price to the ASDV," Richardson said.

"I need that—-"

"Control, Sonar, Master nineteen is increasing speed and coming about fast," Sorenson announced. He must be doing twenty knots."

"Ground Hog, this is Mother, OVER. We have a destroyer bearing down on us. Recommend you hold on," Scott said.

"Control, Sonar, Master nineteen entered our baffles," Sorenson reported. "He is closing fast."

Scott shouted into the mic, "All hands standby for explosions."

The destroyer's active transmissions grew faster and louder. The ominous thrashing of the destroyer's screws could be heard over the active sonar.

"Five hundred yards and closing," Varney reported pulling his seat belt tighter.

Scott glanced at the crew manning their stations. Nothing appears to rattle them, he thought. It's a waiting game.

The destroyer's transmissions grew closer, louder, and more menacing with each passing second.

Scott wondered if he made the right decisions.

"They're about to pass over us," Varney said grabbing the handle on the cabinet in front of him.

"Conn, detecting splashes," Sorenson reported his voice lower than normal. The noise from the destroyer was nerve-ranking.

Three loud thumps bounced off *Buffalo's* hull.

Scott heard the scraping sound of an explosive bomb sliding down the starboard side. "Hold on," Scott shouted, grabbing the periscope rail with both hands.

The explosion was deafening. The shockwave pushed the sub hard to port.

Scott waited anxiously for the alarms to sound indicating damage to his ship.

"Hold two more splashes off our bow," Sorenson shouted above the thrashing noise.

"Brace yourself," Scott shouted as two more explosions rocked the ship.

The violent shock wave pushed *Buffalo* forty degrees to port.

A loud bang aft of Control shook *Buffalo* violently as the boat healed over. A shrill alarm sounded.

"Captain," Jeff Obermeier shouted, "The *ASDV* is gone."

"What? OOD, All Stop," Scott ordered. "Are you sure?"

"Yes, Sir," Obermeier responded looking at the flashing red light next to the fathometer.

"Engineering, damage report," Scott ordered, trying to appear calm. He was afraid he might have killed the crew aboard the *ASDV* and the woman he loved.

"Captain," Dennis Fender replied. "No damage reported."

Scott grabbed the overhead phone. "Ground Hog, this is Mother. Report!, OVER." Scott waited for a response, knowing Janice was locked in the *ASDV*. "Ground Hog, this is Mother, OVER," he repeated his anxiety level increasing every second.

Static filled the speaker in the overhead.

"Raise the search periscope," Scott ordered. "I want to verify the submersible is no longer sitting on our back." He flipped down the handlebars and placed his eye on the rubber eyepiece. "The *ASDV* is not attached to the boat. Sonar, where is that Goddamn destroyer?"

"Both destroyers are heading away from us," Sorenson said.

Scott looked at Varney. "They had us cold. It doesn't make sense they would just leave."

In the *ASDV*, Norris shouted into his mic, "Mother, this is Ground Hog, OVER." Static filled his speaker. The Master Chief keyed the switch again. "Mother, this is Ground Hog, OVER." He looked at Janice. "Let's hope *Buffalo* can find us. For now, let's inspect the submersible."

Norris got up and left the Control room and entered the SEALs compartment. He looked at the wet suits, fins, and masks lying on the deck. The engineer's toolbox was turned over and their tools scattered across the deck. He saw a man placing a compress on the forehead of one of his coworkers.

"Everyone all right?" Norris asked.

"Yes, Master Chief. Just some bruises and Charlie hit his head," The First Class Engineer replied.

"Hang tight. We'll get back on *Buffalo* once we restore power."

"XO, turn this submarine around, and move back along our previous track," Scott ordered. For six tense minutes, Scott waited for Buffalo to swing around and move along her previous course.

"All Stop. All back slow," Scott ordered. He stepped away from the periscope and stared at the large monitor hanging on the bulkhead. "There she is," he said. The *ASDV* was sitting upright on the bottom. Air bubbles were seeping from under the hull. "XO, try reaching them again," he said, not taking his eye off the screen. Please God let them be safe.

"Commander Walsh to Control," Scott called on his 1MC.

"Ground Hog, this is Mother, OVER," Varney repeated. " Ground Hog, this is Mother, OVER."

"OOD, maintain steerage along the *ASDV*," Scott ordered.

"You wanted to see me, Captain?" Walsh, the SEAL Commander, appeared.

"I may need your help," Scott said, "Please remain in Control."

"Mother, this is Ground Hog, OVER."

Scott heard Janice's voice. "Thank God," he mumbled. "Ground Hog, what is your condition? OVER," he asked.

"We're all okay except for a few bruises and cuts. The hull is intact. The blast caused the seal to the lower hatch to leak. We closed the two watertight doors and pressurized the Lockout Chamber to keep it from flooding,"

"Can you repair the seal?" Scott asked.

"No. We don't have a replacement," Norris jumped in.

"Master Chief, can you lift off the bottom and return to *Buffalo*?" Scott asked.

"No. When I apply power to the screw the master circuit breaker snaps open. We only have emergency lighting."

"I'll move *Buffalo* forward and take a look," Scott said. "OOD, increase speed to three knots." He trained the periscope aft of the *ASDV*. "Damn! Master Chief, speaking into the speaker above his head. The shroud is bent and pressing against the blades. There is an angle iron jammed in between the screw and the shroud."

"Captain, there is only one way to return to *Buffalo*," Norris said.

"What's your recommendation?" Scott asked.

"Commander Walsh and I must remove the angle iron and shroud," Norris said. "I'll inject air into the ballast tanks and raise the submersible. Send him over as soon as possible."

Chapter 5

ASDV- Dark Shadow; Persian Gulf -

"Commander Walsh, there are four struts welded to our hull," Norris said. They're about three inches wide by three-quarter inches thick. We can ditch the shroud by cutting them. Once the propellor is free and assuming the screw turn we should be able to return to *Buffalo*."

"We're sitting on the sea floor in one hundred eighty feet of water. How in the hell do you intend to cut the struts?" Janice asked.

Norris, replied, "I will raise the *ASDV* to sixty feet from the surface. The commander and I should complete cutting the struts and return to the *ASDV* in less than sixty minutes."

Mother, this is Ground Hog, OVER. Captain, do you have eyes on the shroud?" Janice asked.

"Ground Hog, that's affirmative, OVER. Let's see what happens when you lift off the bottom. The angle iron should fall onto the seabed," Scott suggested. It better, he thought, or were in real trouble.

"We have nothing to lose," Norris said talking to Walsh. "Here goes." He released the lock on the two-three hundred-pound weights which anchored the submersible to the bottom. He then added air to the ballast tanks.

Janice looked at the depth gauge. "She is starting to lift," Master Chief. As the submersible noise lifted Norris and Janice heard a scraping sound through the hull.

"Ground Hog it's working. The angle iron is sliding out from between the shroud and the propeller." Scott said, looking through the periscope.

Norris stopped the rise sixty feet from the surface.

"Ground Hog, the angle iron has fallen away from the shroud and landed on the ocean floor, OVER," Scott said relieved it was no longer impairing the screw.

"Commander, we should not have to decompress if we can complete the job in fewer than sixty minutes," Norris said getting up out of his seat. "Let's start."

"Sounds like a plan. We'll suit up and prepare to leave the submersible," Walsh said.

"Mother, Commander Walsh, and I will remove the covering. I'll contact you once done, OVER," Norris said. "Janice, take my seat and open the battery breaker," pointing to the switch over her head.

Janice followed Norris's instructions. The lights and ventilation went off, and emergency red lighting snapped on.

"That's normal," Norris said. "Commander, follow me leaving the forward Control Room and opening the door leading to the rear chamber. Once the sealed compartment opened, the lower escape hatch started leaking salt water. Norris quickly secured the door.

Walsh opened the watertight door into the SEAL compartment and saw the engineers working on the leaky valve.

Norris moved to a panel near the deck and opened the cover. "Commander be careful the leads from the batteries are hot," Walsh said.

"I thought as much," Walsh replied.

"OK Commander," Norris said. "Hand me those rubber gloves and the copper U bar from the storage locker."

Walsh pulled the gloves and bar from the locker and handed them to Norris.

The Master Chief pulled the rubber glove on his right hand. He then placed the insulated handle in his right hand and carefully inserted the bar into the panel recess. "Got it," withdrawing the bar. He closed the panel door.

"All right, Obi-Wan, not too bad," Walsh said smiling.

Norris laughed. "Well, Grasshopper, we will remove the cable in the Lockout Chamber so I can cut the struts and remove the shroud blocking the propeller screw."

"Okay," Walsh asked, "What do you want me to do?"

"Wait here," Norris said, leaving the SEAL compartment and reentering the Control Room. "Dr. Lace, once Walsh and I are outside—-"

"Is it necessary?" Janice asked, concerned for their safety.

"I'm afraid so. Don't worry. You know how to handle this crate." Norris smiled confidently at her. "Once we're outside, I'll clamp the grounding lead. Commander Walsh will tap three times on the hull when ready to start cutting. I need you to open the auxiliary power breaker to the welding terminal."

Janice nodded. "Is that the red button above my head?"

"Yes! Just press the button. This will provide power to the cable in the Lockout Chamber." Norris smiled. "We should not take long in the water, assuming no unforeseen problems. When I'm done, Walsh will give three more taps signaling you to press the button off."

"OK, got it," Janice said.

Norris nodded. "We'll reenter the submersible and test the motor. Any questions?"

"Won't the light from the cutting torch attract attention from the surface?" Janice asked.

Norris rolled his tongue over his teeth. "Good question. If we were cutting at night, it would be likely, but it is mid-afternoon, making it less probable. We can't keep sitting here and doing nothing. We have no choice."

Norris headed for the SEALs compartment. They both grabbed a tank and diving gear. They suited up and headed for the Lockout Chamber.

After securing the inner and outer watertight doors, Walsh checked if Norris was ready.

Norris gave a thumbs-up and flooded the compartment. The tepid water rose slowly filling the entire space.

Walsh bent down and opened the escape hatch. They both dropped through the opening and immediately inflated their vests, remaining just under the submersible.

Walsh pressed his finger against the mic around his neck. "Radio check."

"Hear you loud and clear," Norris responded. "Let's start," grabbing the power cable dangling beneath the open hatch and finning to the stern of the *ASDV*.

Walsh grabbed the cable and followed Norris.

"There they are," Varney said, looking at the monitor as Scott trained the periscope camera on the men coming out from under the submersible. He saw them approaching the screw.

Varney saw Norris pull down on the propeller. It had movement. Excellent it was not frozen.

Scott turned his attention to Mike Walsh. He saw Norris pointing to the side of the hull. Walsh moved over where Norris was pointing and connected a clamp to the hull. He held a steel hammer in his hand.

Norris grabbed hold of the shroud and prepared to start cutting. "OK, Mike, bang on the hull three times," he said.

Scott saw the Commander hit the hull three times. Now what? He thought.

Janice heard the three bangs against the hull. She pressed the red button and sat back. The lights dimmed in the cabin.

Norris waited several seconds before attaching the welding rod to the welding clamp. He dropped the protective visor over his mask and started to cut.

Walsh turned away from the blinding light.

Norris held up one finger when the torch went all the way through. He then proceeded to cut the second stud.

"Norris has cut the first stud and is starting on the second," Scott announced. "Wait he just moved to the third stud. This is going faster than I thought."

"Sorenson, do you hold any close contacts?" Scott asked.

"No close contacts," Sorenson said.

Scott saw Walsh move closer with the light as Norris aimed his torch at the third stud.

"Commander, before I cut the fourth stud, turn off your light, and hold the shroud with both hands."

Walsh waited for Norris to move to the fourth stud. He placed the light in the pocket of his vest.

Norris started cutting. "Hold on! I'm about through," he said, ready to drop the cutter and grab the shroud. "Don't let it fall!"

Scott saw Walsh grab the shroud and pull back from the weight. He was struggling to keep it from dropping on the propeller.

"I'm losing it," Walsh shouted in his mask.

"Okay! Lift and ease the covering off the studs," Norris said. "Keep it away from the propeller."

Continuing his running commentary, Scott announced. "They are starting to lift the shroud away from the propeller."

Walsh and Norris struggled to keep the shroud from falling on the screw. Each man was breathing hard on their air.

"Christ that must be heavy," Scott said watching both men lift the shroud over the propeller.

"Easy, Commander," Norris said straining to hold the shroud. "A little more." He urged, guiding the shroud up until it was free. "OK!" He shouted as he struggled to hold the shroud away from the propeller. "Let it fall." They both watched it sink to the bottom.

"The propeller is clear," Scott announced.

"Okay, signal, Dr. Lace," Norris said, gulping air.

Walsh banged three times.

Janice turned off the power.

Norris pushed down on the screw and felt it move freely. "Let's return to the submersible."

"Looks like there good to go," Scott said. "The propeller moves freely," watching Norris turn the screw around.

Both men swam to the submersible pulling the cable behind them.

Scott and Varney saw the men disappear under the *ASDV*.

Norris entered the lockout chamber first and started winding the cable on the spool.

Walsh fed the cable through the opening, entered the chamber, secured the hatch, and turned the lock.

After the water drained, they entered the SEALs' compartment and stripped off their rebreathers and dry suits.

"Good work, Commander," Norris said as they toweled down. Grabbing the intercom, Norris ordered, "Dr. Lace switch the power back on."

The lights in the compartment switched from red to white and the air started to circulate through the vents.

"Master Chief," the engineer announced. "We have repaired the seal. I'll install a new valve when we return to *Buffalo*."

Norris nodded and handed Walsh his gear. "You men get the rags out of the foot locker and wipe up the floor."

"Thank you, Commander," Norris said and returned to the Control Room.

Janice stared questioningly from her seat. "Can we return to Buffalo?" She asked.

"We'll soon find out setting down and prepared to start the thrusters. "Piece of cake," he said, smiling at Janice. "Let's try her out."

Janice thought of Scott and could not wait to return to the submarine.

Scott and Varney saw the submersible retract her anchors. "She is still leaking air," Varney said.

"Let's just get her back on Buffalo. We'll deal with a hatch once she is fastened to the hull," Scott said.

"Here we go," Norris eased forward on the joystick. The submersible shifted and no longer anchored to the bottom. The whine of the electric motor filled the cabin. She felt the submersible start to move

"She's holding," Janice said, seeing the speed indicator increase.

Norris, eyeing his gauges increased the power of the thrusters. "This is the real test," he said.

The *ASDV* edged ahead and increased speed as it moved down the starboard side of *Buffalo*.

Scott tracked the submersible using the search periscope until she moved out of sight. He waited.

"Let's circle Buffalo and make our approach from the stern," Norris said.

"Ground Hog, this is Mother, OVER," Janice called. "Starting my approach."

Janice saw the red lights flash on her console as the ASDV maneuvered toward the locking pads. The faster it flashed the closer the submersible moved toward the pads. "Hold," Janice said as the flashing light turned to solid green.

"Touchdown," Norris exclaimed, hearing the hatch cover lock around the opening.

"Thank God they are safe Tom," Scott said. "I'm going aft. You have the Conn. Let's return to K-901's last track. We must determine if that sub is heading for the Gulf of Oman to attack the carrier group." He prayed his gut feeling was wrong.

Chapter 6

USS Buffalo; Persian Gulf –

"Captain, destroyer classified Master nineteen is slowing and changing course," Varney announced, watching the bearing dots on the screen.

OK, where the hell is he going? Scott thought.

"Control, Sonar, Master nineteen just entered our baffles," Sorenson reported. "She just went active."

Scott looked at the XO. "She must have been passive and searching the entire time we were retrieving the *ASDV*. I bet we are in for another lashing."

Scott heard the Iranian ship's active transmissions grow louder. The ominous thrashing of the destroyer's screws filled the void between each transmission.

"One thousand yards and closing," Varney said, monitoring the readings in the fire control console. "They're going to pass over us."

"Standby for more bombs," Varney announced over the 1MC.

"Conn, detecting splashes," Sorenson reported, sounding anxious.

The crew's eyes followed the scraping sound of an explosive device sliding down the sub's hull.

"Hold on," Scott shouted, grabbing the periscope rail with both hands.

The explosion was deafening. It picked up the sub and tipped it hard to port.

Alarms sounded, indicating damage to his ship.

Scott ordered, "OOD hard right rudder."

"Hold two more splashes off our bow," Sorenson shouted.

"Brace yourself!" Scott shouted as two more explosions rocked *Buffalo*.

The violent blasts from the near hits rocked Scott and the crew. Some of the younger men looked up with frightened eyes.

"Engineering damage report," Scott ordered.

"Captain," Engineering Officer Dennis Fender replied. "Waiting for all departments to check in."

"Let me know as soon as possible," Scott said, holding the rail.

Varney announced, "Passing zero nine zero, one hundred, one hundred ten, one hundred twenty degrees——"

"OOD, steady on course one hundred thirty degrees," Scott ordered. "Now we wait, XO, to determine if finding us was just a fluke or if they've been tracking us."

Sorenson's eyes looked at the three black smudges on the monitor.

"Sorenson, you still with us?" Master Chief Jack Norris asked.

"What? Yes— yes, Master Chief," Sorenson replied, moving his cursor to a new contact that caught his attention.

"Captain, all departments reported no damage—except for some broken glassware," Fender said.

"Thanks, Dennis," Scott said, breathing a sigh of relief. "That was too close." He glanced at Varney.

"If they were depth charges, we might be sucking water from the Gulf now," Varney replied.

Scott nodded. "Sorenson, update on Master seventeen."

Sorenson pressed the headphones to his ears. "Master seventeen, K-901 is opening. If she remains on her current heading, she will arrive at the Northern Straits in an hour." He sighed. "Master nineteen is coming around. We may be in for another pounding."

"Sorenson, any other high-speed contacts?" Scott asked.

"Negative, Captain," Sorenson replied.

"Captain, let's get out of here," Varney said, observing increasing Signal-to-noise (SNR) numbers.

Scott nodded. "I agree, but I don't want to risk attracting their attention. Only one destroyer is interested in us now." He stopped to think. "If the Captain of Master eighteen believed he detected an enemy submarine, he would have called it in. Both destroyers, not just one, would be working us over." He glanced at the surface picture on the automatic plotting board. "I think there would be a shit-load of surface craft sitting on top of our position," he said, pointing to the board. He looked at Varney. "We'll wait them out."

"That's a bit risky. Don't you think so? We could make a run for safety."

Scott frowned. "That's an option, but we can't outrun their destroyers." He listened intently as the transmissions grew louder. He knew this had to be his decision. "We'll remain at our present course and speed."

Varney nodded, secretly worried Scott was taking a significant risk with the lives of the crew. The recently reinstated officer had been lucky so far, and he hoped his luck would last.

"Sorenson, give me an update on the two destroyers," Scott said.

"Master eighteen is opening. Master nineteen is increasing speed and continues to close," Sorenson reported.

Scott shot a puzzled look at his XO. "Why would Master nineteen increase speed if he knows we're close?"

Varney replied, "If he suspects an enemy sub is near, speeding up increases the flow noise across his hydrophones. Detecting us would make it near impossible."

Scott nodded. "Good point Tom."

"Conn, Sonar, picking up another submerged contact off our port quarter. Range one thousand five hundred yards and opening. Classified Master twenty," Sorenson announced, interrupting Scott's conversation with his XO.

Scott looked at Varney. "Sonar, are you telling me there is another submarine?"

"Yes, Captain," Sorenson replied.

"Are you sure it's not Master Seventeen?" Scott asked.

Senior Chief Richardson replied, "Master twenty came out of our starboard baffles—"

"Sonar, get me the classification of the new submarine," Scott ordered, studying the fire control console.

"Captain, it's a Dolphin Class submarine," Richardson replied.

"Hell, can it get any more crowded around here," Scott muttered. "OOD, All Stop. We'll let him move ahead and fall in astern."

"Captain, Master nineteen has slowed and is changing course. It appears he may be trying to intercept Master twenty," Varney said.

Scott smiled. "We got the hell out of that bind. That Captain showed up at the right time."

"Master twenty is opening, and Master nineteen is on an intercept course," Sorenson reported, wiping his forehead.

"Mr. Price, having fun yet?" Master Chief Norris asked, noticing the younger man's panicked expression.

"Is it always like this?" Price asked, keeping his eyes on the sonar screen.

"No. But don't worry about getting bored. Our deployment in this 'fun' zone is just getting started," Sorenson replied with a slight smile. "Captain, it's becoming harder to identify the enemy from all the background noise."

"Understood," Scott replied. "I'm sending you some help."

"You wanted to see me, Master Chief?" Janice interrupted after entering sonar.

"Yes, Dr. Lace. Thank you. Can you help Sorenson distinguish the broadband contact from the background noise in this area?" Richardson asked.

"Yes Master Chief," she replied, sitting at the console next to Sorenson.

Sorenson wasted no time explaining to Janice the difficulty differentiating contacts from the background noise of the many commercial ships in the heavily trafficked area.

Janice leaned over. "Let's see if I can help. Master Chief, request the OOD conduct a baffle clear."

Price looked puzzled.

Janice explained, "I need to determine what threats might still be shadowing us."

Price looked worried. "Do you think they are still here?" he asked.

"You're in the 'fun' zone," Senior Chief Richardson replied. "Anything can happen."

Chapter 7

USS Buffalo; Persian Gulf-

Scott maneuvered *Buffalo* cautiously away from the destroyers for four intense hours. His goal was to move as silently as possible into deeper water. Every stray sound aboard his craft caught his attention as the crew remained at their stations, all fully aware of the danger of not maintaining Ultra-Quiet.

Sorenson broke the silence. "Control, the destroyer's active sonars have shut down." He looked again to be sure. "The ships are slowing."

The tension in Scott's back and shoulders immediately lessened. He glanced at Varney. "It looks like the games are over for today." He checked his screen. "Let's close to two thousand yards and regain contact with the Iranian *Kilo, K-901*." He spoke into his mic, "Engineering, restart air conditioning. It's hotter than hell in this boat." He wiped the sweat from his face and neck. The men sitting at their stations were soaked from sweat, but safe. "They did well, Tom," he said, drawing a lung full of cool air from the overhead vent.

Varney nodded. This captain is a cool customer, he thought. Captain Whitfield was right he tends to take risks. But they seem well thought out before he acts. I can learn a lot from this man.

"Control, Sonar, K-901 has started her diesel," Sorenson reported. "She appears to be moving in between the two destroyers."

"Sonar, anything on Master twenty?" Scott asked.

"Analysis reports the Dolphin submarine is an Israeli boat," Varney replied.

"I don't remember ever hearing of Israeli submarines operating in the Persian Gulf. Did we receive any intel as to why they are here?" Scott asked.

"No I haven't seen any messages alerting us the Israeli are operating in this ocean," Varney said.

"Sonar is the Dolphin boat still around?" Scott asked.

"No, Sir. She was heading toward the Straits," Janice replied.

"Thank you, Dr. Lace," he said. "XO, let's remain in K-901's baffles. Match her speed and course. We need to determine what her intentions are."

"Aye, Captain," Varney replied, "Navigator, chart K-901's course."

Scott said, "XO, with K-901 on the surface, with the two destroyers above us, contacting the Fifth Fleet is impossible. We'll wait until we reach open water and are safe to break radio silence to inform the fleet of the mines. Let's hope the Fifth Fleet did not have the mines removed we've reported already."

Varney looked puzzled. "I don't understand, Captain. Why would you not want those mines removed?"

"If they did, it would be a dead giveaway that there is a submarine operating in this quadrant," Scott answered. He saw that Varney understood. ."I don't know about you, Tom, but I can't wait to see what's next," he said.

As if reading Scott's mind, his phone buzzed.

Sorenson spoke in hushed tones. "Sir, it may be nothing, but we were monitoring underwater transmissions of K-901. A lot was incomprehensible—but the name Admiral Jujair—"

You said Admiral Jajair? Scott interrupted.

"Yes, Sir, I distinctly heard the name Admiral Jajair,"

"Did you catch the message? Was he congratulating the Captain for their war game?"

"Sir, a lot was garbled and lost over Gertrude, but I heard *Carl Vinson* Group mentioned."

Scott's interest spiked quickly. "Are you sure he said, *Carl Vinson*?"

"Only once, but yes. I thought you should know right away," Sorenson replied.

Scott shot a worried glance at Varney. "Thank you. See if you get anything else."

Varney saw the look on Scott's face. "More fun, Captain?" He asked.

Scott leaned close to his XO. "If sonar was correct and they intercepted a fragmented message between Jajair and K-901, yes."

Varney got serious quickly. "Captain, *Carl Vinson* Battlegroup is expected in the Gulf of Oman. If I'm not mistaken, they don't have a submarine attached to the group.

"I've never heard of a battle group heading into the Persian Gulf without one or two submarines searching her forward area," Scott said. "Any ideas what the Iranians are intending if they sent the Kilo south?"

Varney thought for a minute. "We hear her running her diesel engines, therefore, we can assume she is charging her batteries. If K-901 intends to sail south she would have sufficient power to lay mines at the Southern Strait and return north without surfacing."

Scott thought about what his XO had said. "OK! What type of mine do you think she carries?"

"Good question Captain. I believe torpedo mines. They are the most likely weapons to use against the fleet. As we saw in the Persian Gulf they placed torpedo mines in strategic areas along the commercial lanes."

Scott picked up his phone. "Radio, Captain, check our latest messages and tell me when the *Vinson* Battlegroup expects a submarine escort." He held his hand over the mouthpiece.

Weathers' voice shot over the phone. "Captain, *Carl Vinson* will not have a submarine for at least five days."

"Shit," Scott said, glancing at Varney. "Are you sure five days?"

"That's what the message states, Captain," Weather said.

"Thanks." Scott was deep in thought. "The battlegroup could be in big trouble, Tom." Moving over to the chart table. He studied the waters in the Straits of Hormuz and the Gulf of Oman.

"Tom, if K-901 remains in the Persian Gulf, we can sit here and continue to map their mines. But if she enters the Straits of Hormuz, we must follow." He thought of Janice and hoped the Iranian sub would not force his hand.

Varney knew where Scott was leading. He knew the danger and chose his words carefully. "Captain, our orders are to remain in the Gulf, monitor for mines, and collect intelligence on the movement of the Iranian submarines—"

"First which Gulf are you referring to? Second, you forgot our orders also state to maintain track of Iranian submarines in and around the Straits of Hormuz and the Gulf of Oman," Scott replied.

"We could radio the *Vinson*," Varney suggested.

"And say what? The battle group is in jeopardy of being attacked. We have no proof. We don't know if K-901 will head to the Southern Straits." Scott frowned. "XO, you forgot our most important order: maintain radio silence and avoid detection. Tom, we are not here." He scratched his forehead. "Our primary order is to not provide Iran any indication that an American vessel is in their corner of the world. We don't want to give them an excuse for starting a war."

Varney nodded, knowing Scott was right.

"But, you and I, know an Iranian sub in the Gulf of Oman threatens that entire group." He let out a deep sigh. "Tom, if we break radio silence, the surface ships will pick us up on their electronic countermeasures. They could easily triangulate our position. With all the Iranian surface and subsurface traffic, we can't risk being detected." He surveyed the crew. "Let's hope this is a false alarm, but my intuition tells me if Jujair mentioned *Carl Vinson*, he had a damn good reason." He looked at Varney for a reaction but his XO was stone-faced. "I don't like it, but if K-901 heads toward our carrier group, I think the best thing to do is to follow and pray. If I am wrong—"

Varney interrupted. "Sir, with respect, you are knowingly countermanding our orders—"

Scott felt a bit annoyed. "XO, which order do you suggest I follow? We can remain in the Persian Gulf and let the carrier be defenseless, or follow K-901 and possibly prevent a disaster that could lead to war?" He ran his hand through his black hair. "If following K-901 is countermanding my orders, I'll accept the consequences of my actions. I take full responsibility." He tried to look confident. "For now, let's maintain track of K 901 and see what she does." Scott smiled. "I don't see another way. That group and all those aboard will be sitting ducks if that sub reaches them."

"You think Admiral Jujair intends to prevent the fleet from entering the Southern Straits," Varney asked.

"It seems possible. He did mention the battlegroup," Scott said. "Let's play it cool for now Tom. If K-901 enters the Straits, or we pick up more chatter about the *Vinson* from the Iranians, I will have no alternative but to follow her down into the Straits."

"Yes, Sir," Varney replied, grateful Scott had to make the decision.

"You have the Conn. I'm going to get some rest," Scott said and left Control. Once he was away from the others, his shoulders sagged. He was dead tired and worried. He entered his stateroom, and thought about contacting Janice, but was too tired for even that. Pulling down the back cushion of his couch, he lay down on the leather seat and closed his eyes.

No sooner did he fall asleep than the growler woke him up. He glanced at his watch. "Captain," he said and yawned.

"Captain, K-901 submerged. She is leaving the Persian Gulf," Varney reported.

"Where are the two destroyers?" Scott asked.

"They both appear to be heading toward the Naval Base," Varney said.

"What is the status of the repairs to the *ASDV*?" Scott asked.

"The engineers are still having problems with the leaky hatch," Varney said.

"We'll leave her aboard. I don't want to risk the lives of our team," Scott said. "If Washington disagrees with my decision, I will take the hit. We must protect the fleet from an attack." He glanced at a photograph of Janice. I should have left her home, he thought. This could be one hell of a rough ride.

Chapter 8

USS Buffalo; Gulf of Oman, Fifty Miles South of Musandam–

"Officer of the Deck, ahead one-third, make turns for ten knots," Scott ordered.

The OOD relayed the order to the Diving Officer of the watch "Helmsmen adjust speed to ten knots.

"Aye, Sir," the planesman said.

"Now we wait, Tom," Scott said, glancing at the wall clock. "You up for something to eat?"

"Yes, Sir. I could eat a horse," Varney replied.

Scott laughed. "But first get a message to Fifth Fleet now that we are outside the Persian Gulf."

"Do you want me to inform them we have left the Gulf?" Varney asked wondering how much Scott was willing to reveal.

"Yes, tell them I'm in pursuit of an Iranian submarine heading for the Battlegroup in the Gulf of Oman. Indicate I felt it was imperative to support and protect the Battlegroup until her supporting submarine arrives."

"I'll also add the *ASDV* has a seal leak and is under repair," Varney said.

"Yes, do that, and please, bring the draft to my stateroom."

"Yes, Sir," the XO said, heading to radio.

Scott was washing up when he heard a tap on his stateroom door, followed by Varney and First-Class Weathers entering. The XO handed the draft to Scott.

Scott read the message, signed it, and gave it to Weathers. "Send it."

"Yes, Sir," Weathers said and left.

"You mentioned eating a horse, Tom. I'm afraid you'll have to wait until we return to Guam. Midrats are on the menu, which means whatever the cook dreams up from today's leftovers," Scott said.

"Then let's see our surprise," Varney replied enthusiastically. "I see Lt. Morton is working with Senior Chief Richardson weeding out potential contacts from the background noise," he said as he walked through the corridor.

Scott replied. "She and Richardson work well together. A second pair of eyes always helps."

Varney smiled. "Morton will make an excellent officer."

"It's up to us to convince her to remain in the Navy. Let's get a hot meal under our belts," Scott said.

Scott and the Executive Officer went down the ladder and entered the wardroom.

"May we join you?" Scott asked the men already eating.

"Of course," Ltjg. Terry Washington replied.

Culinary Specialist Second Class Brady hurried in with a tray of steaming bowls of vegetable soup, ham sandwiches, and pastry. The smell of fresh-baked strawberry Bear Claw filled the room.

"Thanks, Brady," Scott said, diving into his soup. "Compliments to the cook." He bit into his ham and Swiss sandwich. "Not bad at all," he said to Varney.

"Do you think we'll reacquire K-901, Captain?" Engineering Officer Dennis Fender asked between bites of his sandwich.

"The question is not 'will we,' but 'when,' engineer," Scott replied. "How are things in the reactor spaces?"

"I suspended all but essential maintenance activity while we run silent," Fender said.

"I think this is a good time to allow the men some relief from engineering drills," Scott replied.

"I agree," Tom said. "The men have worked hard."

A knock on the wardroom door was followed by Weathers carrying a packet of satellite pictures and a report. "Captain, I just downloaded this file."

"Have our messages been sent out to Fifth Fleet?" Varney asked.

"Yes, Sir. Right after I downloaded these pictures," Weathers replied.

"Thanks, Weathers. Tom, let's finish our sandwiches in my stateroom." Scott led Varney back to his quarters. He sat down at his desk and had just picked up the documents when the messenger of the watch knocked twice and stepped into the room.

"Sir," Petty Officer Sorenson says, "We've got him."

"Here we go, Tom," Scott said, hurrying out of his room, followed by the XO.

"I have the Conn, Mr. Wilkinson," Scott said, eager to take command. "Sonar, are you positive it is K-901?" He looked at the bearing dots stacking up on the Fire Control Console.

"Yes, Sir," Sorenson responded over the overhead speaker. "It's our K-901, for sure."

"XO, station the Fire Control Tracking Party. Make your depth. Belay that. Nav, sounding?" Scott asked, recalling hitting a seamount and wanting to avoid a repeat of that earlier incident which caused him to lose his last command.

"Twelve hundred feet," Nav reported.

Scott smiled. "Officer of the Deck, make your depth three hundred feet, speed seven knots. XO, designate Sierra eighty-one, Master twenty. Now, you bastard, let's see you try and shake me."

Scott felt the deck tip as Buffalo started to dive deeper.

"Passing one hundred feet," the OOD reported. "Coming to three hundred feet."

Varney had a solution two minutes after *Buffalo* turned onto her third leg. "Target, range four thousand yards, speed six knots, course one hundred eighty degrees," he reported.

Scott glanced at the Attack and Weapons Consoles. "Verified," he said.

"How long do you intend to follow K-901, Captain?" Varney asked.

Scott appreciated Varney's concern. "I intend to maintain track of this *Kilo* until *Carl Vinson*'s submarine arrives. Officer of the Deck, make turns for six knots."

"Conn, Sonar, *Kilo* is turning, crazy Ivan," Sorenson announced. "Looks like she decided to check her baffles, Captain."

Scott saw bearing dots slew across the screen. "OOD, drop ten turns. Give him room to maneuver." He waited impatiently for Sonar to announce that K-901 had returned to her previous course. "Time, XO?"

"Coming up on three minutes," Varney responded.

Scott sensed the uneasiness of the men. The enemy sub's maneuver placed *Buffalo* in a precarious position. He could no longer determine the distance on the fire control console between each boat. All he could do was reduce speed and allow the other sub to open.

"Time?" Scott asked, his neck stiffening from tension in his shoulders and back.

"Four minutes," Varney responded, concerned the two boats were closing each other.

"What the hell is taking him so long?" Scott hissed.

"Control, contact turning starboard, returning to the previous course."

Scott heard the sigh of relief from the men standing by their stations. The tightness in his shoulders subsided. The sub was moving away. "Maintain Ultra-Quiet," he ordered. "Let's close to within two thousand yards."

Buffalo resumed tracking K-901, closing silently astern of her baffles.

After a while, Scott turned to Varney. "You would think, XO, our friend would opt to remain close to the southern end of the Straits," he said, trying to figure out where his prey was heading.

"Captain, Sonar holds a broadband contact, designated Sierra eighty-two on the same course as K-901. Sounds like a large tanker."

"XO, generate a range and speed on the new target," Scott ordered.

Five minutes after *Buffalo* steadied on her second leg, Senior Chief Russell reported, "Sierra eighty-two, eight thousand yards, speed five knots. If K-901 continues on her present course and speed, she'll close Sierra eighty-two in thirty minutes."

"Control, target slowed and is preparing to surface," Lt. Morton reported.

Scott looked puzzled. "I can't figure this guy out. Did he go all this way just to shadow a tanker? OOD, prepare to come to periscope depth. XO, it looks

41

like he's closing the tanker's stern. Any idea why?"

"No idea, Captain," Varney responded, watching the readouts on the tactical display.

"Come right, ten degrees. We'll open five hundred yards off *Kilo's* starboard quarter, just inside her baffle region."

"Captain completed baffle clear. No close contacts," the OOD reported.

"Proceed to periscope depth, slow and easy," Scott ordered.

Buffalo began to creep toward the surface.

"Up scope." Scott stood before the number two scope and turned the training handles. "Bearing, Mark?"

Varney announced, "One-three-zero degrees."

Scott pressed the button under his right thumb.

"Five seconds," Varney reported.

"Down scope," Scott announced, stepping down and walking over to review the images. "*W/T Seed* is the name on the tanker's stern." He sighed. "The big question is, why is this sub following a crude oil carrier?"

"She's a big one," Varney remarked, staring at his monitor.

Scott pulled down a copy of Jane's Fighting Ships from the bookcase. He flipped through the section on tankers. "Here," he said, placing the book on the Dead Reckoning Table. "Iran purchased the ULCC tanker in 1999. Deadweight tonnage is four-hundred twenty thousand tons; one thousand two hundred forty-six feet long with a draft of eighty feet. She can carry over a half-million tons of oil." He let out a low whistle. "Wow! We have ourselves a supertanker."

"She riding too high to be carrying half-million tons of oil," Varney said. "So why is she down here? And why is K-901 now trailing an empty supertanker?"

Scott stepped back onto the pedestal and raised the periscope. He turned it to the last bearing of the tanker. "Down scope," he ordered. "Sonar, do you still hold K-901?"

"Yes, Sir, but the noise from the tanker's screw is beginning to mask K-901's shaft rub," Sorenson replied.

"Up Scope!" Scott observed the *Kilo's* periscope disappear below the surface.

"She's going down." He turned to Varney. "OOD, make your depth two hundred feet and speed seven knots. Helm come right ten degrees. We'll remain one thousand five hundred yards off the tanker's starboard beam."

"Depth two hundred feet and speed seven knots. Helm come right ten degrees," the OOD repeated.

"Skipper," Sorenson announced, "lost K-901 due to the increase in the thrashing noise of the tanker's screw."

"Thanks, Sorenson," Scott responded. "OOD, you have the Conn," Scott said, "XO, please join me in my stateroom?"

Entering Scott's stateroom, Varney pulled up a chair. The captain opened the safe and retrieved the recent satellite pictures. "It doesn't make sense, Tom. Why send a sub all this way to track a tanker?"

"That's the same question I've been asking," Varney replied

"We'll remain in the Gulf until I find out why K-901 was ordered here. I'm convinced the Battlegroup is in danger."

Chapter 9

National Geospatial-Intelligence Agency; Dahlgren, VA –

Colonel Bill Johnson was sitting at his desk when Technical Sergeant Wallace knocked on his open door.

"Morning, Sergeant," Johnson said, placing the report he was reading down on his blotter.

"Colonel, I just completed analyzing the new pictures from the KH-4B Corona strategic reconnaissance satellite," Wallace said.

"Find anything interesting?" Johnson asked, knowing Wallace was one of those whose instincts were uncanny.

"Sir, I was looking over the pictures taken in the Gulf of Oman this morning and noticed a large supertanker heading toward the Arabian Sea," Wallace said.

"That seems normal," Johnson replied. "I believe that's the route if they are heading to Australia, Burma, or Malaysia."

"I agree, but satellite pictures taken over the last two weeks show this tanker traveled two hundred miles down into the Gulf."

"And?"

"That same supertanker reversed course and headed back toward the North. It has done this several times in the past two weeks," Wallace said.

"Are you sure it's the same tanker?" Johnson asked becoming interested.

"Yes, Sir." He placed several photographs in front of the Colonel. "You can see for yourself. *W/T Seed* was the name painted on the tanker's stern."

"Let's have a look," Johnson said.

Wallace handed the additional satellite photos to the Colonel.

Johnson spread the pictures across his desk and studied them in silence. He examined the date and time printed at the bottom left of each photo. "I see what you mean, Sergeant. The question is, why?" He placed another image under the magnifier but returned to the one he had just removed.

"Okay, Sergeant, let's have it. Why did you bring this to me?"

"I think it's strange that a tanker would travel back and forth in the center of the Gulf of Oman."

"And?" Johnson asked, knowing his Sargent had not finished.

"Colonel, I believe the Iranians placed their tanker in an excellent location to monitor our battle groups entering and leaving the Persian Gulf."

Johnson looked at Wallace, then back at the pictures. His jaw tightened as he digested Wallace's conjecture. "Okay." He leaned forward. "I want you to continue to monitor the tanker. I'll contact the Director and give him a heads up."

"Sally, get me Dr. Ure on the phone." The Director of the National Geospatial-Intelligence Agency, Sam Eliot, asked.

Waiting to speak to Jack Ure, Eliot reread the newly received report and scanned the satellite pictures. He dialed the CIA agent stationed at the Creech Air Force Base in Nevada.

The phone rang twice before Mark O'Connell answered.

"Mark, Eliot."

"Yes, Sir, how can I help you?" O'Connell asked.

"Mark, I know it's a bit unusual to ask, but do you have any drones in the air near the Gulf of Oman?"

"No, Sir. All our drones are down for servicing."

"Thanks," Eliot hung up.

"Sir, Dr. Ure is on the phone," Eliot's secretary announced over the intercom.

Eliot picked up the phone. "Jack, I got a call from Colonel Johnson in our surveillance group. He reported they are tracking an Iranian supertanker in the Gulf of Oman.

"And I can't see where that concerns me at this time," Jack Ure said. "My focus is in the Persian Gulf."

If I recall, you forwarded an internal memo notifying me that you were conducting an undercover operation in the Persian Gulf. Is that operation still ongoing?"

Jack hesitated and then replied. "Yes, Sir. I'm closely monitoring the Iranian mining operations and submarine deployments. "But again you are referring to the Gulf of Oman. I don't see where it concerns me," becoming frustrated by the call.

"If I'm not mistaken the *Vinson* Battlegroup is currently in the Arabian Sea and due to continue to the Persian Gulf over the next two weeks," Eliot said. "It would seem to me that with this supertanker traveling back and forth she might be waiting for the carrier group."

"I see your point. But for now, I have bigger problems in the Persian Gulf," Ure said.

"Well, I just wanted to voice our concern and let you know we will continue to monitor the tanker," Eliot said.

"Thanks for the call. Let me know if there are any further developments. "Dr. Ure hung up and continued reading Scott's last status report in the Persian Gulf. I don't think there is a need to inform the President, he thought. I see no threat to the *Vinson* Battlegroup.

Chapter 10

USS Buffalo; Gulf of Oman –

"Tom we've been waiting over four hours for K-901 to reemerge from under the tanker.

Scott checked the time on the digital clock. "OOD mark, your depth, and speed," Scott ordered.

"Depth three hundred feet, speed six knots," Lt Jeff Obermeier reported.

"XO, let's parallel the tanker's track. I want to search forward of the oiler. I agree with you something's not right. Sorenson, have you regained contact on K-901?" Scott asked.

"No, Sir," Sorenson replied. "From what I've seen on my sensors he hasn't moved from under the tanker."

"So where is he?" Varney asked as minutes passed.

Scott looked worried. Has K-901 gotten behind us? He thought.

"OOD execute a baffle clear," Scott ordered.

Varney looked at Scott. "Do you think K-901 came about and is trailing us?"

"It's either that or he is still under the supertanker," Scott responded. "Even if he was conducting an underwater survey he's been under the tanker too long. I don't have a good feeling about this."

Scott felt the submarine turn to starboard as she allowed sonar to search behind her.

"Control, Sonar, our baffle area is clear. No close contacts detected," Sorenson reported.

"Well, we know K-901 is not behind us. So she is either under the tanker or she has given us the slip. Which one are you betting on XO?" Scott asked.

"Even money. I'll bet on the tanker," Varney said.

"OOD come left ten degrees. The new course, three hundred forty-five degrees, make turns for eight knots. Make your depth two hundred feet. Well check under the tanker," Scott said. He waited as *Buffalo* closed under the tanker's hull. "Up scope." Bending his 6' 4" frame, Scott rotated the handlebars. "I don't get it. No shapes or shadows. Dive, mark your depth every fifty feet," Scott said, focusing on the tanker's hull.

"Passing one-hundred fifty feet," the Dive Officer reported.

"Make your depth one hundred feet," Scott ordered, continuing to rotate the periscope, ensuring the water above was clear. "What the hell? "Stop the rise. No wonder we couldn't find the submarine. Take a look, XO. She's inside the tanker's hull."

Varney stared into the periscope. "I can't believe it!" He looked at Scott. "What a perfect way to conceal a submarine."

Scott smiled. "Looks like my hunch paid off."

Varney nodded. "You were right, and I still can't believe the sneaky bastards would try a stunt like this."

"The question is why?" Scott replied. "Why go to the trouble of using a supertanker to hide your submarines unless you intend to attack our ships."

Scott rotated the scope so he could see the rear of the tanker. He peered at the giant white claws securing the submarine. He took pictures of the interior and *Kilo* tucked inside as he rotated the periscope. "From what I can see, XO, this tanker is like our submarine tenders. It may be capable of repairing, refueling, loading weapons, and providing food stores while a sub is concealed inside." He shook his head. "*Vinson* won't suspect a tanker concealing a submarine."

"I wouldn't," Varney said. "And because of the location of the tanker, the Iranian submarines don't have to snorkel or surface to recharge their batteries."

Scott looked at Varney. "OOD, down scope. Make your depth three hundred feet. Once clear of the tanker, reverse course and open four thousand yards off the tanker's starboard side. Bring us up to periscope depth. I want to send a message. Tom, we need to discuss what to send to Fifth Fleet and *Vinson*. Let's go to my stateroom and review the pictures once more."

Scott switched on the monitor and pressed play on the video recorder in his stateroom.

A picture of the *Kilo* clamped by the huge claws inside the tanker filled the screen. Every fifteen seconds, a new picture appeared.

Scott was absorbed in studying the images. He realized what he was looking at posed a significant threat to the carrier. The question was, how would he prevent the Iranians from attacking *Carl Vinson*?

"Captain," Varney said. "We both know the implications of what the Iranians are doing with this tanker."

Scott looked up. "If the Iranians want to mine this end of the straits, this tanker can conceal their submarines. It can also restock them with torpedoes, mines, and recharge their batteries," he replied. "What if they are loading torpedo mines as well as floating mines?"

"Then they can get away with an attack because they can report our ship struck a mine," Varney said. "Or release a torpedo mine. Who would know? The tanker makes the sub—"

"More than one," Scott interrupted. "Take a look at this." He triggered the next photo. "She is capable of carrying two submarines simultaneously. Damn them."

Varney examined the magnified image. "By concealing two boats, she can initiate attacks against our fleet without us even knowing there is a threat. The question is, how can we stop the Iranians from attacking our ships?"

"The answer is strike first—hit 'em where it will hurt and not leave a trace against the US," Scott replied.

"How can we do that and not leave a trace?" Varney asked.

Scott had to think. "Tom, there is a way. It's risky. We can have Walsh attach a mine on the hull of the *Kilo*—"

"What?" Varney interrupted, "We received no orders authorizing you to launch an attack on an Iranian submarine. Remember the rules of engagement—"

"I am well aware of the ROE, Tom. But if the fleet is in danger of attack,

I will not hesitate to attack first." Scott took a deep breath and blew it out slowly to calm down. "Tom, before I consider placing a bomb under K-901's hull, I want you to draft a message and get this out to Fifth Fleet and the *Carl Vinson* at our next satellite pass."

"I'll write it up and send it out right away," Tom said and hurried out of the room.

Scott sat and continued to cycle through the photos. He leaned back against the couch and closed his eyes to rest. The vibration of the boat lulled him to sleep.

"Captain, OOD, radio has suffered an electrical surge in the communication equipment."

"What?" Scott shook the sleep from his eyes. "Did you say radio reported a problem?"

"Yes, Sir," the OOD replied.

"I'll be right there," Scott got up and left the room. "Weathers, report," Scott demanded, entering radio.

"IT1 Lock reported that after loading the buffer and pressing the transmit button he smelled a burning odor," Weathers said.

Scott could smell the foul odor still lingering in the room.

"Petty Officer Lock shut down the equipment and opened the cabinet doors to find several transmitters and receivers burned," Weathers said.

"Did Fifth Fleet and *Carl Vinson* get my message?" Scott asked.

"I don't know. We have no way of telling until we repair the equipment."

"How long will it take to repair the units?" Scott asked.

"I won't know until I determine the extent of the damage," Weathers replied.

"Alright. Report back to me when you find out," Scott ordered.

Weathers was already at work.

Scott left radio and headed for Control. I fear *Vinson* is heading into a trap, he thought. He wondered how many more submarines were waiting to ambush the Battle Group.

"Tom, you heard we cannot send or receive communications?" Scott asked, entering Control.

"Yes, did our message get to the Battle Group?" Varney asked.

"Weathers can't say. If it didn't, *Carl Vinson* could be sailing into a trap," Scott said.

USS Carl Vinson, CVN 70; Northeastern Arabian Sea–

Rear Admiral Clint Dussault, Commander Carrier Strike Group-One, was in command of the *Carl Vinson* Battlegroup, the Navy's third Nimitz-class supercarrier. Dussault stepped through the doorway to the 08 levels above the carrier flight deck and proceeded to his flag chair. Since graduating from the Naval Academy, he had spent his entire adult life in the service of his country. Now, at fifty-two, he was set to retire in one year.

"Attention!" Chief-of-Staff, Captain Jim Wills, announced the Admiral was on the bridge. He then walked to the coffee mess, drew a cup of black steaming coffee, and returned to the Admiral. "Good morning, Sir," he said, handing his commander the hot mug.

"Morning, Jim," Admiral Dussault replied, taking his first cup of the morning. "What's scheduled for today?"

Selected as the Admiral's aid, Captain Wills had just completed a tour as Commander of a F/A-18E Fighter Squadron. He began briefing Dussault on the scheduled aircraft launches, the status of the battlegroup refueling operation, and the planned rendezvous with the Amphibious Assault Group at sixteen hundred. "It's a busy day, Sir," he said.

"Where is the Amphibious Assault Group now?" the Admiral asked.

"Strike Group One is in the Arabian Sea, off the southern coast of Oman, conducting amphibious assault exercises with Kuwaiti, Oman, and Saudi forces," Wills replied.

A Marine rushed onto the bridge, saluted, and handed the admiral a Top-Secret file.

"Hold on, Jim," Admiral Dussault said, opening the folder. He looked surprised when he discovered a blank page. "Jim, get me the communication center."

"Yes, Sir." Wills picked up the phone.

"Commander Winkel speaking."

"Hold for the Admiral," Wills said, handing the phone to Dussault. "Commander Winkel, Sir."

"Commander, I just received a message from *Buffalo* with no text nor accompanying pictures."

Winkel replied, "That was all I received. We checked several times, and I have tried to inform *Buffalo* we did not receive the message. There has been no reply as of this minute."

"Keep trying, Commander. *Buffalo* would not break radio silence if the information were not critical," Dussault said.

"I will keep trying to establish contact with *Buffalo*," Winkel replied. "Hopefully, it is just a glitch."

Dussault put down the phone. "I don't like it, Jim. Contact Captain Newhouse and have him slow the fleet down to ten knots. I have a bad feeling Scott was trying to warn us. We'll delay entering the Southern Straits until he reestablishes communication."

"Jim, get an E-2 Hawkeye in the air." He slammed his fist on the chair's armrest. "I want to know what the hell is ahead of us. Have him closely search the area in case *Buffalo* is on the surface."

Wills checked his clipboard. "Sir, a Hawkeye, call sign Super Fudd-2, was launched this morning."

"Where is he now?"

"He is stationed above the Hormoz Straits, two hundred fifty miles from our position."

"Has he reported anything suspicious?" Dussault asked, leaning forward.

Wills pulled up the latest report from the reconnaissance plane. "The crew reported sighting only small fishing boats and the normal stream of commercial ships. There was a report of an Iranian supertanker moving north toward the Straits. Hawkeye's Tactical Radar Operator has been tracking the same tanker moving north then turning south for several hours."

"Did he provide a reason?"

"No, Sir," Jim replied.

"Inform the pilot to keep reporting the location of the tanker. I want to know why that tanker has been remaining in the area. Any word when the *Cincinnati* will arrive?"

"In two days," Willis replied.

"Is that all, Jim?"

"Yes, Admiral," Willis said and left the bridge.

The Admiral stood and looked down at the flight deck. Two F-35C Strike Jets were ready to launch. "I must know what I'm sailing into. Not having an accompanying submarine to search the waters ahead places my ships at risk."

Chapter 11

The Office of the President; Washington, DC—-

"Mr. President, Dr. Jack Ure, and Secretary Richards are waiting in your outer office," Beverly Yancy announced over the intercom.

"Thanks, Beverly, please send them in," President Washburn said. What does the CIA and Naval Secretary want at this early hour? He questioned.

"Mr. President," Jack Ure, said as he hurried into the Oval Office. In his hand, he gripped a classified report. Raymond Richards was close on his heels.

"Jack slow down and catch your breath," the President said. "Both of you, take a seat and grab a cup of coffee."

"Mr. President Fifth Fleet has not been able to contact *Buffalo* since they received an incomplete message five hours ago," Jack Ure said.

"Did they provide a reason?" The President asked.

"No, Sir," Raymond responded.

"So you have no idea where Scott is do you?" The President barked.

"Sir, the last message from Scott indicated he was leaving the Persian Gulf and following an Iranian submarine K-901 down the Straits of Hormoz," Richards announced.

"Didn't I order Scott to remain in the Persian Gulf?" Washburn asked.

"Yes, Mr. President," Jack Ure replied.

"So, now you're telling me he is charging off to the Gulf of Oman," Washburn snapped back.

"Scott would not leave the Gulf unless he had a good reason," Richards said. "Why he is following the Iranian submarine is still unknown."

Washburn glanced at Jack. "There is something you're not telling me."

Richards sighed. "Sir, the *Vinson* Battlegroup is heading in that direction—"

"Does Scott know the Battle Group was ordered to the Persian Gulf?" The President interrupted.

"I believe he does," Raymond replied. "But I don't know for sure."

"So you are not sure?" Washburn asked.

"I'll have to recheck his messages to verify *Buffalo* was notified of the carrier's orders," Raymond said.

"Jack, I'm getting the impression you're concerned for the battle group?" The President asked.

"Having *Buffalo* in the area will keep us better informed of their intentions once communication is reestablished," Richards interjected.

"I agree," Dr. Ure said.

"But you won't know until you can contact Scott," Washburn said, frustrated.

"Scott may have sensed the danger to the fleet. We don't know if he warned *Vinson*—" Ure began.

"So," Washburn said, deep in thought, "You think Scott did not break radio silence because he didn't want to reveal his location? Is that right?" The President asked, looking at the blank pages.

"It's the only explanation," Raymond said.

"Raymond, let's assume Scott ran off to the Gulf of Oman pursuing K-901. He did not get permission because he did not want to break radio silence. Do I understand your position?" Washburn asked, giving both of his advisers a stern look.

"Yes," Richards replied. "We selected Scott to command *Buffalo* because he is a risk taker. We all trusted his ability to make decisions while putting his ship and crew first."

Ure nodded. "Sir, we believe Scott has a good reason for his actions—"

"He damn well better. If he causes an international incident all of our asses will be in a sling," Washburn said. The President looked at the two men sitting in his office. "Both of you get the hell out and find Scott. Don't return until you tell me where he is and what he is doing."

USS Buffalo: Gulf of Oman –

Scott stood in Control and aimed his eyes at Walsh. "Commander, now that the *ASDV* is operational, I need you to have your men check their equipment." He lowered his voice. "Mike, you can expect new orders, and I want you prepared."

Walsh shrugged. "Any idea what that mission will entail?"

"Not yet," Scott replied. *I have no intention of revealing my plan to take out K-901. Jujair would not have mentioned the Vinson group without a damn good reason, he thought.*

"Whatever you need, we'll be ready," Walsh said, leaving for the SEAL's quarters.

Scott entered the Radio to receive an update on what caused the power surge. "Weathers, have you identified the problem?"

"We have removed the main power converter and found there was a short in the unit. The printed circuit boards normally supplied by twelve volts were hit by an electrical surge causing damage to the printed circuit boards," Weathers concluded. "Now that we know what caused the problem, we can replace the power converter and repair the boards."

"When will communication be restored," Scott asked.

"Within twenty-four hours," Weathers responded. "The men are working as fast as they can, Captain."

"OK! Please keep me informed on your progress," Scott said and left Radio.

Scott returned to Control and stood next to Varney. "Weathers stated it would be another twenty-four hours before we can transmit and receive our traffic. At this point, we are on our own, Tom, and my priority is to protect the fleet."

"If we don't reestablish communication Fifth Fleet and the Squadron will assume we have suffered a casualty and sunk," Varney said.

"That's a problem we'll have to face in twenty-four hours if we don't get the equipment repaired," Scott replied.

"Are you still hell-bent on placing a mine on K-901," Varney asked in a low voice.

"If necessary. When and if the time comes, you and I will work out the details. I think we need to neutralize the submarine inside the tanker," Scott said. "For now, I want you to continue drilling the Fire Control Party in case we must launch an attack on K-901, or in case the *Kilo* launches an attack on us or *Vinson*."

Chapter 12

USS Buffalo; Gulf of Oman —

Scott was in his cabin when the call came.

"Captain, regained contact on *W/T Seed*," the XO announced over the CO's intercom.

"I'll be right there." Scott grabbed his notebook and shut his door. Being alone had given him time to think. He felt ready, impatient to begin what he knew might result in a difficult decision, one that could risk his career. Entering Control, Scott walked over to the chart table. "OOD, clear baffles. XO, let's find out if sonar is correct." He leaned toward Varney. "I want to know if submarines are lurking around the tanker."

Varney nodded. "They could be on either side of the ship or inside."

After an extensive search of the surrounding area, Sorenson reported no close contacts. The area is void of Iranian submarines.

"OOD make your depth one hundred thirty feet," Scott ordered. "I want to close the supertanker," Scott ordered.

"Conn, no close contacts," Sorenson again reported.

"Permission to come to periscope depth?" the OOD, Lt. Jeff Obermeier asked.

Scott glanced at the Automatic Plot Board, a visual of *Buffalo's* contacts. He studied their position relative to his course. "Permission granted," he said as the Control party brought *Buffalo* to sixty feet.

"Hold visual on *W/T Seed*," the XO reported.

"Very well," Scott responded.

"Captain, picking up another narrowband tonal off our starboard beam,"

Sorenson announced.

"Classification?" Scott asked.

"Wait system is analyzing the data. A *Qaaem* class diesel submarine, Sorenson said. This contact just popped on our sensors from nowhere."

"Bearing?" Scott demanded, surprised by the appearance of the second submarine.

"Two-seven-zero degrees," Sorenson reported. "The contact appears to be heading for the tanker."

"Confirm contact ID?" Scott asked.

"Performing another diagnostic on the narrowband tonal. Got it! Contact verified as a *Qaaem* class submarine," Sorenson reported.

"Sonar, please explain how the hell that submarine got behind us?" Scott asked, rotating the periscope toward the bearing.

Chief Richardson responded, "I can't answer that, Sir. The *Qaaem* wasn't there when we cleared our baffles an hour ago. I can only speculate that the submarine stayed close to the coast using the fishing boats or next to the tanker to mask her tonals."

Scott continued to follow the *Qaaem* as the submarine closed the tanker. "If I had to guess, she intends to join K-901, XO." He saw the *Qaaem*'s periscope disappear.

"Captain detecting grinding noise coming from the tanker," Sorenson announced, switching his speakers to Control.

"That answers what the captain's intentions were, Tom," Scott said. Scott and the XO moved over to the chart table.

"I recommend we continue following the tanker. Our last report placed *Carl Vinson* Battlegroup three hundred miles to the south," Varney said.

"That was two days ago. Who knows where she could be today? It looks like the two submarines are along for the ride," Scott surmised. "I don't like it XO. The Iranians wouldn't have a supertanker and two submarines in the Gulf for no reason."

"They have a reason. We just don't know what it is," Varney said. "It doesn't make sense that K-901 would remove her torpedoes and replace them with mines. The area is too large to establish a choke point, and the

Straits would offer the Iranians a better location to place a barrier if that is their intention.

Scott kept studying the chart. "Let's continue trailing the tanker and see if your assumptions are correct. I'm going to my quarters to rest, Tom. Let me know when the tanker reverses course."

"Yes, Sir," Tom replied.

Scott entered his stateroom and lay down. Exhausted, he fell asleep the minute his head hit the pillow.

The squawker next to Scott's head jerked him awake. "Captain, the tanker has reversed course and is heading north," the OOD, Lt. Obermeier announced.

"Thanks, Lt. Continue following the tanker and call me when she reaches her northern boundary and turns south."

"Yes, Sir."

Scott lay awake, looking at the overhead. His mind was racing. "What are my orders? Remain in the Persian Gulf, not the Gulf of Oman," he mumbled. *Is the carrier my concern? Vinson has protection from her surface ships and aircraft. If so should I remain south and wait for the Kilo and or Qaaem to leave the supertanker? Are the Iranians intending to mine the Southern Straits? What a perfect location to place their weapons. Who would know Iran was responsible for releasing a torpedo mine at the carrier?* Scott took a deep breath. Too many questions. Not enough answers. Unable to sleep, Scott got up and headed for Control.

"XO," Scott asked, "How long before the tanker heads south?"

Varney looked at the chart. "Ten miles. The tanker just reduced speed," he replied.

"Control, picking up grinding noises again," Sorenson reported. "That has to be those clamping arms pulling away from a sub's hull," he said.

"This is the Captain! I have the Conn." Scott stepped up on the periscope platform, grabbed the handlebars, and looked into the eyepiece. "Talk to me, Sorenson!"

Sorenson replied, "Cavitation increasing. A submarine is leaving the nest, Captain."

"Is it K-901?" Scott asked

"Too early to tell due to the thrashing noise from the tanker's screw," Senior Chief Paul Richardson replied.

"Captain, K-901 is leaving the tanker," Sorenson said.

"Can you maintain track of her?" Scott asked.

"Yes, Sir, we have a good signal to track," Sorenson replied.

"Tom, let's follow K-901 to determine if she is heading to the Straits."

"You believe she is intending to lay mines, Captain?" Varney asked.

"Yes. If I'm correct she has replaced her torpedoes with floating and torpedo mines," Scott replied.

"And the *Qaaem*?" Varney continued.

"We'll have to wait and see if she joins K-901," Scott said. "I see only two options if they intend to stop the Battlegroup. First placing floating mines across the Southern Strait would slow the ships down, but not stop them."

"And their second?" Varney asked.

"Lay torpedo mines and trigger their release when the carrier crosses the minefield. The latter is the best of the two. As you said, the Iranians can claim they were not responsible for the attack. Our ships were warned not to enter the Southern Strait."

"It falls on us to notify the Battlegroup of their mining operations. I'll be damned if I will leave the Battlegroup unguarded," Scott said in a tart voice.

Chapter 13

USS Buffalo; Gulf of Oman –

"May we join you?" Scott asked as he and the XO entered the wardroom. The ongoing midnight watch was eating Midrats, a mixture of leftovers from lunch and dinner.

"Please do," Weapons Officer Steve Wilkinson replied.

Scott looked down at the table at the men and women eating. His eyes lingered at seeing Janice talking to Dr. Fred Stone. How much longer do I have to wait before I can wrap my arms around you, he thought. I was such a fool to walk away. Getting the Navy to issue the university a million-dollar grant for your support was an excellent idea to get you back in my life. I will never let you go.

"Captain—- Captain," Lt. Obermeier said.

"What, sorry I was —-"

"How do you know the submarine is carrying mines?" Obermeier asked.

The XO intervened. "During our excursion under the tanker, we saw torpedoes removed and mines loaded," Varney said. "If she places those mines in the Southern Straits, *Carl Vinson* could be in jeopardy of being attacked. I—"

The phone rang under the table next to the Captain's knee, interrupting the conversation. Scott pulled the phone from the cradle. "Captain."

Janice saw Scott's forehead crease. "I'll be right there. XO, please join me."

As Scott entered sonar, Sorenson was announcing that K-901 was maneuvering from her previous course. "I heard?" Scott said, looking over Sorenson's shoulder.

"Captain, I think the target is reversing course. At first, I thought it was just another baffle clear, but K-901's turning radius is much broader," Sorenson added.

"Let me know," Scott said, leaving Sonar and entering Control.

"Senior Chief Russell, what was the range to K-901 before she changed course?" Scott asked.

"Five thousand yards," Russell answered, reading the dial on the Attack Console.

"OOD, let's back off," Scott ordered. "We'll hold our position until we are sure she is heading into the Straits. Call me when he returns to base course, I'll be in the wardroom."

"Yes, Sir," Lt. Obermeier replied.

The two engineers from the Naval Underwater Warfare Center were discussing Hunter's test results while waiting for the Captain.

Dr. Mehman, the Iranian defector, sat nearby reading a novel the XO had given him. His information had proven invaluable in helping Scott and the SEALs destroy the nuclear weapon facility.

Patricia Morton and Janice were reviewing the results of their last acoustic test. Patricia was finding it hard to concentrate with the tap, tap, tap from Lace's pencil.

"Are you okay, professor?" Morton asked with a smile like a Cheshire cat.

Janice looked up. "Sorry. I was lost in thought."

Lt. Morton grinned. She had watched Janice become tense every time she saw Scott.

"Good morning," Scott said. He noted the two women had developed an excellent working relationship. He wondered if they had become friends.

"I must talk with all of you now." Scott sat down and looked into each person's eyes, staring a moment longer at Janice. "As you know, I'm remaining in the Gulf for the near future."

"Which Gulf are you referring to?" Dr. Thomas asked.

Scott ignored the comment. "Up until two hours ago, we were tracking a submarine, K-901. Suddenly, it disappeared. Nearby was a supertanker, W/T Seed. At first, we didn't think much about it. But then we observed K-901 emerging from under the tanker."

"I don't understand, Captain," Janice said.

Scott nodded. "I didn't either, but we believe the tanker is a support ship for the Iranian navy." He shrugged. "We found K-901 inside the tanker. Weapons were being transferred from the tanker to the submarine."

"The submarine was inside the tanker?" Janice asked.

Scott nodded.

"Why are you so concerned about this K-901?" Lt. Morton asked.

"Before I answer your question, I must ask you to read and sign the Disclosure Letters the XO is placing in front of you," Scott said.

Scott and Tom Varney waited for the people to read the letters.

"To answer your question," the XO continued. "During the next 48 to 72 hours, this ship and crew might have to defend American Forces. What transpires on board this ship must not be disclosed to anyone. Your signature at the bottom indicates you understand what I just told you. Are there any questions?"

Scott asked, looking directly at Janice. He quickly brought his attention back to the group.

They all shook their heads.

The room fell silent as each person read and signed the Non-Disclosure Letters.

"Okay, please hand them back to the XO for his signature."

"Now that we discovered an Iranian supertanker used to transport and supply submarines, I'm concerned that there might be an attack against the carrier as she enters the Straits. A well-placed torpedo from one of her torpedo mines could cripple a ship."

"What concerns me is we found not one, but two diesel submarines in the area," Scott continued. "The XO and I agree the second submarine could be locked inside the tanker and loading torpedo mines right now. I'm sure each of you understands my position. If I'm required to defend the fleet, from an attack I will not hesitate."

"What you are saying is if the K-901 launches an attack at the carrier, you would counter and launch your torpedoes?" Dr. Stone asked.

"Correct," Scott replied. "I will have no alternative. Until the carrier's support submarine arrives *Buffalo's* job is to protect the ships."

"If you hear Man Battle Stations, Torpedo," Varney said. "I want you to sit in the wardroom unless directed elsewhere. Just sit tight. For now, go down and make sure your equipment is secure."

"Captain, Sonar, K-901 has reversed course."

"Hold any other questions until later," Scott said, as he and the XO left the wardroom.

Janice reflected on the time she signed a similar NDL three years ago while assigned to *Buffalo*. She had never realized the tremendous responsibility and pressure Joe was under. *I know he is ready for a fight. I only hope it doesn't cost him his career.*

Chapter 14

K-901; Southern End of the Straits of Hormuz –

"Captain Karini, we are entering the Southern Straits," Lieutenant Nouri Norouzi reported, looking down at the navigation chart as he spoke.

K-901 call sign Ali Biba just completed her transit to the southern border.

"XO, surface the boat. We will top off the batteries while we wait for new orders."

"Captain, do you think it is wise to give the Americans the opportunity to detect us from their satellite?" the XO questioned.

"Satellite? I'm not interested in what the eyes in the sky see. I'm waiting for the American submarine trailing me to expose himself."

"There has been no report from sonar that we have detected an American submarine," the XO said.

"True, but I have had a nagging feeling an American boat has followed us. The only way to determine if my suspicion is correct is to surface and wait. If I were the American Captain, I could not resist checking out what he found. It is a good time to top off our batteries before returning to the tanker," Captain Karini said. "It's better they see us at this location. I don't want them sniffing around the tanker when we return to load torpedoes."

USS Buffalo; Straits of Hormuz –

Scott entered Radio as First-Class Weathers received an update on the repairs to the communication system.

"Captain, I'm afraid the repairs will take another five hours. The damage caused by the electrical surge was more extensive than we initially reported. Once we complete our repairs, we will reboot the system to ensure all equipment is working."

"Great! I want you to resend our message traffic as soon as the equipment has been tested. Carl Vinson needs to be warned."

"Yes, Sir," Weather replied.

"Captain to Sonar," Sorenson called.

"Report," Scott said, leaving Radio and stepping into Sonar.

"The contact slowed. Wait! Now she's blowing ballast tanks, and her diesel just came online," Sorenson said.

"Conn, OOD come left to zero-nine-zero, speed five knots," Scott ordered, returning with the XO to Control. "He must feel pretty sure of himself surfacing and exposing his location. Navigator, when does the satellite KH-11 pass over again?" he asked.

"The next pass will be in seven hours, Captain," Obermeier replied.

"OOD come to PD, drop fifteen turns," Scott ordered. After clearing the baffles, he raised the search periscope and found K-901 sitting on the surface. "Down scope," he snapped, hoping his periscope remained undetected. "The surface is as smooth as glass."

"It doesn't make sense. Why the hell would he surface?" The XO asked.

"It does if he intends to remain underwater for an extended period. To attack any of our surface units, he will need to charge his battery bank to provide the power he'll need," Scott said. "Either way, we're the big stick here to pound his sorry ass if he intends to launch an attack against our ships. God help him and his crew if it comes to that."

"Control, we detected a thirty-hertz frequency and a thirty megahertz high-frequency radar designated, Shark Gill and Mouse Roar, the intelligence operator reported.

"Now we know why we have not seen nor heard the destroyers in the past two days, Tom. They're patrolling the southern portion of the Straits." Scott said. "Not only must we dodge their submarines, and mines, but also their destroyers. It looks like the fun just got started."

Hawkeye 'Super-Fudd 2; Straits of Hormuz —

Jettisoned off the carrier *Vinson,* Hawkeye Super Fudd 2 circled twenty-five thousand feet, above the straits of Hormuz. The pilot's sensor operator heard an audio alert. He had been monitoring over one hundred square miles of the ocean's surface of the Persian Gulf and the northern Straits of Hormoz. The warning from a surfaced submarine was just another dot on a full scope. This dot radiated a signal from a Russian radar, NATO designated Mouse Roar. He keyed the target information to the plane's data link and sent the target parameters to *Carl Vinson.*

K-901

Captain Karini stood on the bridge, watching the submarine's bullnose push aside the dark sea. The air was fresh, crisp, and absent of land dust created by the many storms this time of year. He felt the bow rise and fall with each long groundswell. The breeze, created by K-901's headway, gently brushed against his face. He placed the binoculars to his eyes and scanned the horizon. He saw a distant masthead light.

"Captain, our electronic surveillance sensors detected the radars of our destroyers to the north," the OOD announced from Control.

"They are searching the Straits for American submarines," Karini responded. "OOD, inform the operator to keep his eyes open. We might catch an American shark lurking around."

"Yes, Sir."

The Captain listened to the deep throbbing of the exhaust from the twin five thousand KW propulsion motors echoing off the surface. It is a perfect evening to capture the essence of Allah, he thought not realizing his XO, Lieutenant Commander Pejman, had climbed up to the bridge.

"Captain, our radar operator reported intermittent radar contacts off our port bow," Pejman said.

"Looks like we caught the shark, XO." Karini raised his binoculars again and peered far over the bow.

"Lookouts keep a sharp eye," Pejman called to the men above him. "Captain, your hunch was correct. The Americans have arrived."

"The important question remains unanswered: Have they been trailing us from the Supertanker?" Karini asked.

"I doubt if they suspect our trap," Pejman said.

"We'll need to be more vigilant," Karini said. "Radar, do you still hold an intermittent contact?" He asked over the intercom.

"No, Sir. The last contact was at four thousand meters (4,300 yds)," the operator reported.

"Captain, we just received a communication from Vice Admiral Salehi," a seaman said, handing him the message board.

Karini read the contents and handed it to his Executive Officer. "It appears our orders have arrived, XO. We are to lay eighteen floating impact mines and six torpedo mines on an east-to-west axis across the entrance to the Straits. Once placed, we're to return to the Great Prophet, *W/T Seed*, and reload torpedoes. Our government has decided to follow through on its threats and close the Straits."

"Captain, the batteries are topped off," the engineer reported over the ship's intercom.

"Very well, clear the bridge. OOD, prepare to submerge. Dive, Dive, Dive the Captain shouted." The clanging of the dive alarm resonated throughout the submarine.

The officers and lookouts descended the ladder to Control.

"XO," Karini said, stepping down from the ladder. "Set Ultra-Quiet and proceed to one hundred meters (328 ft). Let's hover to allow Sonar to search the waters around us. We might get lucky and verify an American submarine is sniffing around."

"With Allah's help," Pejman replied.

Karini nodded. "And the ears and eyes of our sonarmen," he added.

"Captain," Pejman said moving over to the plotting table. "I have designated the first mine as King Pin. The second mine is one thousand eighteen hundred meters (1,968 yds) from the first along a zero-nine-zero baseline." The XO marked the mines on the chart. "The next mine, I would place one thousand eighteen hundred meters west and the next one thousand eighteen hundred meters east. We will soon have all eighteen mines in the water."

"Excellent!" Karini said.

"It will make it more difficult for the enemy surface ships to locate and destroy in a sawtooth pattern. With the mines at the entrance, we will control the Straits. Insh'Allah, God Willing," the XO said.

"And where would you suggest we deploy the six torpedo mines? Forward or behind the floating mined?" Karini asked.

"Suggest they are placed forward of the minefield two thousand yards apart in the center of the Strait," Pejman suggested.

"That will allow us to control the center," Karini said. "I like the idea of the mines across the entrance and the torpedo mines resting on the bottom. The downside of this will be if the Americans discover our mines before the enemy carrier arrives."

"True. But the mines will still act as a deterrent, delaying the American Naval forces from entering the Straits," Pejman said. "And if they find out what can they do?"

Karini smiled. "Okay. Let's move to the center and prepare to launch the torpedo mines first. Once we complete laying all our mines, we must maintain Ultra-Quiet as we return to *W/T Seed*. Vigilance and stealth are the keys to our success."

"Yes, Sir," Pejman said, glancing at a new report. "Captain, the intermittent contact reported earlier has to be an American submarine," he said. "The American carriers normally travel with one or two submarines for protection."

"Sonar, take one more sweep of the area and report all contacts," Karini ordered. "XO, prepare to launch our mines once we know the area is clear."

"Yes, Sir." Pressing down the switch to the torpedo room, "Torpedo room standby to launch torpedo mines," Pejman announced.

Karini was anxious to attack the carrier as she entered the barrier. Allah be praised he whispered, hungering for the kill.

USS *Buffalo*

Scott received the report that K-901 was descending to three hundred feet. "OOD send a Messenger through the boat to verify Ultra-Quiet conditions are still in effect."

A hush fell over Control as the ventilation system was shut down.

The XO noted that critical equipment was still operating. With the air conditioning off, he felt the temperature begin to rise.

"Engineering, switch main reactor cooling pumps to slow speed," Scott ordered.

"Control, main coolant pumps are at slow speed," Dennis Fender, the ship's engineering officer, replied.

"Torpedo room, this is the Captain. Flood tubes one through four."

"Conn, Tubes one through four flooded, equalized, and outer doors open," Chief Torpedoman, Juststone reported.

"Weapon parameters entered and waiting for the order to release," Varney said.

"Very well," Scott replied. "Now we wait. Radio, is the communication satellite still overhead?"

"Yes, Sir. Captain. For another ten minutes," Weathers replied. "All communication with Fifth Fleet and *Carl Vinson* has been restored."

"Did our backlog of messages get released?" Scott asked.

"Yes, Sir," Weathers responded. "We are downloading our message traffic from the satellite now."

"OK! Inform your men great job. Bring me our traffic as soon as possible." Scott said. *Scott knew a reprimand from Washington for leaving the Persian Gulf would be forthcoming.*

"Control, Sonar, K-901 is on the move," Sorenson announced over the sound-powered phones.

"Officer of the Deck, send duty personnel throughout the ship to alert the crew to Man Battle Stations, Torpedo," Scott ordered. He waited for Control personnel to arrive and assumed their battle stations. The room soon filled with 20 additional men.

"K-901 is on a heading of one hundred degrees, five knots," Varney announced.

"Range to target?" Scott asked.

"Four thousand yards and closing," Varney replied.

"Let's stay in his baffles and maintain a one thousand five hundred yard separation. We will remain at Battle Stations until we can determine his intentions," Scott said. He felt his back start to tense up.

"Picking up hydraulics. Sounds like the sub outer doors are opening," Sorenson announced with alarm.

Scott waited, ready to give the order to launch a spread of Mk-48 torpedoes. He looked around Control. He knew from previous events the men were as tense as he was, and the heat in the room did not help. As for himself, his shoulders were in a knot, and his back was dripping wet. Still, he waited. Would K-901 launch a torpedo at *Buffalo*?

Janice and Patricia grabbed their robes and ran forward to the wardroom. They arrived just three seconds after the two NUWC engineers.

"Oh, Shit!" Patricia shouted, running back out.

"She forgot Dr. Mehman," Janice explained.

Two minutes later, Lieutenant Morton reentered the room with the Iranian physicist in tow.

"What is happening?" he asked, an anxious look on his face.

"Yes, what is happening?" Dr. Stone asked, looking around the table.

"Sonar has been tracking K-901 for the past eight hours. The submarine is preparing to launch either a torpedo or a mine. I was talking to Sorenson when he detected what appeared to be outer torpedo doors opening," Dr. Thomas said, the tension in his voice. "The CO appears to be taking significant risks," he added.

Janice looked angrily at the engineer. "Captain Scott is a risk-taker but not reckless. The safety of the crew and the boat will always be his main concern."

Dr. Thomas was taken aback by the forcefulness of Janice's defense of Commander Scott's current actions. "I meant no offense," he said.

"I think we are all a little uneasy at the possibility of what might happen," Patrica said.

"Do you think Captain Scott will attack?" Dr. Mehman asked.

"Only if they launch at us," Janice replied. "I bet the submarine is lining up to deploy torpedo mines in the Straits. What better place to attack and sink our naval units?" She thought of Scott and what he must be going through. All of their lives depended on his decisions. "I have every confidence, the Captain will make the right calls," she said, hoping the others believed her.

Chapter 15

The Office of the President—

"Mr. President, I have Admiral Armstrong sitting in my office," The President's secretary announced.

"Send him in, Beverly," Washburn said, interrupting his conversation with Dr. Ure.

Admiral Armstrong entered the room. "Mr. President, you asked me to notify you when I receive a message from Commander Scott."

"Well? Let's have it," The President snapped. "Does he give a reason why he failed to contact this office?"

"Scott reported he had a fire in the radio and lost all communication," Armstrong said. "He also stated he was still in the Gulf of Oman—"

"What? Did you say? He's still in the Gulf of Oman?" The President interrupted. "He is not in the Persian Gulf as he was ordered? Scott had specific orders to remain in the Gulf and collect data on Iran's mining and submarine operations. Contact Scott and order him back to the Persian Gulf."

"Yes, Sir, but first I recommend you read this message before I issue that order," Armstrong said, handing the President the communique.

The President started to read the report when Jack Ure interrupted. "Mr. President, Commander Scott must have had a good reason to disobey orders and leave the Persian Gulf."

"He damn well better, or I'll have him court-martialed. He found what?" Washburn exclaimed still reading the report. "What does this mean?" he asked Armstrong.

"The *Kilo* he was tracking disappeared and Scott found it inside a supertanker," Armstrong said, handing Washburn the photos."

"Submarines inside a tanker?" Washburn said. He studied each picture. He let out an exasperated sigh as he handed them to Jack Ure. "Damn the Iranians. Do they want to start a war? They could attack our ships without us knowing they were near. Where is this supertanker now?"

Dr. Ure interrupted. "The Gulf of Oman. The National Geospatial Agency reported the ship has been transiting up and down the Gulf for several weeks."

"I'm just finding out about this now? The President asked. "You knew about the supertanker, Jack?" Washburn asked.

"Yes, Mr. President. I was notified by the Director of the Agency. I felt there was no need to bring it to your attention."

"Anything that involves Scott or the Gulf must be brought to my attention. Understood?," Washburn demanded.

"Yes, Sir, Ure replied. "At the time I didn't know the tanker was being used to transport Iranian submarines. I thought it was just what it appeared to be, a run-of-the-mill tanker. Nothing more," looking slightly embarrassed.

"Again keep me informed of anything pertaining to either Gulf."

"Mr. President, now that Scott has found a *Kilo* locked inside the tanker, he must remain in the Gulf and determine what their intentions are," Armstrong said. "A second submarine known as the *Qaaem* is now also inside the tanker."

"You're telling me there is another Iranian submarine inside the tanker? When did you—"

Dr. Ure interrupted. "Scott is currently following the *Kilo* north. He believes the Iranians might place mines across the Southern Straits leading into the Straits of Hormuz."

Washburn's face reddened as he again looked at the pictures. "Admiral, countermand my previous order. Scott must remain in the Gulf of Oman. Have him report if Iran mines the Southern Straits."

"Yes, Sir," Armstrong acknowledged the orders.

"Mr. President," Jack Ure again interrupted. "I need to remind you..." He scribbled a note on his pad and held it in front of Washburn. "Of your next meeting."

Turn off the recorder, Ure's note read.

"Yes, Yes, I almost forgot," Washburn mumbled, getting up and walking around his desk. He reached under the left corner and switched off the recorder. "Damn, that was close," he said. Reading further Washburn asked, "Did Scott suggest how he was going to prohibit the Iranian submarine from attacking the fleet?" flipping through several pages of the message.

"No, Mr. President. Scott understands the Rules of Engagement. I don't believe he would take it upon himself to initiate an attack on the ship of a sovereign country," Dr. Ure stated.

The President tapped his pen as he thought of the repercussions of Scott attacking an Iranian submarine. Keep me informed of Scott's movements. I will not authorize an attack on an Iranian submarine unless there's a damn good reason."

Chapter 16

USS Buffalo; Straits of Hormuz –

The temperature in Control was becoming unbearable. Watchstanders were sweating profusely. No one moved or said a word. Scott wondered if the *Kilo's* Captain had detected his presence.

"Control, hold a loud water noise coming from K-901," Sorenson announced,

"Is it a torpedo?" Scott asked, ready to react if needed.

"No, Sir. K-901 just deployed a mine," Sorenson replied.

Scott breathed a sigh of relief, *Buffalo* was not under attack.

"Senior Chief Russell, mark our position on the DRT and place a note, floating mine," the XO ordered, stepping away from the weapon console.

"Captain, K-901 is changing course to the north," Sorenson reported.

"Where the hell is he going?" Scott asked, seeing the bearing dots move across the screen.

"K-901 is slowing," Sorenson announced. "Captain, he just launched another mine."

"She is changing course again," Senior Chief Russell reported. "Heading south this time. It appears he is laying a sawtooth pattern," he said while marking the third mine on the chart.

"XO range and speed to the target?" Scott asked.

"Two thousand yards, speed six knots," Varney reported.

"OOD, make your depth two hundred feet. Let's remain in his baffles and under the mines," Scott ordered.

Buffalo continued to monitor the deployment of eighteen mines.

"Captain, K-901 is changing course, increasing speed, and heading south," Sorenson reported.

"K-901 has deployed eighteen floating mines in a sawtooth pattern across the entrance of the Straits," Scott said, looking at their location on the chart.

"Captain the *Kilo* is moving toward the center of the Strait in front of the floating mines," Sorenson reported.

"What is he up to now?" Scott asked turning to Varney.

"Maybe he's maneuvering to launch additional mines," Varney responded.

"Weapon launch! Weapon in the water!" Sorenson shouted.

"Standby tubes one and two," Scott ordered trying to appear calm. Inwardly his anxiety raged.

Varney raised his hand, to release the torpedoes on Scott's command.

"Talk to me, Sorenson," Scott ordered.

"Weapon heading south and diving toward the sea floor. Wait! The torpedo just shut down," Sorensen reported.

"He's launching torpedo mines, Skipper," Varney said.

Scott breathed a sigh of relief. "Damn, that was close. I was seconds away from launching a pair of Mk-48 torpedoes."

Over the next forty minutes, sonar reported that K-901 launched five additional torpedo mines.

Scott monitored each weapon as it was marked on the chart. The tension in his back and shoulders never let up.

"Captain K-901 has increased speed to eight knots," Senior Chief Jack Russell announced, reading the output from the Fire Control Panel.

"I think K-901 may be returning to the tanker to reload," Varney said. "Recommend we secure from Battle Stations, Torpedo, Captain."

"I agree," Scott breathed a sigh of relief. His shirt was soaked from sweat. "Dr. Lace and Lt. Morton report to Control," Scott ordered over the 1MC. He looked up just as both of *Buffalo*'s female passengers entered.

"Captain, you sent for us?" Janice asked.

Scott aimed his eyes at Janice. "I want to send a message informing the fleet of the locations of the mines we recorded on the Dead Reckoning Trace (DRT). Would both of you work with the second class and provide the best guess of the drift pattern based on taking account of the wind and current in this area."

"Are they floating mines?" Janice asked.

"Yes. There are two sets of mines. Eighteen floating and six torpedo mines. The location of each mine is recorded on the DRT." He handed Janice a sheet of paper. "Here is the latest weather report for this area."

"Okay, Joe, uh, Captain, we'll start right away."

Scott ignored the slip. He looked at Lt. Morton. "Once the two of you have calculated the drift of the floating mines, provide the report to the XO."

"Nav, when is our next satellite pass?" Varney asked.

"Our satellite will be within range in ten minutes," Lt. Jeff Obermeier replied.

"OOD, conduct a baffle clear before we raise the antenna," Scott ordered. "Tom, when you receive their report, let's link up with the satellite. Address the message to *Carl Vinson,* Fifth Fleet, and Squadron Fifteen. OOD you have the Conn. I'll be in the wardroom."

In the wardroom, the Weapons Officer, Steve Wilkinson, and Scott discussed the mines launched by K-901. "If I am correct in the number of mines recorded on the DRT she can't be carrying any torpedoes. I am willing to bet K-901 will need to return to the supertanker and reload," Scott said.

"If so, it makes our job much easier knowing where she intends to go," Varney added. Having the submarine locked inside of the tanker would make it easier if we wanted to place a limped mine on her hull, he thought.

"Captain to Sonar," Sorenson called over the intercom.

"Let's go, XO," Scott said, hurrying out of the wardroom and up the ladder to sonar.

"I just lost the target," Sorenson said. "One minute the K-901 was off our port beam, the next the tonal disappeared. I think she secured her electric drive and is drifting."

Scott returned to Control. "OOD, all stop," he ordered. "XO, have all departments verify personnel not on duty are in their racks. Do we know why she stopped?" he asked.

"Maneuvering! Did anything happen in engineering that may have caused a noise transient?" the OOD asked.

"No, Sir— belay my last. The Duty Watch Supervisor just reported the off-going engine Room Upper-Level duty machinist knocked off a heavy valve onto the deck plate. It might have resulted in a noise spike," the Engineering Officer reported.

"How long do you intend to drift?" the XO asked Scott.

"We'll wait until he moves," Scott replied. "I don't want to give away our position."

K-901: *Straits of Hormuz –*

"What did you hear, Torsi?" Captain Karini asked his leading sonar technician. His anxiety grew as he waited for Torsi to complete his passive search.

"Not sure. I thought I heard a bang moments ago off the starboard beam. It might have been an anomaly."

"Keep looking. There have been too many irregularities. There may be another submarine in these waters. It could be an Israeli or an American predator," Karini said, returning to Control. "OOD, let me know when we reach forty meters (131 feet). Chief of the Boat (COB), deploy the floating antenna. I want to collect our message traffic," he ordered. "Pejman, do you ever get the sense that someone is watching us? I feel the eyes of an American submarine boring through our hull."

"Yes," Pejman responded, "I fear it's been too quiet. To my knowledge, an American Battlegroup always has an accompanying submarine searching the area ahead of their ships."

Turning to his XO, "Where is their Battle Group located?" Karini asked.

"Our last report placed the ships in the Arabian Sea, three hundred miles from our location," Pejman replied.

"That would place them two hundred miles from the tanker," Karini said.

"Correct depending on if the tanker was to the north. The battle group would be much closer when the *W/T Seed* is in the southern quadrant," the XO said.

"I know you are out there, Madar Ghahbe, motherfucker," Karini mumbled. His anger and frustration grew at not detecting the predator he felt sure that was shadowing him. "*So, we play the game. Who will make the first move?*"

After two hours, K-901 reached forty meters.

Sonar kept sweeping the area, reporting only broadband noise from passing fishing boats and commercial shipping.

Returning to sonar, Karini asked. "Anything?"

"No, Sir, but until we maneuver I can't check our baffles," Sonar Technician Specialist Pahlavi said.

"Keep listening," Karini ordered, aggravated at not detecting the submarine. "Once we reach thirty meters (100 feet), I will maneuver the boat to allow you to search our baffle region," he said, leaving for Control.

"OOD, continue to hold until we reach thirty meters," Karini whispered the order, then headed for the wardroom.

The Captain, drinking hot mint tea with his Executive Officer, told of the time he had patrolled the mouth of the Straits of Hormuz in search of American nuclear submarines. "I don't think their skipper expected us to be waiting in the area. He was at periscope depth with their communication masts extended."

"Were you able to detect any radiated noise?" Pejman asked.

"Yes, but only when we closed to within one thousand yards. Even then, sonar could not maintain solid contact with the American submarine. After the boat submerged, it didn't take long before we lost him."

The phone buzzed from under the table.

"Karini," responded the CO placing the receiver next to his ear.

"Captain, we are at thirty meters," Lieutenant Norouzi reported.

"Very well. Has sonar detected any further contacts in the area?" the Captain asked.

"No, Sir," Norouzi replied.

"Lieutenant, conduct a ninety-degree baffle clear to port and starboard, then make your depth one hundred twenty meters (393 ft), speed seven knots, and lay a course to return to the tanker. The time has come to show the arrogant Americans that Iran will defend our sovereign waters. I want all divisions to prepare for battle."

"Allah be praised. Allah be praised," the officers kept shouting.

"I will enjoy hearing the sounds of an American ship imploding as it sinks to the bottom of the sea," the XO said.

Chapter 17

The Office of the President; Washington, DC –

"Mr. President, Dr. Mohammad Yazdi is here to see you," Mrs. Yancy announced.

"Does he have an appointment?" Washburn asked wondering why the Iranian Ambassador would call without an appointment.

"He does not," Beverly replied. "He demands to see you now."

"He demands?" Washburn hesitated. "Alright send him in, Beverly," The President said not looking forward to a meeting.

The tall, overweight Iranian ambassador entered the Oval Office.

Washburn had been meeting with Sally Wheatfield, the Deputy National Security Advisor, Dr. Ure, and Ian Williams, the President's Chief-of-Staff. They were discussing the Iranian mining in the Persian Gulf when Dr. Mohammand demanded a meeting.

"Mr. President," Dr. Mohammad Yazdi spoke in a hurried voice.

"Tea or coffee, Mr. Ambassador?" Sally Wheatfield offered as Margaret Rice Secretary of State entered the office.

The ambassador waved his hand dismissively. He had not acknowledged any of the members of the President's staff. "I'm here to inform you my government firmly believes the United States is responsible for the attack on our weapons facility."

"Mr. Ambassador, I can assure you my government was not involved in any attack," President Washburn responded, becoming impatient.

"Mr. President," the Ambassador continued. "I think we can dispense with your government's denial, don't you?"

"Mr. Ambassador, I was as surprised as your government was when I learned of the attack—"

"You should not be. Your Special Forces were responsible," the Ambassador replied loudly. "Our government is well aware of the clandestine operations of one of your submarines operating in the Persian Gulf. That weapon facility was developing conventional torpedoes. Yet your government seemed to overlook that fact and destroyed it without regard for the consequences."

"Consequences? Again, I will state my government was not responsible for the attack on that facility." Washburn countered. "Mr. Ambassador," the President, started to respond—

The Ambassador raised his hand, stopping the President in mid-sentence. "I am here to inform your government Iran is closing the North and Southern Straits of Hormuz."

"Your government is preventing access to international waters?" Washburn asked.

"You are mistaken, Mr. President," The Ambassador said. "The Straits of Hormuz are not in international waters. The international Courts ruled the waters between Iran on the northern side of the Straits and Oman on the southern side are sovereign waters. Under international law, such Straits are territorial waters of the adjoining nations."

"My government has never agreed with the ruling," Washburn said.

"It makes no difference whether your government agrees. The water, the seabed, the air above - all is the sovereign territory of those coastal states. At present, our navy is mining the Southern Straits. You can inform your Naval ships they enter at their own risk. Iran will not be responsible if any of your ships are sunk or damaged by mines."

"I disagree —"

"Good day," The Ambassador said leaving the room.

Washburn watched in disbelief as Ambassador Yazdi left. Not accustomed to people having the final word, he looked up at Sally Wheatfield, letting out an exasperated sigh. He pressed the button on his intercom. "Beverly recall the Security Council," he ordered.

Security Council Meeting—

"My meeting," The President began, "with Ambassador Yazdi did not end well. Iran has closed the Straits of Hormoz to all military traffic. Thanks to Scott, we already knew the Iranians were mining the Southern Straits."

"Mr. President, I recommend our foreign embassies and our military bases in the Gulf Region go on alert," General Shaw, Joint Chief of Staff, declared. "I also suggest we move the Amphibious Assault Group into the Persian Gulf."

"I am not sure it would be wise, Mr. President," Margaret Rice argued. "Iran might interpret the build-up as a prelude to the U.S. preparing to launch an attack against them."

"Then I suggest we place our embassies on alert and increase satellite surveillance in the area," General Shaw encouraged.

"I agree, General. Also, increase the number of Marines at our Embassies in that region," Washburn ordered.

"Yes, Sir." The General made a note on his iPad.

"Raymond, notify Fifth Fleet to hold all commercial traffic leaving the Persian Gulf. Do we have enough Naval ships to conduct escort services?"

"No, Sir, Mr. President," Raymond responded. "All Naval units attached to the Northern Battlegroup are one hundred miles south of Kuwait City."

"So, ships transiting the Straits and the Persian Gulf are on their own?" General Shaw commented.

"It looks that way," The President replied. "Jack, notify the commercial shipping companies the Straits are being mined. Inform them the US Navy is unable to escort them."

"Yes, Sir," the CIA director Jack Ure responded.

"This will surely slow down or stop the oil coming to the US," Margaret Rice stated.

"Unless one of you has a recommendation, I don't see, what we can do about this," Washburn said.

The Oval Office of the President—

"Admiral Armstrong, what type of mines have the Iranians placed in the Southern and Northern Straits?" The President asked.

"Floating and torpedo mines. The floating mines can be spotted on the surface. The major problem is the torpedo mines. They sit at the bottom of the ocean and are triggered by an Iran submarine or surface ships," the Admiral concluded.

"Can we eliminate the torpedo mines, Admiral?" Washburn asked.

"There is no way any of our MH-53E Sea Dragon helicopters would be able to locate each bottom mine. The only solution is to search for the antennas attached to each torpedo mine," Admiral Armstrong said. "We must count on Scott to locate the triggering submarine and prevent the boat from releasing a torpedo mine."

"What is your recommendation Admiral," the President asked.

"Scott must eliminate the trigger," Armstrong suggested.

"And how the hell do you suggest he does that?" Washburn asked.

"I guess we'll have to wait and see what Commander Scott intends to do to protect our fleet," Armstrong replied.

Chapter 18

USS Buffalo; Gulf of Oman –

Scott sat in his stateroom with only his desk lamp lit. He thumbed through the photos of K-901 tucked in the belly of the supertanker. His gut told him the Iranian submarine captains were preparing to attack the carrier once the Battlegroup entered the southern straits. Scott realized under the rules of engagement (ROE) not to launch a weapon at an adversary unless attacked first.

He conjectured that the submarines concealed inside *W/T Seed* were a threat to the Naval ships. *Knowing what I believe the Iranians are planning, how do I rationalize placing a mine on the hull of K-901?* "My orders are to track Iranian submarines. Not start a war by attacking their boats," Scott said to himself.

Scott sat back and reflected on why he received command of *Buffalo*. His reputation as a risk-taker, he knew was a significant factor. But how far do I go in placing my crew and the woman I love in harm's way? Attacking another submarine is grounds for a court-martial at the least. Or jail time in Leavenworth never to see the light of day. He shuddered at the thought.

Scott heard a knock at his door.

"Enter!"

"Captain," Varney said as he entered and sat down on a chair. "K-901 continues to head south. We are three thousand yards astern of her, and I estimate she will rendezvous with *W/T Seed* within the hour."

"Tom, I've been sitting here trying to determine how to eliminate K-901 from launching torpedo mines. I'm willing to bet the *Qaaem* is now heading to the Straits to lay additional torpedo mines. We know from Dr. Mehman that those mines have a floating antenna and require an external trigger to launch the weapon. If we allow K-901 to reload and head for the Straits, two submarines will be able to trigger the release of those weapons."

"What are your options, Joe," Varney asked.

"Placing a limped mine on the hull of K-901 or wait for her to attack the carrier."

"I would say your first option counters our orders of rules of engagement (ROE). The second option will end with Washington screaming for your court-martial."

"You and I know if the Iranians launch the torpedo mines, there is nothing we can do to stop them from sinking the carrier," Scott replied. "Tom you and I agree finding each antenna is impossible. Not to mention we would jeopardize being detected."

"I can't let that happen," Scott said in a raised voice hands clinched tight "The Iranians will repudiate any responsibility for the attack on our ships. I'm going out on a limb by stating Washington knows about the mines across the Southern Straits. For now, let's wait and see if Washington or Fifth Fleet has any suggestions after you send what we have found."

"I will go and draft a message with the pictures we have collected," Varney replied.

Scott looked at Varney. "If we don't get a reply in several hours, I must consider my first option and place a mine on K-901. At least we would remove one trigger leaving Qaaem to deal with."

Weathers knocked on Scott's stateroom door and entered. "Captain, we just received this message from Fifth Fleet. Admiral Armstrong will contact you shortly."

"Did the message indicate what he wanted to discuss?"

"No, Sir," Weathers responded.

"Thanks," Scott said, anticipating a rebuke from Washington's dissatisfaction for leaving the Gulf.

"We'll find out soon, " Varney said.

"My guess will be a reprimand for leaving the Gulf," Scott said.

"Admiral Armstrong," Weathers announced, handing the phone to Scott. Weathers left the radio room.

"Commander Scott," The Captain said, speaking into the classified phone.

"Captain, Please clear the room," Armstrong ordered.

"Admiral, only my XO is here."

"Captain, the President, has reviewed your last message and the photos. Your orders are to protect the fleet. How you do this is up to you. You will receive no authorization to attack a sovereign country's property. I understand the importance of neutralizing K 901. At this time I'm not ordering you to launch a weapon unless the Iranian submarine commander launches first. How copy?" Armstrong asked.

"Copy all," Scott replied looking at Tom.

"Good luck, Commander." The line went dead.

Scott just stared at the phone.

"Looks like option one, placing a mine on the submarine, is on the table, Captain," Varney suggested. "There seems there is a fine line between neutralizing and attacking."

"Let's get with Commander Walsh and see if we can come up with an alternate plan," Scott said, leaving Radio.

Scott and Tom Varney were sitting in the wardroom, drinking their first cup of black coffee when Commander Mike Walsh entered.

Scott wondered how Walsh would react once he learned he was ordered to place a mine on K-901.

"Good morning, Captain," Mike Walsh said, sitting down. BM1 Rose sat next to his commander.

"Mike, I might need to neutralize K-901," Scott said. "I believe that the *Vinson* Battle Group is in danger of an attack."

"How do you intend to neutralize this submarine without launching a torpedo?" Walsh asked.

"That's where you come in. I want you to place a limped mine on K-901's hull," Scott replied.

"What? Do you want me to attach a mine on the hull of the Kilo? Have you received orders?" Walsh questioned.

"No, I have not. The decision is mine and mine alone," Scott replied.

Walsh looked at Varney. "Do you agree XO?" Walsh asked. "This action borders on insubordination."

Varney looked at Scott. "I agree with his decision," Varney replied.

Scott continued. "Tom, show Mike the photos."

The XO opened a folder and handed the photos to Walsh.

"I need a way to neutralize the submarine without pointing to *Buffalo*," Scott said.

Walsh accepted the pictures and spread them on the table. He studied each one not saying a word. Petty Officer Rose looked over his shoulder.

"Captain are you ordering me to place a mine on the submarine?"

"Yes, and I will sign a letter stating I was ordering you to place the limped mine on K-901.

"If it's an order I will comply," Walsh said smiling.

"Captain, what is the speed of the tanker?" Rose asked.

"She has maintained a seven-knot headway," Scott replied.

Walsh continued to look at each picture. Finally, he pulled the third photo from the stack. "Captain what do you believe they're removing from the submarine," Walsh asked pointing to the long slender object.

"They're unloading torpedoes," Scott replied.

"What do you think, Rose?" Walsh said handing the photo to him.

"I agree," Rose said looking at the picture.

"What are you thinking Mike," Scott asked.

"You said that you followed the *Kilo* up to the Straits and recorded her launching surface and torpedo mines correct?" Walsh asked.

"Correct," Scott replied.

"Where is the K-901 now? Walsh asked.

"We believe she is preparing to re-enter the tanker and reload her torpe-does," Varney replied.

"Then you have a perfect opportunity to neutralize K-109. Reloading torpedoes is extremely dangerous. Accidents do happen," Mike said.

Scott looked at Tom. "Looks like we have our answer," Scott said. "How do you suggest we proceed, Mike?"

"Captain, I am concerned the laminar flow or turbulence between the tanker's hull and *Kilo* might be a problem in attaching the mine," Rose said.

Scott looked surprised at Rose's comment.

"Captain I have a degree in physics," Rose said.

Scott looked and Varney. "We cannot measure the speed of the water between the two hulls. I assume it is less than seven knots," Varney replied.

"Can you get close enough to place your periscope inside the cavity?" Rose asked. "The Commander could attach himself to the tube as you raise the scope out of the sail."

Scott looked at Varney. "What do you think of the idea, XO?"

"I like Roses' idea," Varney said. "My only concern is the flow between the outer hull and the cavity."

"Mike, we must be cautious when we lift you into the area. If you feel the flow is too fast, signal us and we will lower the mast and bring you back inside the submarine," Scott added. "Also, at seven knots, we are placing a considerable drag on the periscope."

"I recommend you place the sail under the submarine's bow if you are correct about the flow. It would limit my movement and assist me in placing the mine," Walsh said.

"What do you think, Tom?" Scott asked, weighing Walsh's suggestion.

"Let's do it," Varney answered. "The theory is sound. The only question will we succeed?"

"We'll give it a shot, Mike. Rest up; we will initiate our approach soon," Scott said. "XO, let's head up to Control."

Scott waited for K-901 to submerge under the tanker. *Buffalo* closed the stern of the supertanker and waited for the Iranian submarine to become secure inside the tanker's cavity.

Walsh and Rose removed their equipment from the *ASDV* and prepared to enter the forward escape tank. The possible death of K-901 weighed heavily on Walsh.

Chapter 19

USS Buffalo; Gulf of Oman –

"OOD, increase speed to ten knots, come left ten degrees," Scott ordered. "Control room, I intend to parallel the tanker, open ahead of her, and allow her to overtake *Buffalo*."

"Coming left ten degrees, speed ten knots," the OOD repeated.

Scott stood on the periscope pedestal and pressed his eye against the rubber cup. He twisted the handle grip back to high power, searching the water astern. "Helm, 'All Stop'," he ordered. "Make your depth two hundred feet, five degrees down bubble."

"Two hundred feet, five degrees down bubble," the Chief of the Boat (COB) ordered.

COB watched the planesmen slowly push forward on his yolk. "Easy now," he said looking at the level indicator.

Helm answered, "All Stop, coming to two hundred feet," the COB responded.

"XO, are Commander Walsh and BM1 Rose ready to exit the forward escape trunk?" Scott asked.

"Yes, Sir," Varney answered.

"Then proceed," Scott ordered, with his eye pressed against the rubber cup, searching for the tanker's bow.

Mike Walsh turned the ring and pushed open the escape hatch. Both SEALs pulled themselves through the narrow opening into the chamber, then closed and locked the door. Sitting in the escape trunk, they waited for the water to fill the cavity.

"Opening the outer hatch," Walsh said, exiting the chamber.

Scott watched Walsh and Rose work their way up the sail and connect their safety lines to the eye bolts. We'll find out about the current in the cavity shortly, he thought.

Rose connected his communication line that led to the ship's intercom. "Control, can you hear me, OVER?" Rose asked into his throat mic.

"Hear you loud and clear. Are you ready to proceed?" Scott asked.

"Yes, Sir," Rose responded, sitting on the bridge. He waited for the order to help Commander Walsh shoot for the sail.

"Helm, all ahead one-third, make your depth ninety feet," Scott ordered.

"Slow and easy," the Diving Officer said to the plainsmen.

Walsh and Rose hunkered down as they saw the tanker's hull start to overtake Buffalo.

"Christ she is huge," Rose said looking up at the hull.

Scott waited until the tanker was directly above. "Standby," he ordered. "Helmsmen add three turns," he said, matching the tanker's speed as she closed over Buffalo. "Ignore my last order. Helmsmen drop two turns," Scott ordered, seeing the tanker's bow directly above Buffalo's sail. He continued to monitor the tanker's position, ensuring his submarine matched the tanker's course and speed. Any deviation could be disastrous.

The radiated noise from the massive thirty-foot, five-blade propeller slapping the water's surface made it almost impossible for Scott to hear anyone speak. "What do you think, XO? Scott asked. "This is an excellent position to minimize the chance of being detected by workers on the tanker's catwalk." He stepped aside and allowed Varney to look at the Kilo's hull.

"Walsh and Rose should be able to snap those pictures Washington requested," Scott said louder than he normally would.

"Roger that," Varney replied with a slight smile. He looked through the scope, knowing that Scott saying this loudly was meant for other ears.

"OOD, make your depth eighty feet," Scott ordered.

The Plainsmen slowly pulled back on the yoke and *Buffalo* started to creep up toward the tanker's hull.

"Ninety feet, coming to eighty feet," the Chief of the Watch (COW) announced. "Spenser, mind your depth," standing behind the Plainsmen operating the sail plains.

"XO, un-house the attack periscope," Scott ordered, looking up at the bow of the *Kilo* through the search periscope. "Rose, ready when you are," he said.

Walsh felt a tap on his shoulder.

Dipping his head in acknowledgment, Walsh pushed off *Buffalo's* deck. He swam toward the attack periscope. At seven knots, he reached the scope in seconds. Grabbing the tube, he looped the safety line around the mast. Freeing an arm from the mast, he pointed to the *Kilo's* hull.

"Lift away," Rose ordered after receiving Walsh's thumbs up.

Scott moved over to the attack periscope.

Walsh wrapped his arms and legs tightly around the tube as the seven-knot current pulled against him.

"Stop the rise," Rose announced, seeing Commander Walsh's clenched fist. Rose saw Walsh was in the cavity ten feet under the *Kilo's* hull.

Scott turned the ring back to the off position and then looked into the search periscope to monitor Walsh's movement. He saw the Commander pull the camera from his pocket, snapping several pictures of the submarine's hull. Good, we will need those photos for the intel people, he thought.

Walsh replaced the camera in his pocket and launched himself toward the *Kilo's* bow. His safety line trailed behind. "Not bad so far," he mumbled, kicking hard toward the centerline of K-901. His breathing increased as he pulled hard on the cool air from his rebreather. Reaching the hull below the sub's torpedo room, Walsh paused for a minute to catch his breath. Would the scraping noise be heard through the *Kilo's* hull? He paused. No time to stop now. He removed the scraping tool from his chest pocket and started to remove the scum from the bottom. Having nothing to hold onto he kicked hard as he scrapped to keep his body against the submarine's hull. His breathing increased from the exertion.

Dropping the tool, he unstrapped the mine held against his chest. He removed the cover and pressed the adhesive side against the clean hull. "Ninety minutes should do it," he mumbled, turning the bezel to ninety.

"Ok, so far," Scott said to Varney as Walsh pulled a camera from his pocket and started snapping pictures as he swam toward the *Kilo's* stern. Once past the sail, Walsh grabbed his tether and pulled himself hand over hand back onto the bridge of *Buffalo*.

"Got him!" Rose announced, grabbing Walsh's arm.

Breathing heavily, they waited for *Buffalo* to descend before returning to the escape hatch.

"You seem to have trouble keeping up against the hull as you cleaned the scum," Rose said.

"Between the water flow in the cavity and trying to clean the hull, I found it almost impossible to keep in front of the spot I was working on," Walsh said. The two SEALs waited on the bridge anxious to get back inside. They saw Buffalo start to descend away from the tanker.

"It won't be long now," Rose said.

"Make your depth one-hundred fifty feet, speed nine knots," Scott ordered.

"All Stop! Forward compartment standby to retrieve our men. Let me know when they're secure in the chamber. Weps, how long must they decompress?"

Weps looked at the digital clock counting down. "They just got back in time. Decompression is not required, Skipper. They were out and back in less than sixty minutes. They're good to go!" Wilkinson responded.

Rose disconnected the cable to the ship's intercom. He followed Walsh forward. Lifting the lid, both men dropped into the chamber and secured the opening. Walsh turned the valve applying air to force the water from the compartment.

Both men leaned back against the wall, waiting for the water to drain from the escape trunk. "That wasn't so bad," Walsh said and removed his mask and mouthpiece, still breathing hard as they waited to get out of the chamber. He switched the red night light to white and settled back against the wall trying to become comfortable. His breathing slowed.

"Commander, how much longer are you going to volunteer for every hazardous mission you can find?" Rose asked in a cordial tone.

Commander Walsh had thought about what Dr. Lace said the other day. *She was correct in her assessment of his activities over the past year. He had been pushing himself, hoping the pain after the loss of his wife and child would be erased. Unless he opted for a lobotomy, that would never happen. It was time to give up the ghost and move on.*

"Why do you ask?" he questioned.

"Samantha and I want to start a family, and I can't agree to children if I continue to support the type of missions you volunteer for," Rose said.

"You could apply for a transfer," Walsh replied.

"Don't think so. I like my job, and I don't want to break up the team," Rose said.

"You can inform the men this was my last mission, and I intend to take Dr. Lace's advice. Apply for a desk job and date Lt. Morton," Walsh said.

"You're kidding?" Rose replied, a smile appearing across his face.

"Admiral Westfield asked me before this mission if I was interested in running an extension of SEAL Team Six in Guam. As a member of Admiral Westfield's staff, I can direct them to the hot spots in the Middle East," Walsh said, waiting for the hatch to open. The Commander looked at his watch. Seventy minutes before the bomb goes off, he thought.

Scott waited outside the chamber door as Mike and Rose exited. "Mike, addressing Commander Walsh, it looks good from where I stood," Scott said.

"Here is the camera with the pictures. If there is nothing else we will go change and get dressed," Walsh said.

"Thanks, Mike," Scott said returning to Control.

"Lieutenant Powers, bring us five thousand yards astern of the tanker." We need to get behind the blast, he thought.

Chapter 20

USS Buffalo; Gulf of Oman –

"Captain, thirty minutes remaining," the XO announced, seated on a chair in Scott's quarters.

Weathers knocked on the stateroom door and entered. "Sir, here is Commander Walsh's thumb drive of the photos he took from under the *Kilo's* hull."

Scott inserted the drive into his laptop. He and Varney studied the underside of the enemy submarine.

"Those massive claws holding the *Kilo* are padded," Tom said. "Did you notice the bottom of the tanker can be closed? Our intelligence people would not have known the tanker had a retractable bottom."

"Your right. I missed that. They must have a way to drain the water once the doors close," Scott said. "Which means they can conduct repairs on the hull at sea."

"Look at the anechoic tiles under the submarine's machinery spaces. They're working hard to reduce the radiated noise," Varney said.

"Tracking their submarines has proven more difficult, and now we know why. We'll pass this up the chain of command. We need to inform them that Iranian silencing efforts are working. Hell, if it weren't for the shaft rub, we would have had difficulty detecting and tracking that *Kilo*," Varney said.

"The *Qaaem* submarine is homegrown, and I fear their radiated noise will be nill," Scott replied.

"I'm betting on Sorenson to find the *Qaaem*. He hasn't let us down yet," Varney said, looking at the video of the tanker's approach over *Buffalo*.

"Wait, go back to the last picture," Scott said. "Look at that," he said, pointing to a line of bright lights extending along the starboard side of the submarine. "Are those weapons there loading?"

Varney leaned closer to the screen. "I believe you are correct, Joe," Varney replied.

"Excellent timing on our part, don't you think?" Scott said enthusiastically. "Tom, we can use this picture to corroborate our story about what caused the explosion.

"I agree, Captain," Varney said.

"Tell Weathers to keep these photos until I direct him to transfer them to the intel people."

Varney nodded in agreement, then said, "Damn lucky, no one spotted our hull from the W/T Seed's catwalk."

Scott nodded. "That's why I chose to have the tanker close over our position. With our overall length of three hundred sixty-two feet, placing our sail directly under the bow of the Kilo covered our stern."

"Great idea. I wondered why you allowed the tanker to run over us," Tom remarked, glancing at the wall clock. "It's almost time, Captain. Should we warn Sonar of the pending explosion?"

"No, that would be a dead giveaway Walsh planted a mine on the submarine's hull. I'll head for sonar to see if Sorenson has an update on the Qaaem."

"What level of damage should we expect from the charge?" The XO asked.

"The sealed Semtex-shaped charge should produce a hole under the battery compartment," Scott said.

"If they're fast charging their battery banks, there should be enough hydrogen in the battery wells to create one hell of an explosion," Varney said. "I hate to think of how many sailors will die choking on the Sulfur dioxide gas."

"We can only hope they're venting the gas," Scott said. "If the Hydrogen explodes the crew won't have to be concerned about the Sulfur dioxide gas."

"I agree," Tom replied, still looking at the photos cycling on the screen.

Scott and Varney left his stateroom and entered the sonar three minutes before detonation.

Scott stood over Sorenson and looked at the operator's screen. "Anything on the *Qaaem* you held earlier?" Scott questioned.

"Captain," Senior Chief Richardson replied. "Sorenson has not been able to regain contact. I suspect the Iranian submarine has sailed toward the Southern Straits."

Scott kept glancing at the clock above the console as he spoke to the duty section. "The XO and I will—"

K-901; W/T Seed; Gulf of Oman –

The loading party aboard K-901 stood next to the third torpedo waiting to lower the weapon into the torpedo room.

Karini stood thirty feet above the men against the railing, scrutinizing the work. He knew loading and unloading weapons was always a critical task. Safety was paramount. He watched the Weapons Officer, manual in hand, checking the men were following procedures to load weapons safely. Looks good from here, he thought.

The third four thousand-pound torpedo resting at a forty-five-degree angle was held fast by the three men holding restraining straps. He knew they were waiting to lower the next weapon in the torpedo room.

In two more months, my dear, I will be retired. I'm looking forward to spending time with you and our Grandchildren, Karini thought just before he heard a tremendous explosion. He saw the bow of his submarine shift slightly, ending his reflection of days with his family.

Seconds later, a second explosion fueled by hydrogen gas blew a funnel of searing red flames from the forward torpedo loading hatch up against the tanker's ceiling. The intense heat from the flame and black smoke filled the upper cavity. The white-painted bulkheads and ceiling started blistering as the flame rose. Fire crawled like an angry beast across the ship's overhead. The roar of escaping gas from the blast filled the ship's cavity. Knocked off his feet, Captain Karini lay stunned on the catwalk.

The three men holding the securing lines of the third torpedo were knocked to the deck, stunned by the blast. They were aflame, screaming in pain. One man was hurled into the water and disappeared.

The concussion from the two explosions rocked the submarine. No longer restrained by the men, the third torpedo slid down the guiding rail into the torpedo room.

Unlike the contact torpedoes of WW II, the current weapons usually would not explode on impact. Damaged from the heat and striking the steel deck, the torpedo exploded. The bow ripped wide open, followed by another massive fireball.

Death was instantaneous for the crew members in the torpedo room and the damage control party fighting the fire.

Unable to stop the water flowing into the forward compartments, the XO announced, "Abandon ship" over the ship's internal speakers.

Rushing water rapidly filled the submarine's three forward berthing compartments. Sailors, overcome by smoke, and anoxic gas scrambled up the ladder to the Control room. Those not overwhelmed by the cloud of chlorine gas fought to escape as water surged behind them. Men rushed down the passageway, choking from the smoke. They climbed out of the submarine and collapsed on the burning deck. Panic replaced years of training as they sought to save themselves.

Alarms throughout the supertanker blared. The tanker's Damage Control Parties struggled to extinguish the fireball mixed with the deadly vapor.

The men on the walkways were knocked to the deck when the massive claws shifted with the explosions.

K-901's forward nylon mooring lines snapped from the weight of the water in the submarine's bow. The lines slashed across the submarine's deck. A sailor standing near the sail fell to the deck screaming, legs sliced at both knees.

As the bow of the submarine sank deeper, pushed down by the weight of the water in the forward compartments, the stern lifted against the tanker's cavity.

The Ships Master had ordered 'All Stop', but *W/T Seed's* forward motion continued for the next twenty minutes, pushing K-901's bow deeper beneath the tanker's outer hull.

Choking from the smoke, Karini picked himself up off the catwalk. His vision blurred from the intense smoke. He saw the devastation around him. "Nooo," he wailed, seeing his submarine fight for her life. Tears ran down his face as he witnessed crew members trying to save themselves when they jumped into the water and the burning oil.

The overhead of the tanker buckled when the submarine's screw sliced into the upper section. Each gigantic claw holding the submarine snapped from the weight of the water.

Karini stared in horror as K-901 bolted upright. The loud, ear-piercing scraping sounds resembled the screams of a sinking ship as if she knew of her imminent death. Her descent to the bottom was quick.

Karini standing on the catwalk looked down through the black smoke at what remained of his men. The bobbing heads of dead men floated in the burning oil.

"Why," he cried, his hands locked around the rail.

"Captain, Captain," the ship's crewman called. "Let go of the railing." The crewman tried to pull Captain Karini back from the blistering heat and the choking black smoke.

Releasing his grip, the shattered captain allowed the crewman to lead him into the safety of the inner passageway. "The Americans did this. They are responsible for sinking my boat," he mumbled. "My revenge will be swift and deadly."

Chapter 21

USS Buffalo; Gulf of Oman –

"Christ, what was that?" Sorenson shouted, rotating in his seat to face the screen. Pulling the right headphones back over his ear, he worked the controls.

"The explosion came from the tanker," Senior Chief Richardson shouted.

"Thank God *Buffalo* wasn't under the hull," Scott said. The captain started to leave when a second, then a third explosion blasted through the overhead speaker. The boat quivered when repeated shock waves pushed hard against *Buffalo's* bow. Scott moved behind Sorenson and saw the imprint of the explosions on his monitor. A feeling of remorse flashed across his face. The footprint from the bow hydrophones confirmed the end of K-901 and crew. Not what he wanted. *I only meant to immobilize her and prevent the Captain from releasing the torpedo mines.*

"The second and third explosions must have been torpedoes cooking off," Sorenson said.

"I concur," Senior Chief Richardson replied.

"Wait," Sorenson said. "I hear snapping and groaning noises beneath the tanker. Sorenson pressed his hands against the earphones. He turned around, facing the Captain and the XO, his face solemn. "I hear creaking and popping noises, Sir. Wait! She's breaking up." He paused, "The hull just imploded. She's gone."

"What?" Scott exclaimed, the shock evident in his voice now.

He caught his XO's sad expression. *I just committed 52 men to their deaths.* "Let me know if anything else develops, Senior Chief." He turned to Varney,

"Let's go."

Scott and Varney left Sonar and headed for his stateroom where they could talk out of ear shots of the crew.

The red night lights gave Scott's room a subdued effect that reflected both men's somber mood.

"Let's get off a message informing SUBRON 15 and Fifth Fleet of the explosion we detected while tracking W/T Seed, Tom," Scott said.

Varney sighed. "I'll draft the particulars and bring it to you for approval." Tom Varney sensed Scott regretted having to destroy K-901 with its loss of lives. "Sir, No ship's captain takes pleasure in taking a life," he said, trying to ease Scott's sense of guilt. "Neither of us foresaw the sinking of K-901. If Sorenson is correct, Walsh's mine triggered several torpedoes to explode. You and I did not foresee the torpedoes exploding. They say war is hell, but I don't think the CO of K-901 would hesitate a second to launch a torpedo at us or our ships if ordered."

"I agree, Tom, but up to this point, I've never sunk an adversary. I did not intend to sink this one." He sighed. "There's no sense dwelling on what happened," Scott said.

"I'll go draft the message," Varney said, leaving Scott's stateroom.

Scott sat in the near darkness, trying to relax when a knock on his door disrupted his catnap. "Enter!" Scott said, letting out an exasperated sigh.

Janice walked in, closed the door, and sat beside him. "Are you okay, Joe?" She asked, knowing the Kilo sinking weighed heavily on his mind.

"What do you mean?" he asked, trying not to reveal his feelings.

"It doesn't take a rocket scientist to understand what happened an hour ago. I know you, and you're trying desperately to rationalize the sinking of the Kilo. Unfortunately, it is what you had to do to protect the fleet, crew, and me," Janice said, speaking quietly.

"How much do you know?" Scott asked, wondering if she knew more than she should.

"Let's say, for argument's sake, Mike Walsh and Rose were not just out swimming around taking pictures."

"If I weren't so crazy in love with you, I'd toss you out on your ear," Joe responded with just the faintest hint of an ironic smile.

"You didn't answer my question," Janice said, looking directly into Scott's eyes as she reached for his hand.

"I could never hide anything from you. Could I? You're right, of course. I've been sitting questioning my decision to immobilize an antagonist."

"You did what you had to do to save *Buffalo* and the other ships in the Battle Group, and for that matter, us. You could have left me in Hawaii and never seen me again. I know why you got the navy to bring me aboard—"

"What are you talking about? I didn't do anything—"

"Let's be honest. You're not fooling anyone but yourself. I knew how you manipulated the navy to get me onboard. I tried to convince myself not to come, but I had to come." Janice smiled. "I love you, Joe. This time aboard has allowed me to understand the man I fell in love with."

Scott sat back in silence, staring at her, thinking what to say when he heard a knock on his door.

Varney entered. "Sorry, Captain, I didn't know you were —" He smiled when he saw Janice. He shut the door and took the empty chair.

"I was just leaving, XO," Janice said, starting to rise.

"Wait just one minute, please? Are you Dr. Lace, the science advisor aboard this ship three years ago?"

"Yes," Janice replied.

"I'm going out on a limb, and perhaps also out of line, but I take it you two were an item for some time after your last deployment," Varney said.

"Again, yes," Janice smiled, glancing at Joe.

"How did you know?" Scott asked, wondering what had given them away.

"I started adding two and two after the engineer remembered seeing Dr. Lace aboard three years ago. The last time I observed you in the wardroom, you glowed like newlyweds. And you tense up when Janice comes near you, Skipper."

"Is it that apparent?" Janice asked, uneasy at being found out.

"Yes!" Tom said, smiling at both.

Scott and Janice looked at each other. Neither spoke.

Janice broke the awkward silence. "I'm not sure how to turn off the glow, but you can bet I'll work at it, XO. You're correct. We have a long history."

Scott nodded. "I guess we do."

"Don't worry. We're getting married once we arrive back in Guam," Janice said.

"Marriage?" Scott looked surprised. "What did you say?"

Janice smiled. "Oh, I forgot to mention that one small detail." She laughed. "And, oh, yes, one more thing I forgot. Mr. Scott, get this. There can be only one CO while we are ashore. That will be me." Turning to Varney, she added. "By the way, XO, may I call you Tom?"

"Yes, please do."

"Would you ask your wife to be my bridesmaid? You've talked about her often and I think she would make a wonderful bridesmaid for our wedding."

Scott sat in awe. He felt as if he had been torpedoed and didn't know what to say.

Janice started for the door. "Oh, yes, Captain, I emailed my parents informing them of our pending nuptials. Joe, I suggest you do the same." She stopped by the door. "And Commander Scott, I think Tom would make an excellent best man. Don't you?"

Without another word, Janice left the two men staring at each other, trying to take in what she just said.

"That is one headstrong woman, Captain. I hope my wife doesn't learn about your command structure at home."

Scott burst out laughing. "I guess that's what I always liked about her."

"I almost forgot this." Varney handed Scott the draft message for his review. "Congratulations, Joe. I know you'll be very happy together." He smiled and left the room.

Scott sat back and reflected on the surprising turn of events. *Christ, I dreamed of this ever since I saw her again. But are we moving too fast?* He visualized her face, her teasing face. *No, this is what I, no, what we both wanted. Now is the time to move on with our lives.* He closed his eyes.

An hour later, the XO knocked on Scott's door, and entered, holding several sheets of paper. "I drafted an email to Beth explaining she and I are going to be your best man and maid of honor for your wedding." She wrote back, "I hope once the crew gets wind of this, *Buffalo* doesn't become known as the 'Love Boat.'" He gave Scott a warm smile.

Scott looked up at Varney and suddenly began to laugh. The tension hanging like a dark storm cloud over his head had been relieved by this unexpected salvo by Janice. "The Love Boat?" He asked Varney.

"That's what Beth said."

Scott saw a pile of papers on his desk. "I wish it was true, but we have work to do before we can head back to search for the *Qaaem*." He handed Varney the top sheet. "Here, Tom, after reading and adding changes, it's ready to be sent." He forced himself to become serious. "Now that we neutralized the *Kilo* and tanker, we need to locate the *Qaaem*. I have a strong hunch our fleet is still in danger."

"The crew is ready, Sir," Varney said.

"They've done a great job."

After Varney left, Scott lay back on his couch. For a few minutes, Janice made him forget the dangers he was forcing on his crew. He wished she was back with him to help him focus on their happy future. He knew she would not return tonight. She understood the safety of his ship and crew had to come first. As he sank into sleep, he heard the sound of explosions and saw the faceless men, enemy but still human beings, bobbing like broken toys in the blood-red sea. I did that, he thought. I did that.

Chapter 22

The Office of the President; Washington, DC –

"Mr. President, Raymond Richards and Dr. Ure are on their way to see you," President Washburn's Chief-of-Staff Ian Williams announced.

"Any idea what they want, Ian?" The President asked.

"No, Sir. Secretary Raymond stated he needed to see you right away," Williams responded.

Just then, Secretary of the Navy Raymond burst into the Oval Office, gripping a piece of paper. He walked up to the President and handed him the note. Ure followed.

Washburn looked at it and said, "It's about Goddamn time we received a message from Commander Scott." He walked to his desk and flipped off the recorder. "Where the hell is he?"

Richards replied, "In the Gulf of Oman. Commander Scott reports there's been an explosion aboard an Iranian supertanker."

The President continued reading aloud. "According to Scott, the Iranians have been using the supertanker as a submarine pen. A *Kilo* locked inside the tanker was loading torpedoes when the explosion occurred."

"What did you say," Dr. Ure asked.

"A submarine exploded inside an Iranian supertanker," The President repeated. "That's what his report states."

"I called Admiral Armstrong and discussed Scott's report," Raymond said. "The Admiral speculated that one of their weapons must have exploded during their weapon loadout on the submarine. The tanker was concealing the *Kilo* submarine and a ton of weapons."

"Was the supertanker destroyed?" Washburn asked.

"No, Sir," Raymond said. "Scott reported that the tanker is dead in the water, spewing black smoke from her vents on the main deck. He believes the tanker has been neutralized and can no longer support Iran's submarines."

"Well, that's something. At least we won't have to worry about Iran hiding their submarines in the tanker," Washburn said.

"Was the *Qaaem* inside the tanker when the explosion occurred?" The President asked.

"He did not mention the *Qaaem*," Raymond replied.

"Send Scott a message asking if he knows where the *Qaaem* is and if she is deploying mines," Washburn ordered.

"Yes, Sir," Jack Ure responded, making a note on his pad.

"Has Iran reported the explosion and loss of one of their submarines?" Washburn asked.

"Nothing so far, but it might be too early," Williams replied. "I'll keep my eye out for the next release of the Iranian Times newspaper."

"Also a bit embarrassing," Ure added. "Even if they suspect we were somehow involved, they might not want to admit they were this vulnerable. I have my field operatives keeping their ears open for any word of the sinking of the *Kilo*."

"Was this more of Scott's work?" The President smiled. "Did he do something to cause the sinking of the *Kilo* and damage to the tanker?

"As you have read he has reported the explosion. He did not state he was in any way responsible." Jack Ure said.

I don't believe I was ready to court-martial the son-of-a-bitch for disobeying orders and leaving the Persian Gulf." Washburn said, sitting down behind his desk. "Let me see Scott's second message."

Raymond handed him the latest communique.

"Scott says there was another submarine. It got away before the 'accident.'" He looked at the men observing him silently. "Gentlemen," the President said. "We can't let our guard down."

"Does he think the other sub is a threat to the *Vinson*?" Ure asked.

Washburn nodded. "Scott says he needs to find the *Qaaem* and prevent her from launching the torpedo mines."

"I agree," Raymond said. "I trust his judgment. He has not failed us yet. He will do what he has to do to protect the fleet."

The President sat back and thought about how I could keep Scott in Buffalo. Yes! He burst out, placing his elbows on his desk. "Ray contact the Bureau of Personnel and have them issue orders for Commander Scott to remain *Buffalo's* CO for at least two years. Any objections?"

"Not from me," Richards said. "I'll contact BUPERS and change Scott's orders. Mr. President."

"He's got a big set of balls. A good man, a damn fine officer! I want him available if the Gulf erupts into a major conflict," The President demanded.

"Yes, Sir. But the *Qaaem* submarine is still capable of launching the torpedo mines." Richards said.

"What the hell are you doing about the mines?" President Washburn asked.

"I have ordered Avenger minesweepers to sweep the northern area with the help of Sea Dragon helicopters. We are deploying Raytheon's airborne mine neutralization system. I also requested authorization to use the airbase in Oman for crew rest, maintenance, and fueling," Richards replied.

"OK! Jack, any intel on what the Iranians are doing in the Persian Gulf?" The President asked.

"Our satellite pictures reveal the Revolutionary Guard is continuing to mine the northern waters. We've spotted Ships and barges loaded with mines pier-side and along the coast."

"All right. That takes care of the Persian Gulf and the Northern Straits. What about the Southern Straits?" Washburn asked.

"We will have to count on Commander Scott to eliminate the threat at the Southern Straits," Raymond said. "Scott's last message reported the number and placement of the floating and torpedo mines. He has two options. Launch a weapon in response to the *Qaaem* attacking one of our surface ships. His second is to eliminate the floating antennas of the torpedo mines."

"From what I have been told, eliminating the antennas is almost impossible," Washburn replied. "I don't like it. "He is only one man. How wide are the Southern Straits?"

"Twenty-six miles," Raymond answered.

"The *Qaaem* is the key. That submarine can launch torpedo mines. Let's pray he is tracking the *Qaaem* as we speak." Dr. Ure said.

"Ray, when will the Battlegroup enter the Gulf of Oman?" Washburn asked.

"*Carl Vinson* Carrier Strike Group is in the Gulf of Oman and is proceeding north," Raymond responded. "Attached to the group are Carrier Air Wing 17, Destroyer Squadron-1, and the guided-missile cruiser, *Bunker Hill*. Additionally, the *Bataan* Amphibious Ready Group and the 22nd Marine Expeditionary Unit with 1,200 Marines aboard will leave the Suez Canal tomorrow."

"Do you still disagree with not sending a Carrier Strike Group and The *Bataan* Amphibious Ready Group to the Persian Gulf?" The President asked.

"Yes, Mr. President," Raymond said. "I suggest the *Bataan* Amphibious Ready Group and the 22nd Marine Expeditionary Unit remain in the Arabian Sea for the near future.

"OK Ray," Washburn replied. "Let me know what happens. Thanks, everyone." The President got up, ending the meeting. Well, the day is still young, he thought. Will Iran lose another submarine?

Chapter 23

USS Carl Vinson, CVN 70; Gulf of Oman –

"Anything from Scott?" Rear Admiral Clint Dussault asked his Chief-of-Staff, Jim Wills, who had just entered his stateroom.

"Yes, Sir. I just received this message," Captain Jim Wills said, handing the board to the Admiral. "Scott sent the location of the minefield and the types of mines Iran deployed."

"Has Captain Newhouse seen this?" Clint Dussault asked as he flipped through the pages.

"A copy is being sent to him," Wills responded.

The growler sounded on the bulkhead.

"Admiral Clint Dussault's quarters, Captain Wills speaking. Yes, Sir."

"Admiral, Captain Newhouse," Wills handed the phone to Dussault.

"Morning, Clarence," the Admiral said.

"Have you read the current message from Scott?" Newhouse asked.

"Yes! Have the coordinates been entered on our tactical boards?" Dussault asked.

"They just finished," the CO replied.

"Excellent! I'll meet you in the Combat Direction Center (CDC) in a few minutes."

"Jim, let's look at the minefields mapped out by Scott's team. We need to see what the Battle Group is heading into," the Admiral said.

Admiral Dussault and Captain Wills took the elevator down three decks and entered CDC. They paused after entering the classified space to let their eyes adjust to the darkness. They then proceeded to the three large tactical screens attached to the forward bulkhead. The IT operators sitting in front of the screens were entering the coordinates of the mines.

Admiral Dussault and Captain Will stood in front of the middle screen scrutinizing the shoreline. The Admiral noted the light tan-colored sand dotted with light saddle brown streaks indicating mountain ridges blanketed both sides of the Gulf.

"I don't believe how blue the water is," he said. Looking at the deep blue water leading up to the Straits of Hormuz separated the two landmasses.

"Lieutenant, please display the mines you entered on the tactical screen," the Admiral asked.

The operator selected a point off the coast of Diba Al Fujairah located in the northeast part of the United Arab Emirates. "Here are the Iranian floating and torpedo mines, Sir."

Admiral Dussault moved closer to *Vinson's*, CO. "How does it look, Clarence?" He asked.

"Not good, Admiral. You can see the area is loaded with torpedo mines and floaters." He pointed to the screen. "Scott pinpointed the torpedo mines, but the location and number of the drifting horned mines' is anyone's guess. They could be anywhere depending on the wind and current." He shook his head. "*Buffalo's* science advisors provided the mines' original locations. Dr. Lace and Lt. Morton, both oceanographers, calculated the drift of each mine based on the environmental conditions in the area as best as they could. Dr. Lace—"

"Dr. Lace?" Dussault said. "I was not aware *Buffalo* had a civilian aboard."

"Dr. Lace was transferred from the University of Hawaii at the request of Commander Scott. They worked together when Scott was operating with the SEALs in the Gulf three years ago."

"Classified Operations?" the Admiral asked.

"Yes, Sir," Newhouse answered. Black Ops. I was unable to find out anything on the operation or what Buffalo was involved in."

"Then I guess, the Dr. is qualified."

"Eminently so. But we're still working with unpredictable variables. We can't say for certain exactly where the Iranian mines may have drifted. That makes them very dangerous to any ships in the area."

"How far are we from the minefield?" Dussault asked, staring at the tactical picture on the screen.

"Distance to the Straits is three hundred fifty nautical miles, seventy-two hours if we remain at our current speed of twenty knots."

"That doesn't give us much time. Ask your environmental and meteoro-logical people to study Lace and Morton's calculations and update the mine locations based on current conditions," the Admiral ordered. "Is the *Bataan* Amphibious Ready Group still involved in exercises?" He asked.

"Yes, Sir. Petty Officer Jefferson," Newhouse addressed the young IT sitting in front of the GeoPlot. "Please, pull up the current location of the *Bataan* Amphibious Ready Group."

Within seconds, the air picture with symbols representing the Amphibious surface units was displayed.

"Admiral, the upper right of the screen displays the ships attached to *Bataan*, their latitudes and longitudes, distance from us, course, and speeds. The red symbols represented a hostile, blue friendly, and white neutral." Petty Officer Jefferson said.

"As you can see, the *Bataan* Amphibious Ready Group is still off the coast of Oman, Admiral," Newhouse said. "Our potential threat, *W/T Seed*, has been neutralized. It is two hundred seventeen nautical miles north of our current location. The message from Commander Scott stated the supertanker was on fire, and a torpedo explosion in the tanker destroyed one *Kilo* submarine. Additionally, Scott reported he was maintaining contact on the burning supertanker and a *Qaaem* class Iranian submarine. He stated the *Qaaem* has remained in the area and is maintaining contact with the tanker."

"At least Scott knows where the *Qaaem* is at present," Captain Wills said.

"Lt. show us the position of the *W/T Seed*," Newhouse asked.

The Admiral and Captain Will watched as the junior officer shifted the screen to another location.

"Sir, *W/T Seed* is located, moving a yellow pointer across the screen and placing it on a red symbol. Buffalo's last message placed Scott here near the tanker."

"Let's hope Scott can maintain track of the *Qaaem*. *Buffalo* is the only deterrent we have at present," Dussault said. "Has the E2 Hawkeye picked up any Iranian surface contacts?"

"Sir, shifting the picture further north. They have reported two Iranian destroyers near the north end of the Strait," the Lieutenant said.

"At least we don't have to be concerned with the destroyers releasing the torpedo mines," Dussault said looking at the screen.

"We still don't know how many Iranian submarines are stationed at the mine barrier along the Southern Straits," Captain Jim Wills said. "Scott is tracking the Qaaem. What other boats doesn't he know about that concerns me."

"I agree. What weapons does the *Qaaem* carry?" Dussault asked.

"She carries a Type 53 torpedo and surface-to-surface missiles. The Pentagon estimates that the one thousand-ton submarine can only carry fifteen torpedoes. They are unsure of the number of surface-to-surface missiles," Lt. Martin replied.

"Order the Fleet to set condition ZEBRA, and secure all watertight doors and hatches. Once we close the Straits, I believe an attack is imminent once we enter the minefield," The Admiral said.

Chapter 24

USS Buffalo; Gulf of Oman –

Scott was looking at Janice while listening to the OOD's phone call interrupting what he hoped would be a peaceful interlude in the wardroom.

Janice watched the concern grow on his face. The frog's feet increased
around his eyes. She knew the news was concerning him.

"I'll be right there," Scott said.

Janice sensed that what was about to happen would place *Buffalo* in harm's
way. *God, not another fight, Joe.*

Scott looked apologetically at Janice. "I have to leave." He turned to Varney.
"Please join me, XO," he said, getting up from his chair and hurrying out of
the wardroom.

Varney followed as Scott headed for Control. After the sinking of K-901,
Buffalo remained off the tanker's starboard bow of the damaged supertanker.

"The explosion must have been severe in the cavity of the tanker, Tom,"
Scott whispered as they headed for Control. "Black smoke continues to pour
from her starboard vents."

Varney nodded. "I agree. The black smoke is a good indication that the
tanker suffered considerable damage."

"We can assume for the near future, the tanker will not be able to hide their
submarines," Scott said.

"Nor supply them," Varney said. "I would assume *W/T Seed* will return to
the yards for repairs."

"With K-901 and the tanker no longer a threat," Scott said heading for
Control with Varney. "We need to go after our next target," entering Control.

"OOD, make your depth three hundred feet."

Scott noticed a surprised expression on the OOD's face.

"Problem, Nav?" Scott asked, preparing to house the search periscope.

"You might want to take a look, Captain," Lt. Obermeier said, stepping away from the periscope.

Scott spotted a sail emerging from the water, followed by the submarine surfacing. "I'll be damned. The *Qaaem* just surfaced in front of us. He's moving toward the tanker's starboard side. What are you doing?" Scott asked out loud, continuing to peer through the periscope.

"Ten seconds, Captain," the XO announced, eyeing the clock above the video feed from the periscope.

"Down scope," Scott ordered, staring at the picture on the monitor with the XO.

"What's he up to, XO?" Scott asked.

"No idea, but I'm sure we'll find out soon," Varney responded.

"Up scope," Scott ordered. "I see a small boat being lowered from the tanker. Three men are sitting in what appears to be a motorized whaleboat. Down scope!"

"One man appears to be an officer," the XO said, replaying the video record.

"Up scope!" Scott pressed his eye against the black rubber buffer but quickly pulled back. "Down scope!" he ordered. "I think they caught us, XO. A man in the boat's stern pointed in our direction."

"Are you sure?" Tom asked.

"I'm afraid we'll know soon enough." Scott grabbed his mic. "Sonar, you want to explain how the hell the *Qaaem* arrived undetected by us?"

Senior Chief Richardson replied, "She must have come through our baffles. That's the only explanation I can offer, Sir."

"Captain, we haven't cleared our baffles in over two hours," Varney said in defense of the sonar team.

"Damn it," Scott shouted. "That won't happen again. Sonar, any distinguishing lines from the new submarine?"

"We got a fifty-five Hz line signal level of ten dB before she lit off her diesel engines. The signal fluctuated when she went from a beam to a stern aspect,"

Sorenson replied.

"Well, that gives us something to work with," Scott said. "Designate Master twenty-one a *Qaaem* class and feed the bearings to fire control."

"Looks like we found the second trigger, Captain," Varney said. "The question is where is she going."

"She'll head for the Southern Straits and lay more mines is my guess. The real question to ask is when are the Iranians going to launch an attack. OOD set Ultra Quiet."

Qaaem Q-100: Gulf of Oman –

"Welcome aboard," Captain Atash Naceri, CO of Q-100 said, addressing Captain Karini, CO of K-901. "I received a message from Vice Admiral Salehi requesting you contact him once we can surface. I assure you it won't be anytime soon."

"Coming to three hundred feet," the Diving Officer reported.

"Roger that," the XO said.

"Thank you, Atash. I wish it were under different circumstances," Karini responded, still reeling from losing his ship and crew. He wore white gloves to cover the burns on his hands. The cream on his face helped the pain, but it was still there, a throbbing reminder of his lost ship and crew.

Naceri led the way to the wardroom. "One of our lookouts thought he detected a periscope feather off our stern during your transfer," he said.

"I am not surprised. How soon will their Battlegroup arrive?" Karini asked, anxious to attack and sink an American carrier.

"Our fishing fleet estimates twelve hours," Naceri responded. "I'm preparing to attack the carrier the second the ship crosses the torpedo minefield."

"I think if a periscope was spotted, it must be an American nuclear submarine operating ahead of their units," Karini said. "I believe that submarine has been shadowing me for the past week. It was responsible for the sinking of my boat," Captain Karini said with a bitter taste in his mouth. Karini dropped his voice. "Any further developments following the attack at our weapon facilities?"

"No, Sir," Naceri answered. "Our government is still assessing the damage and the number of deaths due to the radiation." He frowned. "Our President issued an order closing the Straits and subsequently released a statement to the world's press to that effect."

"It is time we did something," Karini said.

Naceri nodded. "I received orders to head toward the entrance and deploy my torpedo mines—"

"You stated you were preparing to attack an American ship. Did you receive orders?" Karini asked, looking for revenge on the sinking of his submarine.

Naceri shook his head. "No, but if the Americans transit through the minefield, I will release a torpedo mine at their carrier. It will appear the American ship triggered the weapon. An unfortunate accident wouldn't you say?"

"Allah be Praised," Karini replied, excited at the prospect of sinking one of the American's high-value assets.

"Allah be praised," Naceri repeated. "I believe such action reinforces what the news media reported. Iran will protect our sovereign waters. All Naval and commercial ships will enter the Southern Straits at their own risk."

"Excellent!" Karini exclaimed. "Your action against the Americans will help resolve the death of my crew. They will have not died in vain."

Naceri placed his hand on Karini's shoulder. "My sympathies, my friend." He dropped his hand. "I intend to remain here and recharge my batteries before heading toward the Straits. We will arrive several hours before the American carrier."

"And what of the American submarine?" Karini asked.

"If there is an enemy submarine, he is likely waiting to see what we do," Karini responded with a supercilious attitude. "The American nuclear submarines have tried to detect our submarine. My boat has the most advanced silencing tiles on her hull."

"Do not underestimate this one," Karini said and let out a yawn.

"You are exhausted. Please use my stateroom to rest. I will call you when we near the entrance to the Straits," Naceri said. "I'll send a messenger promptly when we establish communication with Vice Admiral Salehi."

"Thanks, Atash. I will take you up on your offer," Karini said leaving Control and heading for the stateroom. "My hands hurt like hell," he mumbled, staring at the bandages as he entered the room and sat down. All he could think about was the death of his submarine and crew. He could still hear his men screaming and calling for help in the inferno of burning oil. How could this have happened, he thought. His crew conducted weapons handling and loading monthly. He had seen nothing to alert him of a potential problem as the weapons party prepared to load the third torpedo. Was it one of the two torpedo mines left in the torpedo room? No, the first explosion did not appear to be caused by a weapon. "But what did cause it," he mumbled, praying he would not hear the screams of his men as he slept.

"The American submarine will pay. I will get my revenge even if I must relieve the CO of his command," Karini said with a bitter taste in his mouth.

Chapter 25

USS Buffalo; Gulf of Oman –

"Helm left ten degrees," Scott ordered. "Range to the *Qaaem*, XO?"

Two thousand yards and opening," Varney said. "She appears to be conducting another baffle clear. Target is continuing left.

"What are you up to this time," Scott mumbled, his eyes following the bearing dots on the fire control screen. "Obermeier, how far are we from the entrance to the Straits?"

"One thousand yards," Obermeier said looking at the navigation chart. "The floating minefield is two thousand yards from the torpedo mine barrier."

"Control, Sonar, detecting outer doors opening," Sorenson announced over the sound-powered phones.

"Let's remain in her baffles, XO," Scott ordered. "I believe he intends to place torpedo mines this is the area."

"Did they detect us?" Scott asked knowing his silencing program had been extensive.

"Not a chance. We've been in her starboard baffles for the past eight hours," Varney replied.

Scott saw Senior Chief Russell entering the latest target parameters into the Fire-Control Console. "XO, what are the odds he is launching a mine and not a torpedo?" he asked Varney.

Varney sighed. "I'm betting torpedo mines, Captain."

Scott eyed the penciled track of the *Qaaem* on the DRT. He compared them with the charted track on the vertical board. "He is still closing the torpedo mine barrier—"

"Weapon in the water! Weapon in the water! Down Doppler," Sorenson shouted.

Scott gripped the rail thanking God the weapon was not directed at Buffalo.

"It's opening away from *Buffalo's* location," Richardson said. "Speed and tonal trace confirm they launched a torpedo mine."

"Well, that answers that question," Scott replied.

For the next two hours, the *Qaaem* launched nine more torpedo mines along the entrance to the Southern Straits. The Navigator recorded the launch time and the location when each weapon shut down on the sea floor.

"This confirms it, XO. Their submarines are deploying torpedo mines in preparation for the arrival of the Battlegroup," Scott said. "If those mines are like the weapons we found in the Gulf, then there are ten floating communication buoys on the surface. Send out a message that we still hold the *Qaaem*, and she has deployed ten torpedo mines at the entrance to the Straits. Weps," he said, speaking now to Lt. Wilkinson. "Continue developing and maintaining firing solutions on the target. Provide the OOD with the required course, speed, and range information. I want *Buffalo* to match the *Qaaem's* every movement. That guy's not going to lose us."

Qaaem Q-100 –

Karini felt better after getting some rest. He found Captain Naceri in Control. "What is your status?" He asked.

"I am pleased to report ten torpedo mines were seated along the seabed. Each will respond to our signal when we are ordered to attack the carrier," Naceri said, sounding as if he were seeking praise from the senior officer.

"Excellent," Karini replied. "I can't wait to hear the sound of our torpedoes racing toward the American carrier. Has sonar reported any contact with an American submarine?"

"No, Sir," Naceri responded. "We remain vigilant. I instructed the Senior

Sonarman to change operators every two hours to keep fresh eyes on the screen. Now, we wait for the American carrier group to cross the first torpedo barrier." He smiled. "Just think, Captain, we will be able to damage, perhaps sink one of their high-value units without them suspecting it was a torpedo and not a mine."

Karini nodded slowly. "I remind you, according to the message I received yesterday, escort ships are flanking the carrier, searching the waters ahead. Remember, you will be vulnerable to attack by their helicopters or forward screen ships if you are detected. You must be no further than forty-five hundred yards from any one of the antennas. "

Naceri replied smugly, "Exactly, Sir. They will have to find us first. And I will not make that easy for them."

USS Buffalo –

Scott and the XO were sitting in the wardroom having lunch. *Buffalo* continued to track the *Qaaem* after she launched her mines. "I counted eighteen floating mines and sixteen torpedo mines, on the chart, Tom," Scott said.

Varney grimaced. "It's impossible to neutralize those torpedo mines?" He asked. "Sixteen is a lot even for us to handle."

Scott nodded. "At present, the *Qaaem* is the only boat capable of triggering those weapons. Eliminate the *Qaaem* and the *Vinson* Battlegroup will be safe to transit the Strait of Hormuz. As far as the floating mines they're on their own."

A knock on the door interrupted their conversation. IT1 Weathers entered. *What now?* Scott thought.

"It's official," Weathers said handing over a message board.

Scott lifted the lid and read the message. After initialing the page, Scott handed the board to Varney.

Varney looked around the wardroom, pausing when his eyes met Janice's.

Janice didn't want to think about what was coming next. Her heart dropped into her stomach and bounced back in her throat. "Is it bad news?" she asked.

Varney smiled. "I am pleased to announce that Captain Scott is to remain *Buffalo's* CO for the next two years." They couldn't have picked a better officer, he thought.

Scott looked at Janice, wondering how she would take this news. She nodded her acceptance with a smile.

Janice remained silent as the officers shouted their congratulations.

"I have a woman who loves me and a Navy that needs me. I could not have planned this if I tried." He wanted to say something to Janice but with everyone around that had to wait.

"The Navy came to their senses," Varney said. "Great news, Sir."

Weps smiled. "The Brass realized their error," the engineer said. "You deserve it, Sir."

Scott stood. "Thanks, Dennis, Tom, and everyone. I was hoping I would complete a full tour of *Buffalo.* She's a fine ship, and the officers and men are exceptional. I couldn't ask for a better crew."

Just then, the buzzer sounded from under the table. "Here we go, XO," Scott said. He whispered to Janice, "We'll talk later." He rushed from the room and headed for Control with Varney behind him.

"Report!" Scott asked, entering Control.

"Sir, the *Qaaem* is taking up station in the center of the Strait," Lt. Obermeier said. Varney studied the charts. "Sir, she is east of the torpedo mines. It appears she is setting up to attack."

"Messenger go throughout the boat and announce Battle Stations Torpedo," Scott ordered. He prayed the Iranian Captain did not intend to attack an American Naval Ship.

Chapter 26

USS Carl Vinson; Gulf of Oman –

Captain Newhouse knocked on the Admiral's stateroom door and hurried inside. "Admiral, I just received this from Scott. He reports he detected the *Qaaem* deploying ten torpedo mines along the entrance to the Southern Straits."

"Danm it!" Slamming his coffee mug on the table angry at the news. He reached for a towel to wipe the coffee from his hand. "How many did you say?"

"Ten, Sir," Newhouse replied.

Captain Jim Wills walked in with the Admiral's message board. "Sir, a message from—"

Dussault looked up with a grim face. "I already know."

Newhouse exploded, "Does Iran think they can mine the Southern Straits without repercussions?"

"They may be that foolish," The Admiral responded. "Get this information to the Combat Direction Center. Have them delineate the danger zone for each mine." He turned to Wills. "Jim, contact Fifth Fleet. Request Scott remain in the area until our accompanying submarine arrives." He shook his head. "If things blow up, I want Scott protecting my ships."

"Yes, Sir," Wills replied, making a note on his iPad.

"Do we know the range of these torpedoes?" Dussault asked.

Newhouse replied, "Our intelligence community states between six thousand to eight thousand yards. I recommend extending the Torpedo Danger Zone around our ships to ten thousand yards."

Dussault nodded. "I want a line drawn ten thousand yards out from the torpedo mine barrier. To be on the safe side, factor in a fifty-knot speed for each weapon. Instruct the Intel team to record the location of these weapons. I want it ready when I arrive at the CDC. Thanks, Gentlemen," dismissing Captains Wills and Newhouse."

Dussault sat in his flag office in silence after washing his hands from the coffee he spilled. His orders were to relieve the *USS Abraham Lincoln* CVN-72 in the Persian Gulf. He was already two weeks late in relieving the Battle Group. Scott needs to neutralize that Iranian submarine or I will be forced to sail the group through the mine barrier. Those weapon antennas must be destroyed or the *Qaaem* sunk. I don't much care how it is done.

Stepping into the darkened CDC, the Admiral walked over to the status board. It displayed all surface, sub-surface, and aircraft placements within *Vinson's* Battle Space. He noted each unit's fuel status and search sector. He paid special attention to the group's helicopter detachments knowing they were part of his front-line defense. He surveyed the room. Each crew member was doing their job with maximum efficiency. Some were busy entering data and updating tactical displays. He addressed the Lieutenant in charge. "Would you please display the location of the new mines along the Strait?" He asked.

"Yes, Sir." The officer ordered a nearby operator to display the mines. "Admiral," Lt. started to explain, "The exact location of the floating mines was initially reported here." He pointed to the red symbols on the screen. "Unfortunately, that information is twenty-four hours old. Their location now may be different." He faced the Admiral. "Captain Scott has provided us with the location of sixteen torpedo mines. You can see they were placed across the entrance. It looks like one hell of a trap, Sir."

Captain Newhouse entered the space as the Admiral was receiving information on the mines. Dussault pulled Newhouse aside. "Do you believe Scott can eliminate the *Qaaem* from triggering a torpedo mine?"

"I do given time," Newhouse replied.

"He has got to, or we can't possibly bring the Battlegroup into the Straits," Dussault responded. My orders are to get the ships into the Persian Gulf. Unless Washington orders us to remain in the Gulf of Oman, that's what I intend to do. Scott hasn't failed us yet."

Studying the ship status board Newhouse had a sinking feeling. "Admiral, two of our support ships only have 40 percent of their fuel remaining," he said. "We need to refuel those ships before we continue to the Southern Straits."

"You're right! Let's get it done while we have time," the Admiral. replied. "That buys us a little time to let Scott do what he has to do. Let's slow the fleet down until all the ships' fuel tanks are topped off. I do not intend to enter the Southern Straits until the torpedo mines have been neutralized. Wills, collect my senior officers and have them report to the Flag Bridge Conference Room."

Rear Admiral Clint Dussault entered the Flag Conference Room. Having been told not to stand, the officers remained seated. Taking his seat in the middle of the semi-oval brown mahogany table, the Admiral waited for the Culinary specialist on duty to fill their coffee cups. To Will's left sat IT1 Cousins, sitting in front of a large LED screen. He was busy updating the status of the units inside *Vinson's* Battlespace.

Rear Admiral Dussault had hand-picked each Tactical Team member after assuming command of Carrier Strike Group One the previous year. With a collective knowledge base of over one hundred eighty years backing him up, he felt confident in executing the orders to keep the Straits and the Persian Gulf open to naval and commercial shipping. This was not the Admiral's first flag assignment. However, he was still excited at having the opportunity to command a Battlegroup of this magnitude with decisions that could have global repercussions. He felt he was the right man for the challenge. "Gentlemen, let's start," Dussault said. "Chuck, as Commander of Strike Warfare, why don't you take the lead?"

"Aye, Sir," Chuck Reed stood and headed toward the screen showing the upper half of the Gulf of Oman and the Straits of Hormuz. "At present, four F/A-18C Super Hornets are patrolling the entrance to the Straits. The yellow circles denote the Combat Air Patrol search sector. Each flight pattern overlaps the search sector of the four aircraft to ensure maximum sensor coverage. In addition, there is one E-2C Hawkeye early warning aircraft stationed two hundred nautical miles ahead of the carrier."

"Anything else, Chuck?" The Admiral asked.

"Yes, Sir, the Hawkeye on-station reported a build-up of Iranian high-speed patrol boats near the Musandam Peninsula and the Bandar-e-Abbas Naval Base. Based on our previous experience, I expect they are developing swarms to attack our ships and enforce the blocking of shipping channels."

"Their constant disruption is already evident to the commercial traffic entering and leaving the Gulf?" Dussault added, not pleased by this news.

"Sir, tankers and commercial shipping are starting to back up along the southern entrance to the Straits near the eastern Iranian coast. The same holds to the northern entrance between the Musandam Peninsula and Jazieh-ye Larak island."

"Have there been any reports other than from Scott of mining in the Straits?" Dussault asked.

"Yes, Sir, Fifth Fleet reports that the Gulf is being mined all along the northern waters."

"Tempers will soon start to boil over and the shooting will commence. Let's hope that the other side fires first," the Admiral said. "Thanks, Chuck. Commander Gary Langdon, you're up next."

"There is not much that I can add, Admiral. I recommend repositioning the E-2C farther into the Gulf to monitor the Straits of Hormuz. Also, I recommend two MH-60 LAMPs Seahawk helicopters patrol our forward ships while the carrier heads north."

"How many Seahawks are attached to the group?" Dussault asked.

"Six are currently operational with two down for maintenance," Commander Langdon responded.

"And the number of Seahawk Detachments per screen ship?" The Admiral asked.

"Two, Admiral," Langdon said. "Each ship can place one Seahawk in the air and one under a maintenance schedule."

"Do each carry acoustic hydrophones?" Dussaule asked.

"Yes, Sir. Also, each Seahawk can carry two weapons and can be configured with a module of sonobuoys."

"It appears we have ample coverage of the forward area?" Dussault said, staring at the tactical display with the locations of each surface and air unit on the screen.

"Yes, Sir," Commander Langdon said.

"Commander, I want two Seahawks in the air 24/7 searching the outer screen. Keep rotating the units. I want them to continue to sweep the area. Also, formulate a plan to have the screen ships carrying LAMPS alternate placing their helicopters in a ready-thirty-minute lift-off. If a ship reports gaining contact, I want them off the deck in five minutes. I'll get the rotary wings in the air now and send a message to the screen ships right away," Langdon responded.

"Commander Connors, what do you see and hear in the Electronic Intelligence, (ELINT) sphere?" Dussault asked.

"The environment has become richer with information with each passing hour. Every analyst is working to collect, decode, and disseminate the information we're getting from our organic sensors to all concerned parties. So far, Signal Intelligence, (SIGINT), hasn't reported any immediate threat recognition signals from the Iranian surface ship radars," Commander Connors reported.

"Any activity from the Iranian missile sites?" Dussault asked.

"None reported at this time, Admiral. We've charted their location. We have not seen any of their radar sites activated."

"Thanks, Commander. I need to know if any aircraft get painted by their radar by even one radar site. If that happens, they'll get an introduction to a Tomahawk up close and personal!" The Admiral warned.

"Captain Riddel, you're up," Dussault said. "Admiral, we maintain the surface and sub-surface units under the Battle Space except for Commander Scott, who is shadowing the *Qaaem* diesel submarine. You are aware that Commander Scott reported ten additional torpedo mines at the southern end of the Straits? When can I expect *Buffalo* to be attached to the Battlegroup?" Captain Riddel asked.

"*Buffalo* will remain under direct orders from Washington. Commander Scott is operating under a Black Umbrella. Please continue." Dussault asked.

"The mines reported by Commander Scott," Riddel continued, "have been placed on the tactical screen behind me. Each mine and torpedo mine is red. Scott reported that with the loss of one *Kilo*, in addition to the *Qaaem*, there might still be another *Kilo* north of the minefield."

"Bob, any sniff from the E-2 or the Combat Air Patrol (CAPs)?" Dussault asked.

"No, Sir," Commander Connors responded.

"Commander in addition to the F-18 how many F-16 Falcon aircraft do you have up on patrol?" The Admiral asked.

"Four F-16s are flying designated patterns north of the Straits of Hormuz," Connors responded.

"Gentlemen, I don't have to tell you what the Iranians have in store for us should we cross the barrier. First, by closing the Straits and informing Washington to keep out, Iran can trigger any one of the torpedo mines and claim no responsibility."

"You said trigger, Admiral?" Commander Langdon questioned.

"Commander Prorock," Undersar Warfare Commander, asked the Admiral. "Would you care to answer Gray's question?"

"The torpedo mines can be actuated by a submarine or surface ship signal. Up to this point, Scott is dealing with one or two Iranian submarines capable of releasing the torpedo mines."

"According to his recent message, he is tracking the *Qaaem* responsible for placing ten torpedo mines in the Straits. Searching for the antennas is like looking for the proverbial needle in the haystack. I believe the only option Scott has is to eliminate the trigger, meaning the submarine," Commander Prorock said.

"As we know, the Rules of Engagement constrain Scott from attacking. Therefore, he must wait for an attack against *Buffalo* or on one of our surface ships," the Admiral said.

"So, going back to your earlier statement, Admiral, Iran will be able to claim no responsibility for damaging or sinking any ships if they use these torpedo mines? Is that their strategy?" Commander Prorock asked.

The Admiral nodded. "Triggering those mines will be from a distance, so it will appear to be the fault of a captain getting his ship too close to a mine rather than a deliberate attack."

"Ingenious and lethal," Commander Langdon remarked.

"Washington and I are counting on Commander Scott to find and eliminate the threat. Scott believes the *Qaaem* that deployed the mines is the one that can pull the trigger." Dussault said. "Continue, Gene."

"The, USS *Fitzgerald* and USS *Decatur* are conducting active sweeps along the outer zone in case another Iranian diesel operates north of the disabled Iranian supertanker. They reported they reached the ten thousand-yard Torpedo Danger Zone in their search sector. I have directed Commander Miller to establish new search sectors ten thousand yards ahead of our position. USS *Churchill* will remain five thousand yards ahead of us."

The USS *Oscar Austin* will search along the coast of Iran, and, the USS *Sampson* and *Russell* were assigned to search behind the carrier.

"Okay! Let's keep processing and fusing the data from all resources. Information transfer will be the key to our success in eliminating attacks against us as we head toward the Straits. Thanks, gentlemen," The Admiral drew the meeting to a close.

When the officers left, Dussault continued studying the status board. "Have I provided adequate protection around my ships," He mumbled. "I've got to get Washington to order Scott to eliminate the *Qaaem*. How Scott executes his orders without causing an international indecent, I leave to him. On the other hand, if I must execute an attack on the Iranian boats without provocation, that order must come from Washington."

Chapter 27

The Office of the President; Washington, DC –

President Washburn stood behind his desk, talking to Ian Williams when Secretary of the Navy Ray Richards burst into the Oval Office with Secretary of Defense Aspen hot on his heels. Beverly Yancy, Washburn's secretary, hurried behind the group.

"Mr. President, I tried to stop them," Yancy said with an exasperated sigh.

Washburn smiled at her. "It's okay, Beverly. Better cancel the rest of my morning appointments. I see by the look on their faces that this won't wait."

"Mr. President," Richards said, pouring himself a cup of steaming coffee. "We received another message from Commander Scott. He informed us, that in addition to the twenty-four mines stretched across the entrance to the Strait, the *Qaaem* class submarine he has been tracking has placed ten torpedo mines in the same area.

Jack Ure spoke up. "Iran's iFirm Persian TV station, controlled by the Islamic Republic of Iran, announced their government has restricted all traffic in and out of the Gulf."

The President's intercom buzzed. "Mr. President Admiral Armstrong is in your outer office. He must speak with you," Mrs. Yancy announced.

"Show him in, please," The President said, wondering if this day could get any worse.

"Mr. President," Admiral Armstrong said as he hurried into the office. "You asked me to keep you up to date on Scott's movements in the Gulf."

"Let's hear his report," Washburn snapped back.

"Mr. President, have you seen the last message from Scott reporting a *Qaaem* submarine has placed ten additional torpedo mines across the Southern Straits?" The Admiral asked.

"Yes, Chuck and Raymond were just discussing Scott's message," Washburn replied. "Have a seat, Admiral. Please continue, Raymond."

"Our Eastern Battlegroup," Raymond said, "has been ordered to remain in the area. I've also ordered all Middle Eastern bases to remain on alert for the next twelve hours."

"What steps have you taken to reduce the tension with Iran?" Washburn asked

"I have moved our Eastern fleet west, away from the area. Recommend we keep *Vinson* Battlegroup in the Gulf of Oman for now," Raymond responded.

"I don't agree," The President interrupted. "I want Carl *Vinson* in the Persian Gulf."

"Mr. President," Admiral Armstrong quickly countering the President's statement. "I believe that would be a mistake. "I recommend that the Battlegroup remains in the Gulf of Oman. Placing the ships in the Persian Gulf would box the fleet in hostile waters. Suggest you wait until Scott can announce that the Straits are safe to enter. If the Gulf blows up, and the Battle Group is attacked Scott is there to respond to any such attack."

"I agree," Chuck Aspin interjected.

"OK, I see your point," Washburn replied. "Continue, Raymond."

"Admiral Dussault has sent an urgent appeal to Fifth Fleet requesting *Buffalo* remain in the area until his attached submarine arrives tomorrow. He believes the Iranian submarine threat to the Battlegroup is imminent. His concern is torpedo mines at the Southern Straits," The Secretary of the Navy said.

"*Buffalo* is not going anywhere. I want Scott to remain in the area, find the *Qaaem* and neutralize that damn submarine if she attacks our ships. Based on Scott's messages, he has made it clear the threat to his carrier group by the Iranians is real. Do you agree, Admiral?"

"Yes, Sir. He reported the *Qaaem* was positioning her submarine in a direct line behind the torpedo mine barrier and was waiting for the first ship to cross into the field of torpedoes."

"So, we also agreed Admiral Dussault believes the Iranian Captain intends to release the torpedo mines against his ships as they enter the Southern Straits?" The President asked.

"Yes, Mr. President," Raymond Richard said.

"Mr. President," Admiral Armstrong interrupted. "Dr. Mehman, the Iranian nuclear physicist aboard *Buffalo*, informed Scott the torpedo mines must be triggered by either a submarine or a surface ship. The satellite pictures we received this morning show the area clear of shipping for one hundred miles. The only trigger is the *Qaaem*."

"Are you suggesting Scott attack the *Qaaem*?" Washburn asked.

"I believe Scott will attempt to destroy as many torpedo antennas as possible. But it's like looking for a needle in a haystack. His only other option is to strike first."

The President remained silent and then sat down. He placed his hands behind his head and leaned back in his leather desk chair.

No one spoke. They waited for Washburn to utter the first word.

Leaning forward, he slammed his hand on his desk. "I cannot be responsible for starting a war," he shouted. "Although," he said in a much calmer voice, "I have the power to authorize Scott to attack the *Qaaem*, I cannot in all conscious attack a sovereign nation without provocation." He sighed. "Raymond, inform Scott to take what action is necessary to protect the Battlegroup," The President ordered, "But not to initiate any hostile action unless he is fired upon first."

"I will send a message right away," Raymond said and left the office.

"Mr. President, you know what Scott will do if the Iranian submarine launches a weapon at any of the carriers' ships?" Chuck Aspen said.

"I'm aware he'll do what he needs to do to protect our ships," Washburn replied. "If our ships are attacked I will inform Iran they must understand the United States will defend our Naval forces."

"Yes, Mr. President," Chuck said.

Washburn shook his head. "Keep me updated when Scott believes it is safe to bring *Carl Vinson* into the Persian Gulf. Send a message to *Carl Vinson* and the amphibious group to remain in the Gulf of Oman until ordered to enter the Persian Gulf," the President said. "Thank you, again, gentlemen as they left his office."

Washburn sat staring out the window of the Oval Office. *Will Scott eliminate the Qaaem and avert a possible war with Iran?*

Chapter 28

USS Buffalo; Southern Straits of Hormuz –

Dr. Mehman sat in the wardroom having lunch discussing countermeasures against the torpedo mines with Commander Walsh and Scott when IST1 Weathers knocked and entered.

"Captain, we received a message from Washington forwarded from Fifth Fleet." He handed the message board to Scott.

Scott read the message, initialed it, and handed it to his XO. "Iran's Ambassador has reminded the President that the southern entrance to the Straits is closed to all military and commercial shipping. The Ambassador further stated that Iranian submarines are patrolling the area to enforce the embargo."

"And our orders?" Varney questioned.

"Continue to track the *Qaaem* and monitor the deployment of mines. We are to take what measures I deem necessary to guard against their submarines' attacking our ships as they proceed north," Scott said.

"Captain, where is the Battlegroup now?" Mike Walsh asked.

"Currently they are one hundred miles off the coast of Muscat in the Gulf of Oman. *Carl Vinson* has been delayed closing the Straits for twenty-four hours," Scott answered.

"Captain, how do you intend to stop the Iranians from launching torpedo mines?" Glen Thomas asked.

"There are two options," Scott began. "First Fifth Fleet has deployed the MH-53 Sea Dragon helicopters to search the area. We provided Fifth Fleet with the approximate location of the mines. I hold little hope of their success in destroying the antennas. We hope that the Sea Dragon towing the sled behind the aircraft will destroy the torpedo antennas."

The second option is to search for the submarine ordered to trigger the release of those torpedoes. If she launches a torpedo, my response to any attack will be with an Mk-48 ADCAP weapon," Scott continued. "My concern with the first option is the noise created by the Sea Dragon as the aircraft flies across the barrier. Their rotor noise will interfere with our sensors and possible detection of a torpedo if fired."

"Dr. Mehman, you stated a submarine or surface ship could only activate the torpedo mine?" Steve Wilkinson asked.

"Correct," Mehman responded. "With the torpedo mine, the submarine deploys a floating box that rests forty feet below the surface. Extended from the box is the antenna wire that floats twelve inches above the surface."

"Our engineers were working on several options to configure the software to react to changes in the magnetic field. All attempts were unsuccessful," Dr. Mehman said.

Scott eyed Commander Walsh. I wonder, he thought

"Captain, your not thinking of my men neutralizing the mines, the depth of the water is too great." Mike Walsh interjected.

Scott smiled. He looked at Tom Varney and Mike Walsh. "The thought crossed my mind. But I agree?"

"For now," Scott continued, "let's get Hunter involved. Control has the location of the mines launched earlier on the chart table. If we're lucky, the unmanned underwater vehicle (UUV) might find a mine with the wire leading to a box."

Chief Juststone slid Hunter into the torpedo tube as Glen Thomas prepared to activate the connection. Next, he attached the spool containing the five thousand yards of fiber optic cable behind the UUV propellers and the other half of the spindle to the breach door. Satisfied, Juststone swung the one-hundred-pound brass door shut and rotated the locking mechanism. He wrote on the whiteboard attached to the door 'UUV.' "Dr. Stone, ready for system checks," Juststone said.

Stone pressed the power switch on the control panel. The system lights switched from red to green and back. He began verifying the acoustic hydrophones, amplifiers, searchlight, rudder, and batteries. "Good to go. The system checks are complete," Thomas said.

"Flooding Tube two," Juststone said. "Control, Hunter's ready to deploy."

Lt. Steve Wilkinson acknowledged, "Very well, open the outer door, Tube two."

"The outer door opened," Juststone reported.

"How do we look, Navigator?" Scott asked.

Lt. Jeff Obermeier leaned over the chart table and placed the opened dividers between the projected points of the first torpedo mine and *Buffalo*. "Distance between mine number one and two is three thousand yards, Captain."

"Very well, OOD, come to 'All Stop'. Torpedo Room, launch Hunter," Scott ordered. "Now, we wait, XO, for the UUV to sniff out the location of the mines."

In the torpedo room, Dr. Stone and Chief Juststone heard the faintest sound of the electric motor start as Hunter left the tube on the way to its next, perhaps most critical, mission.

Qaaem Q-100: Gulf of Oman –

"Captain, I have detected a strange noise off our port beam," Sonar Technician Giv Parsi announced.

"Coming," Captain Naceri responded from Control.

"What do you hear, Parsi?" Naceri asked, standing over his right shoulder.

"There," Parsi said, pointing to the screen. "See the small dark line on the bearing time recorder?"

"Yes, what did it sound like?" The Captain asked, trying to understand what the dark line represented.

"An electric motor," Parsi responded, looking at the monitor as he spoke.

"Electric motor?" The Captain questioned.

"That's what it sounded like," he said, handing the Captain a set of headphones.

Naceri pressed the earpiece against his ear.

Parsi flipped on the recorder.

"I agree. It does sound like an electric motor. It is weak and keeps fading in and out. It cannot be a torpedo, or, for that matter, anything else I have ever heard."

Parsi changed his sector parameters to narrow the search window, picking up additional noise transits as the Captain listened.

"Could it have been a submarine outer door opening?" Naceri asked.

"No, Sir. It does not match the recordings of American submarines opening their torpedo doors. A low thud is normally associated when the door locks open."

Karini had been listening. "There must be an explanation. These anomalies don't appear anywhere. My sonar operators also reported something like what you just described. So, the only rational reason is an American submarine is shadowing us."

"Keep searching and let me know the minute you hear anything else," Naceri ordered.

Returning to Control, the Captain waited for a report from Sonar. "It can't be an American submarine. We left it searching for us back at the tanker," Naceri said to Captain Karini, standing next to him.

"Don't be so quick to assume the American submarine did not follow us here," Karini said.

"I'm not concerned. This new class submarine has been wrapped with sound-isolated pads. All onboard equipment has rubber footing," Naceri replied. "I doubt that an American submarine could detect this boat.

"What about an American submarine attached to the Battlegroup searching the waters in this area?" Karini asked.

"We are too far north. If the carrier has a company submarine, I believe it would remain relatively close to the carrier," Naceri replied.

No, I do not, but there is always a first time," Karini said. "I recommend coming to 'All Stop,' and securing all unnecessary equipment. Confirm all personnel not assigned to a duty station are in their bunks. Let us see if a hungry shark is swimming around."

"Control, I am detecting an electric motor again," Parsi announced.

Naceri and Captain Karini hurried to sonar. They joined the operators studying the broadband line running down the screen.

"Parsi, could it be a shoreline generator from a power station?" Karini asked, frustrated at not being able to identify the source of the unique sounds.

"There is no power station this far south. This sound is off our port beam, away from land. It sounds like fish farts," Parsi said.

"What," Naceri exploded. "Are you toying with me?"

"No, Sir," Sonar Technician Giv Parsi responded, alarmed at his superior's angry tone. "Wait! I just lost the signal again."

Naceri scowled at the operator. "This is not a time for humor. The men on this ship are depending on you." And on me, he thought, as he prayed the Americans did not have a new and unknown weapon that could endanger his ship. "Find that damn sound," he ordered.

Chapter 29

USS Buffalo; Southern Straits of Hormuz –

Dr. Stone didn't realize he commanded Hunter to point directly at *Qaaem* Q-100. He saw the signal-to-noise meter jump twenty decibels on the control panel. "Got something huge! Holy cow!" he uttered.

"Back her down, Fred!" Glen hollered as Hunter's light reflected off a black object directly in her path.

Stone slammed the throttle into reverse. "Hold Hunter's position," Fred ordered. Something black filled the screen.

"What the hell have you found, Dr. Stone?" The XO asked, looking up at the monitor in Control.

"I'm not sure," Stone responded, moving the UUV to the left of the black object.

"Captain, to Control," the XO called using the sound-powered phone.

Resting after a long night on watch, Scott left his stateroom and headed for Control. "What is it, XO?" Scott asked, moving behind Varney, peering at the video.

"In searching for mines, we stumbled across what appears to be a submarine."

"I'll be damned," Scott said. *Kilo* or *Qaaem?*" he asked as Hunter moved along the hull. "Dr. Stone, move Hunter higher," he ordered.

Hunter started to lift along the rounded hull.

"What the hell?" Scott said. "We have found the second submarine." Scott looked at the fathometer. "Sixty-five feet. He's lining up to launch one of his torpedo mines at the carrier."

The searchlight on the nose of the UUV stretched across the deck of the submarine. The light brightened as it reflected off the sail.

"I don't believe our luck," Varney exclaimed. "We have found the *Qaaem*."

"Dr. Stone, move Hunter above the bridge. I want to determine if she is floating a wire," Scott said.

Scott and Varney looked at the monitor as Hunter slowly lifted toward the top of the sub's sail.

"Stop the lift. I see a thin wire extended from the top of the sail to the surface," Dr. Stone said.

"Forget searching for the antennas we have found the trigger. Eliminating her wire will neutralize all torpedo mines for now," Scott said. "If there is another Iranian submarine or surface ship in the area the fleet has a major problem. "Right now we have only one option."

"Destroy the wire?" Varney interjected. "They're not going to like your order," he said with a sheepish smile.

Scott pressed the button on the sound-powered phone. "Chief Juststone, let me speak to Dr. Fred Stone. Yes, Sir. Captain Scott wants to talk to you, Fred." Handing the phone to the engineer.

"Dr. Stone speaking."

"Fred, I want you to secure Hunter to the antenna wire by wrapping the tether around the cable."

"If I do, we might not be able to retrieve the UUV," Dr. Stone responded.

"I want you to destroy the wire using Hunter's onboard explosives," Scott demanded.

There was dead silence.

"Fred," Scott continued. "We can't neutralize all the mines, and we are running out of time. The first ship from the Battlegroup will be in the area in less than three hours. We need to destroy the communication wire that will launch the torpedo mine."

Fred didn't say a word.

"Fred, are you still there? Scott asked.

"Okay. I will maneuver Hunter around the wire," Stone said. Christ, he thought, I can't believe I've got to destroy our UUV.

Scott kept an eye on the monitor as Hunter circled the antenna wire. He saw the minisub stop. The light on the UUV pointed down toward the submarine's deck.

Fred pressed the red button marked detonation in the control box. He saw the clock flash five minutes and start counting down. "Five minutes until detonation," Dr. Thomas announced.

Scott waited anxiously as the clock counted down.

"I wonder how the Defense Advanced Research Project Agency (DARPA) and Naval Undersea Warfare Center (NUWC) will react when we inform them that we destroyed Hunter?" Fred asked Glen.

Scott sighed. "XO let's hope this works," he said.

Qaaem Q-100 –

Captains Karini and Naceri sat in the wardroom, anticipating the arrival of the first American ship.

"We will make our first kill in three to four hours," Naceri said enthusiastically. "I instructed Sonar I was going to allow their advance ships to cross our barrier. Once the carrier enters the trap, we will release our first weapon."

"Excellent. I only wish I had the opportunity to conduct the first att—"

An explosion reverberated through the hull. "What the hell?" Karini shouted and ran for Contol. Naceri followed.

"Report," Captain Naceri demanded.

"The explosion came from the sail," Lieutenant Habibi reported.

"Control, we lost continuity on our communication wire. Trying to reconnect," the IT announced.

"OOD, come to periscope depth," Naceri ordered. The captain watched the planesmen pull the yolk back. He felt the submarine start to rise toward the surface.

"Passing three hundred feet," the Chief of the Boat announced. "Two hundred feet—one hundred feet—Leveling of at sixty feet."

Karini saw the fury in Naceri's eyes. *I pity the poor soul when he finds out who is responsible.*

Naceri turned to Karini. "Damn them! Unless you can reconnect the antenna wire, you will be unable to launch your torpedo mines."

"There's another way to destroy the carrier, Captain," Karini said a sly smile on his face.

USS Buffalo –

"Detected an explosion," Sorenson announced, seeing the dark smudge on the spectrum analyzer. "Q-100 is on the move."

"Here we go," Scott said. "Slow and easy. We don't want to alert them we're following. Pass the word Man Battle Stations, Torpedo. Sonar, talk to me."

"She's coming to periscope depth," Sorenson replied.

"Diving Officer, bring us up to PD. Let's look at what we've snagged, XO," Scott ordered. "Range to target?"

"Coming to periscope depth," the diving officer announced. "Slow and easy boys standing behind the plainsman and helmsman."

"Fifteen hundred yards," Senior Chief Fire Control Technician Jack Russell replied.

"Let's close to one thousand yards, XO," Scott ordered. "I don't want to lose this guy."

Qaaem Q-100 –

Captain Naceri stood on the pedestal, hands on the stainless-steel hydraulic lift ring above his head. "Up scope," he said, flipping down the handles as it lifted from the tube. He rotated the periscope. "No shapes or shadows."

Karini struggled to keep his desire to take over command of the submarine. As a senior officer, he had the right to remove Naceri from command. He prayed Naceri could handle it.

"Scope breaking, watch your depth, Diving Officer," Naceri barked. "I will fix that bastard for sabotaging our weapons."

"Do not let your anger blind you," Karini advised.

Naceri rotated the handlebars three hundred sixty degrees in low power, then switched to high power and circled again. "Down scope," he shouted.

Karini stared at the monitor attached to the bulkhead. "I can't see the wire, Captain."

"It confirms what we know. The communication wire is gone. But how is it a mystery? Helm, make your depth forty meters (130ft)." Naceri ordered. "The loss of the wire will not defeat me. I will launch my onboard torpedoes at the first American ship to cross the barrier. Unlike the torpedo mines, the Russian weapons are wire-guided. Sinking a surface ship is almost assured. Damn them all to hell."

Chapter 30

USS Buffalo; Gulf of Oman –

"Mark your depth," Scott ordered.

"One hundred feet," the Diving Officer responded.

"Make your depth six zero feet, Scott said anxious to see what they caught. "Up scope. Scott stood next to the search periscope waiting for it to rise out of the well. As the handlebars passed in front of him he pulled them down, wrapped one arm around the left handle, and looked into the optical lens. "Scope breaking. XO bearing to the Qaaem?"

"Three zero two degrees," Varney announced reading the dials on the FC Weapon analyzer. Scott continued to circle until he reached the reported bearing. "There she is XO. She appears to have broached. Men are up in the sail taking pictures. Down scope."

Scott waited several minutes before raising the pariscope. "Up scope," Scott ordered. "They're prying a piece of what from the antenna housing?"

"It could be a piece of the UUV," Varney suggested.

"Down scope," Scott announced turning the steel ring above his head. "Messenger find Dr. Glen Thomas and have him report to Control," Scott ordered. "He might shed some light on what they found."

Glen Thomas and Fred entered Control and walked up to Scott and Varney.

"Can either one of you tell us what one of the crew members is holding in his hand?" Pointing to the monitor.

Glen and Fred looked at the screen for several seconds. "What do you think Fred?" Glen asked.

"It's got to be a part of the composite hull of the UUV," he replied turning to Scott and Varney.

"You said the hull?"

"Yes Captain," Fred replied.

"Were there any identification markings on the hull?" Varney questioned.

"None Glen," said. "We purposely did not place any identification markings on the UUV. If that piece he holds in his hand is part of the hull, testing would reveal it is made from composite material. The ingredients are not unique to the US."

Scott looked at Varney. He seemed relieved that the Iranian Captain would not know what caused the explosion. "Again I'm sorry we had to destroy Hunter," Scott said. "Thanks for your input. We'll talk later."

Fred and Glen left Control and returned to the wardroom.

"Tom let's remain at PD. If the *Qaaem* decides to take up station in the middle of the Straits we'll sit off her port baffles and wait."

"What are you thinking Joe?" Varney asked.

"I don't believe the Captain will give up. He has an opportunity to attack the carrier. Unless he is ordered not to launch a weapon at the carrier he will release his torpedoes."

"Drs. Thomas, and Stone, please return to the wardroom," Scott said.

After the engineers returned to the wardroom, Mehman was the first to ask what the captain wanted.

"It appears a part of the UUV was stuck on the top of the sail of the Qaaem," Fred said.

"We found the other submarine?" Dr. Lace asked. Janice knew if there was another submarine there would be another fight to the death.

"Will Captain Scott attack?" Dr. Mehman asked, a worried expression on his face.

"Not unless they launch a weapon first," Lt. Morton responded. "The Captain set battle stations in case the other submarine's CO decides to attack the carrier."

Janice Lace leaned back and closed her eyes. "I'm facing a battle, and I just got engaged," she mumbled.

"Did you say something, Dr. Lace?" Dr. Mehman asked.

"No, I was thinking out loud." Janice felt the tension in her back.

Just then, CS2 Brady opened the door and peered into the wardroom. "Control," he said on his sound-powered phone, "Our ship riders are in the wardroom. Yes, Sir." He turned to those at the table. "The XO wants all of you to remain here until we secure from battle stations. Should you hear the collision alarm, remain seated and hold onto the table. I assume you all know where the emergency air-breathing masks are and how to use them?"

They all nodded.

"Good," Brady replied, left, and shut the door.

No one said anything, but the implication of what might happen in the next several minutes was clear.

"I feel a slight down angle," Stone murmured.

"Yes, I feel it too," Lace said.

"Have any of you experienced a shock wave from an underwater explosion?" Dr. Mehman asked.

Each shook their head.

Lace smiled sympathetically at the Iranian scientist. "Are you worried about *Buffalo* being attacked, Dr. Mehman?" she asked.

"Yes! Is that not why Brady said we should grab hold of the table at the sound of the alarm?"

They each looked at each other. Janice could feel the tension in the room.

"OK, Dr. Mehman, you have our attention. It appears you have something to say," Lt. Morton said.

"As most of you know, water has a much higher density than air," he started. "It is much harder to move and compress making it an excellent conductor of a shock wave from an explosion. So, the slight roll we experienced, was the result of a shock wave from a nearby explosive device."

"I hadn't thought about the effects of an underwater explosion," Stone admitted.

"So what happened?" Janice asked. She remembered feeling the results of an explosion before. As *Buffalo's* Science Advisor two years ago.

"The expanding gas," Mehman continued, "creates a pressure wave, key to the destructive power. This wave has a much greater intensity than most people realize."

"Now think of an exploding warhead in water. The eruption creates a gas globe that expands radially outward until the hydrostatic pressure reaches the maximum distance from the point of the explosion. In this instance, the globe collapses, and another is produced until all the energy of motion is dissipated.

"What happens to the target or *Buffalo* in this case if were attacked?" Thomas asked.

"The pressure created by the blast can rupture the hull of a submarine or surface ship," Dr. Mehman concluded.

"Then, let's hope we're far enough away," Morton said.

"I can only guess what Joe must be thinking as he prepares *Buffalo* for a possible battle," Janice whispered to Patrica. "I wish I could help him."

"Your man is one cool customer. He doesn't seem to get raddled easily," Patrica said with a smile.

Janice nodded. "I have confidence in him."

"I hope that is enough to guarantee our survival," Mehman muttered listening in on their conversation.

Buffalo moved under a cloak of silence through the grayish waters. Operators in Control sat monitoring their equipment. Every sound picked up by sonar was scrupulously analyzed and placed on the DRT trace.

"Sonar, Fire Control, how far has the towed array been streamed?" Varney asked.

"Twelve hundred feet," Senior Chief Richardson replied. "Well beyond our baffle region."

"Who's monitoring the array?" Varney asked.

"I have Price, on the stack," Senior Chief Richardson replied.

"Range to target?" Scott asked Varney.

"Two thousand yards," the XO responded.

"Let's move just outside the starboard side of his baffle area. If he intends to launch an attack on a surface ship, I want to give us a clear shot at his torpedoes. Restrict weapon ceiling to one hundred feet."

"Aye, aye," Varney replied. With a ceiling of one hundred feet, he knew the Mk-48 torpedo would stay fifty feet below the carrier's hull.

Pulling the mic down from the overhead. "Give me an update, Sorenson?" Scott demanded.

"Signal is strong. I just picked up two of our destroyers' active sonars on the intercept receiver. From the dB levels, they are in high power, but still nowhere near detecting us," Sorenson replied.

"Are they interfering with our sensors?" Varney asked.

"If they continue to close they will start to mask our return," Sorenson said.

"Captain message from USS *Carl Vinson*," Weathers interrupted.

"Tom, Check if any action is required," Scott said, as *Buffalo* moved closer to the *Qaaem*'s baffles.

"No, Sir," Varney said after looking at the message. "*Vinson* reported reducing the speed of advance to ten knots and continuing toward the Straits. They also informed us two Sea Dragon helicopters are en route to assist in searching for mines."

Scott nodded. "Weathers, release a communication buoy and contact *Carl Vinson*. Give them our position. Tell them we are tracking a *Qaaem* submarine. Request they secure their active sonar. Report they're interfering with our passive sensors. Also, add we have neutralized the torpedo mines and request they direct the MH-53 helicopters to search north of our position.

"Communication buoy loaded. Ready to launch," Weathers said.

Varney stepped up to the launcher switch and pressed the button. He looked at the launcher light turn from red to green. Buoy away, he said.

"Let's hope they receive the message. That's all we need. Two active destroyers and Sea Dragons interfering with our sensors. Don't they realize their interference could mean life or death?" Scott snapped.

"I'm betting on the two destroyers not responding to your requests,

Captain," the XO said.

Scott said, "My experience tells me hell would freeze over before our guys comply. Let's just focus on maintaining track of that damn submarine."

Varney frowned. He looked up at the intercept receiver. "The SNR levels continue to creep up." He shook his head. "Sir, we've got to get to deeper water."

Scott replied. "We'll wait a little longer to see what our target is up to. I don't want to lose him by going under the sound barrier."

"The way I see it," Varney said, "Our own Battlegroup could mistakenly launch weapons on us. More likely the Q-100 could launch an attack. If we are not going deep let's load a Three-Star Grenade into the signal ejector in case we need it. Lighting up the sky with a phosphorus flare might keep our boys from launching an attack on us."

Scott said, "I agree, XO. Have several flares placed near the signal gun if we need to launch in rapid succession?"

Varney picked up his phone. "Torpedo Room, load, and standby to launch a Three Star Grenade flare on the Captain's command," he ordered.

"Control, Torpedo room, bringing three flares to the aft signal injector," Chief Juststone responded.

"Control, Sonar Q-100 is changing course. Wait! I'm detecting a helicopter's active dipping sonar. It's starting to interfere with my sensors," Sorenson said.

"What now?" Scott muttered his lips tightened worried Sonar would not detect the *Qaaem* weapon launch until it was too late.

Chapter 31

USS Winston S. Churchill; Gulf of Oman –

Lieutenant Braden entered the pilot's berthing compartment and flipped on the lights. "Peterson, get your ass out of the rack. You will be going to a thirty-minute standby in ten minutes. Your turn to bore holes in the sky."

"All right, all right," Lt. Peterson, yelled, jumping out of his rack. "The word is there are one possibly two Iranian submarines in the area," Braden said removing his green flight suit.

"Well maybe I'll get lucky and tag one," Peterson said slipping on his suit.

"Captain," referring to Rusty Smith, CO of *Churchill*, "a message from *Buffalo*. He is requesting we secure active sonar on both forward screen ships," Lt. Tom Ralph the ship Communication Officer said.

"Do it," Tom, the CO ordered. "If we cripple their sensors we are the ones that will suffer from an attack."

"Petty Officer Rydell secure active sonar," Lt. Ralph ordered.

"Going passive," Rydell replied.

"Launch Safety Officer (LSO), place Light Air Borne Multi-Platform (Lamps) 610 in Ready Thirty," Captain Smith ordered.

Lieutenant Will Peterson, his copilot, Lt. Junior Grade Braden Cook, the Airborne Tactical Officer, and a 1st class Aviation Antisubmarine Warfare

Operator (ASO) stepped through the hanger door and climbed into the helicopter.

Four men dressed in yellow fire retardant suits stood by with fire hoses.

Lt. Peterson flipped the switch to start the port engine. He watched the gages as the engine spooled up to the maximum revolutions. A loud whining sound filled the cockpit. Again the pilot reached up and flipped the switch to start the starboard engine. He waited for the second engine to reach its speed and temperature. Satisfied he announced, "Engaging rotors."

"Sea Dipper 610 standing by to launch," Ltjg. Cook reported to the Launch Safety Officer.

"Captain Sea Dipper is ready to launch," the LSO announced.

"LSO, release 610," Smith ordered.

"Lt. Peterson, you have permission to Launch," the Safety Officer said.

Peterson pulled back on the collective lever and adjusted the cyclic control to the left, placing the helicopter off the port side. The two G.E. Turboshaft engines, coupled to a three thousand four hundred shaft horsepower transmission, roared as the helo lifted from the flight deck.

"Sea Dipper," the Airborne Surveillance and Control Operator announced in the Combat Information Center (CIC). "Initial dip position ten thousand yards ahead of our unit."

"Roger," Peterson responded, pushing the collective lever forward.

The nose of the helo dipped as the power was applied. Within seconds, Sea Dipper reached a speed of one hundred thirty knots.

Sitting in front of her radar console, the Operation Specialist (OS) tracked 610 movements toward the farthest-on-circle imprinted with a yellow grease pencil on the radar repeater. She saw the helo hover over the initial dip position.

"Standby to 'mark dip.' Now! Now! Now! Mark dip!" Ltjg. Cook announced, hovering sixty feet above the surface.

"ASO release the dome," Lt. Peterson ordered.

The Aviation Antisubmarine Warfare Operator reached up and tapped the touch-sensitive button on the Dome Control unit, releasing the active/passive hydrophone. The cabin vibrated as the high-speed winch released the sensor from the underside of the fuselage.

"Ball wet," announced the ASO after the hydrophone dropped below the surface. After a brief passive search, the operator announced. "Switching to active." The ASO leaned over and pressed her face on the black rubber tube, covering the scope. She heard the and saw first transmission of the active pulse. Eyes shielded from any external light, she followed the reddish sound wave propagated symmetrically out on her scope to the end of the five thousand-yard search area. "No joy," she announced to the pilot.

USS Buffalo: Gulf of Oman –

Senior Chief Richardson reported, "Control, active dipping helicopter to the west. The Destroyers (DDGs) are opening to the south. The signal-to-noise from the two destroyers is dropping."

"Where the hell is the *Qaaem* heading, XO?" Scott asked.

"Toward the east, out of the path of the surface ships," Varney replied, reading the dials on the Fire Control panel.

"I want to close within two thousand yards of her port baffles. The closer we get, the better sonar will be able to maintain track," Scott ordered.

"Based on her current course, one eight zero, speed four knots she is lining up to close the carrier's position," Varney said, watching the bearing dots on the monitor.

"I believe she intends to launch her torpedo," Scott said. "XO. Ask Dr. Mehman to join us in Control."

Scott was leaning over the chart table when Dr. Mehman entered moments later. "Dr., you mentioned you helped develop the torpedo acoustic warhead. Correct?" He asked.

"Yes," Dr. Mehman replied minutes later entering Control. "What questions can I answer?"

"What distance must the torpedo travel before the warhead is armed?"

Scott asked.

"Two thousand yards is what the fleet ordered for each weapon," Mehman responded.

"Can the torpedoes be adjusted to fewer than two thousand yards?" Scott asked.

"No, Sir. The operators can increase the distance before the weapon arms but can't override the two-thousand-yard safety setting. Captain, you understand the Type 533 weapons are wire-guided." Mehman continued.

"I was not sure, but thanks for providing me the update on the torpedo. Thanks, Doctor. You've been a great help. Please return to the wardroom and remain there until you hear secure from GQ," Scott said.

Varney listened and did not say a word. "I'm not sure I like where you are going with this, Captain," he said.

"I understand your concern XO. I want *Buffalo* one thousand five hundred yards off the port side. That places *Buffalo* well behind the weapon when it arms. Other than a slight dent to our bow, we should suffer no damage. We will remain behind the weapon's acoustic window," he said. She can't attack what her weapon does not see.

Varney sat back. *Would I make this decision?*

"Sir, I recommend we move into the middle of the Strait with our outer doors open. If the *Qaaem* launches weapons, we counter with four Mk-48 torpedoes down the firing bearing. It is not a perfect solution, but if we activate our first two weapons directly astern of their Russian weapons, they will detect the torpedoes and destroy them. Our third and fourth torpedoes will be directed at the *Qaaem*.

"You seem confident in your approach. Have you tried this before?" Scott asked.

"Yes, in New London at the Submarine Officer Advanced Course using the simulator. I tested my idea with targets at various bearings. The target was destroyed in all but one simulation."

"And the weapons fired at a surface ship?" Scott quarried.

"One out of two were destroyed," Varney said.

"I like your idea. It gives us a fifty-fifty chance of destroying their weapons.

forcing the weapons out of each tube. Control felt the ship quiver as each torpedo was released from its tube. The six-cylinder internal combustion engines pushed the two-ton weapons at fifty-plus knots toward their targets.

"Weapons running hot and normal," Lieutenant Wilkinson announced. "Weapons one and two acquired the wakes of the two Russian torpedoes. Weapons three and four shifted to high speed. Hold continuity on all four weapons."

"All head one-third," Scott ordered. This better work, he thought.

Qaaem Q-100 –

"Weapons activated and running directly for the carrier," Lieutenant Azizi, Naceri's XO, reported.

Naceri glanced at Karini, "I have waited years to sink an American ship. A carrier? Allah be Praised."

"Praise Allah," Karini replied hoping they would survive.

"Weapons' in the water!" Parsi shouted over the internal speakers. "We're being attacked!"

Naceri shouted, "Ahead flank right full rudder."

The Weapons Officer reported, "Lost weapon continuity on both weapons."

"Who, what fired those torpedoes? It's not possible," Naceri shouted. "Those are our torpedoes you are hearing Sonar."

"NO! American Mk-48 torpedoes Captain," Praise said panicking in his voice.

"Evade," Naceri screamed. "Give me more speed!"

Karini stood next to the planesmen. He saw Naceri panic when Sonar announced they were under attack. He listened to the active pinging.

"Yes, Sonar was correct, Mk-48," Karini said. He heard the torpedoes shift to a fast speed. The weapons had locked on the *Qaaem*. He knew there was little hope of evading.

Naceri suddenly realized it was hopeless. He could not outrun American high-speed torpedoes. He cast his eyes at Karini and saw him bracing himself for the strike. *I gambled and lost*, he thought listening to the weapon's rapid pulses and the high wine of its propellers. "XO launch countermeasure," he yelled, hoping to save his ship and his life.

Naceri felt his ship shake as the countermeasure was jettisoned from the launcher. He took a deep breath and heard the explosion of the decoy. He prayed the massive ball of air bubbles would fool the American torpedoes into detonating.

"Sonar report!" Yousefi ordered, realizing his life would end soon if the countermeasure did not stop the weapons.

Parsi shouted, "American torpedo reverted to search mode."

Naceri felt a surge of hope.

Parsi screamed, "The second torpedo blew through the noise barrier!"

"Launch another countermeasure," Naceri yelled. Panic had overtaken logic. Getting a grip on himself he turned to Karini and said "At least I will take the damn carrier with me."

"Allah, be praised," Karini cried realizing his life was over. He will soon join his ship and crew. He grabbed the internal mic, Now hear this stand-by for torpedo detonation pushing the collision alarm."

"Strike imminent," Parsi screamed over the collision alarm.

Naceri grabbed the railing and held on tightly. He saw the panic gripping his men as they waited to die.

The rapid pulsing alarm grew louder as the deadly torpedoes bour down on the *Qaaem*.

"I don't want to die," Parsi screamed throwing down his headphones. He sprang for the escape ladder. Grabbing the rungs, he climbed halfway up before the XO pulled him down. Two men joined the XO, holding the crying sailor in their arms. They each looked up to the overhead and waited.

Captain Naceri waited to hear the explosion of his torpedoes. It would be his salvation to die a hero for sinking the American titan. Why did the sound not come? He should have heard it by now. Why? The answer came to him. Somehow, the American Captain tricked his weapons. The carrier survived.

He closed his eyes knowing he was seconds away from his ascension toward Allah. I failed, were his last thoughts.

The water erupted below the *Qaaem's* hull as the torpedo detonated.

The first explosion broke the submarine's back sending a steel rod through Karini's chest. Tons of water flooded Control killing all inside. "You young fool," Naceri, hissed as the water enveloped him.

Chapter 33

USS Buffalo Souther Straits—-

"Captain, the first two torpedoes are locked on the Russian weapons," Varney announced in a higher-pitched voice. "Our weapons are changing depth in response to the Russian torpedoes."

"Range to the torpedoes," Scott asked, displaying no sign of anxiety. He knew this was a critical action. He could not afford to miss. To do so would mean the carrier could be sunk by the Russian torpedoes. Scott looked around the Control room. There were twenty-five men squeezed into the hot room. Except for the sound of the torpedoes the room was relatively quiet.

"Six hundred yards and closing," the XO responded, eyes glued to the weapons readout. "Our weapons are still locked on and adjusting to the Russian weapons course changes."

"Maintain current weapon ceiling of one hundred feet," Scott ordered. "Give me the range to the carrier."

"Fifteen hundred yards," Senior Chief Russell reported reading the digital numbers on the Fire Control Console.

"XO, we can't wait for our weapons proximity fuse to detonate our warheads," Scott said.

"Give it one more minute," Varney replied. "The Mk-48 ADCAP weapons are closing the Russian torpedoes."

"We can't wait much longer," Scott muttered, glancing at the Weapon Control Panel. "Range?"

"Three hundred yards, and closing Captain," Varney replied anxious his weapons were not close enough to avert the destruction to the carrier.

"XO, standby to detonate," Scott said. He counted the seconds.

"Two hundred yards," Varney announced.

"DETONATE!" Scott shouted. "DETONATE."

The XO pressed the detonation buttons on the Weapons Console. The third and fourth Mk-48 ADCAP torpedoes exploded astern of the two Russian weapons. Both communication wires were broken. Each weapon was enveloped in the air globe and pushed down toward the sea floor.

"Sorenson, the status of the Russian weapons," Scott demanded.

"Torpedoes appear to be weaving. The radiated noise from their propellors has become erratic. The sound shifts from high speed, to low and back to high. They are no longer running straight for the carrier."

"The explosions had to have affected the Russian torpedoes," he thought. "Damn," Scott cursed. "Give me something Sorenson."

"Wait!" Sorenson announced. "They're diving toward the ocean floor. Holy cow! They just plowed into the seabed. The torpedo engines are racing. Sonerson looked at the bearing time recorder. The black line disappeared. "The torpedoes engines have shut down."

Scott relieved that Varney's plan worked, turned his attention to his two weapons locked on the Iranian submarine. "Range to our weapons?" he asked.

"Target detonation three seconds," Varney reported.

Hearing the XO's announcement, Sorenson threw off his headset before the two-hundred-pound high-explosive warheads detonated under the hull of the Iranian submarine. Even with the headset off, he heard the powerful blast as the first and then the second torpedo exploded. "Bullseye," Sorenson yelled. "Control, she's breaking up."

Patrica, Janice, the two engineers, and Mehman scurried under the table. They each wrapped their arms around the two steel pipes welded to the deck and held on. They knew what came next from Dr. Mehman's description of an underwater detonation.

"Hold on!" Dr. Mehman groaned, pulling his body close to the pipe.

Janice gripped the table leg, praying Scott was all right.

Patricia thought of Walsh, wondering if his team was secure in the ASDV or their onboard compartments.

"Sound the collision alarm," Scott ordered."Everyone hang on he shouted."
The high-pitched wail of the alarm screamed throughout the ship. It was
soon followed by a sudden gut-wrenching jerk as the first shock wave pushed
massive amounts of water against *Buffalo*'s starboard side. The submarine
lifted sharply and twisted to port. Coffee cups not secure in their holders
crashed onto the deck. Men were knocked to the deck or against cabinets.

"One more," Scott shouted. "Hold on." Scott clasped the stainless-steel
railing surrounding the periscopes as the submarine tilted forty degrees.

The men in Control grabbed whatever was available and held on tight as
the boat rolled violently from the explosions.

Scott felt a second shockwave slam against the hull. *Buffalo* rolled twenty
degrees off-center. He prayed everyone on board was safe. Once, the ship
steadied, he wondered if the *ASDV* was still attached. "Turn off those damn
alarms," Scott yelled. "Damage Control, report."

The Chief of the Boat disengaged the ship's alarms.

The crew was surprised by the sudden silence. Some laughed releasing the
tension they had experienced earlier.

Scott saw several men pick themselves off the deck. "Anyone hurt," he
asked as the men moved to their stations.

Varney walked over to a Petty Officer Clarence holding his head. "Clarence
has a cut on his forehead," he said holding his shoulders to stop the man
swaying.

"Messenger take Clarence to Sick Bay and have him looked at," Scott
ordered.

Sorenson shouted, "The Iranian boat is sinking. She just imploded."

Men assigned to the repair party started moving through the ship verifying
all compartments had not sustained any significant damage.

"Engineering report," the XO asked over the 1MC.

"Waiting for engine room Upper and Lower Level reports," Fender responded."

"Captain. She's gone," Sorenson announced.

Scott felt sad at the loss of so many lives. What a tragic waste, he thought.

He picked up his mic. "Now secure from Battle Stations," he ordered, feeling suddenly very tired.

"Is it over, Dr. Mehman?" Dr. Stone asked, still shaky.

"I believe so," Mehman replied.

"Control, Engineering reports no damage," Fender said.

"Dennis have someone check the ASDV," Varney ordered.

"I'll get right on it, XO," the Engineering Officer replied.

Scott was relieved only two of his men had some cuts and there were no broken bones. He was about to leave Control when Sorenson said, "Sir, we've picked up another contact. Classification unknown."

"Sonar, keep your eyes and ears open. There may be another submarine hunting us."

USS *Winston S. Churchill* –

Captain Smith sat in the Captain's chair on the port side of the bridge. He was just handed a fresh cup of black coffee.

"OOD what is the weather forecast," Smith asked.

"We're moving into a high front. Warn weather, calm seas, and blue skies, Captain," the OOD said.

Smith loved being at sea. He had joined the Navy when he was eighteen as an Enlisted man. Was accepted to the Naval Academy a year later. He never married. The navy was his life and mistress.

"Torpedo in the water!" Sonarmen, First Class Johnston shouted. "No! Make that six weapons!"

"OOD, all ahead flank! Left full rudder," Captain Smith ordered the watch officer on the bridge. "Sound General Quarters (GQ)."

"Sonar give me a bearing to the weapons," Smith demanded.

"Torpedoes are astern of us," Johnston replied.

"Helmsmen belay my last," Smith ordered. "Return to our previous heading." Christ I was heading right into the weapons.

Churchill healed over as the rudder dug into the water turning the ship in the opposite direction.

The OOD stepped over to the 1MC. "This is not a drill! Man Battle Stations, Man Battle Stations!" He pulled down the lever on the red-painted plate marked GQ. The high-pitched, clanging sound resonated throughout the ship. Releasing the lever, the OOD repeated, "Man Battle Stations."

Smith felt the vibration and heard the high-pitched whine from the turbines as *Churchill*'s thirty-three thousand horsepower gas turbines pushed her to thirty knots within seconds. "Give me an update, sonar," he ordered. He knew at thirty knots that the flow noise of the water would mask the hull's hydrophones. He would have to rely on the towed array streaming astern of the ship to detect any weapon closing the ship.

"Weapons are off our port bow. Two torpedoes are racing toward the carrier," First Class sonarman C. Rydell announced. "Captain, sonar detecting one— no wait! Make that four American torpedoes in the water."

"What the hell is going on?" Smith shouted. "Captain, TAO, all departments manned and ready."

Smith glanced at the wall clock. "Not bad. A minute and a half," he mumbled to man battle stations.

"Captain, TAO, after lookout reports two geysers of water exploded skyward one thousand yards off the *Carl Vinson's* stern."

Smith grabbed his binoculars. "What are the Yanks up to?"

"TAO sonar, still tracking two American torpedoes running off our starboard side, down Doppler, opening from *Churchill*."

Seconds later, another explosion erupted three thousand yards off *Churchill's* bow.

"OOD left full rudder, come to course one eight zero degrees," Smith ordered. He prayed the torpedo decoy towed astern, simulating *Churchill's* high-speed screws would draw any other weapon toward its radiated noise.

"Sonar, report," the TAO demanded.

"Lost contact on all weapons. Background noise masking our sensors from the exploding weapons," Sonar responded.

Sea Dipper 610 –

"Sea Dipper 610, break dip and initialize active search five thousand yards from our location," *Churchill's* Airborne Surveillance and Control Operator ordered. The white dot on the operator's radar screen indicated that six hundred and ten acknowledged the order and started to move down the bearing line toward the new search area.

Sighting the disturbance in the water from the underwater explosion, Lieutenant Peterson, 'Dipper' for short, decided to mark his first dip five hundred yards south of the ordered location. Unknown to the pilot, his decision placed him close to *Buffalo's* location. Hovering sixty feet above the surface, the ASO released her teardrop-shaped hydrophone into the water.

"Standby, Mark," the ASO announced, going active. Pressing the transmit button, the ASO placed her head on the rubber cover and waited. Her eyes followed the red acoustic circle sound wave expanding from the center of the screen.

Gotcha!" Hold contact four thousand five hundred yards, bearing one eight zero degrees from our position," she reported to the pilot.

"We got him," Peterson shouted over the noise of the hovering helicopter's massive blades. He turned to his copilot. "Release the torpedo."

"Roger! Weapon away," Ltjg. Cook reported pressing the weapon release button. Six ten lifted slightly when the weight of the weapon was released.

"Peterson keyed his communication switch and announced over the secure net to Churchill's TAO. "Weapon away! I say again weapon away."

Chapter 34

USS Buffalo; Gulf of Oman –

Scott entered the sonar to listen to the sound of the dipping helo. He saw Sorenson pressed his hands against the headphones. His expression on his face changed to horror.

"What is it, Sorenson?" Scott demanded standing behind him..

"Low rotor noise from a LAMPS helicopter," Sorenson reported looking at the intercept receiver. "He just went active."

Scott heard the repeated sound of the active sonar transmissions.

Sorenson heard the transmission switch to a faster pulse. "He's locked on!" Sorenson said looking at Scott and questioning why they were targeted.

"What? Damn, those Rotor Heads," Scott barked. Anger in his voice. Scott stuck his head out of sonar and shouted, "OOD, make your depth six hundred feet, ten degrees down bubble, all ahead one-third, right full rudder. Launch the emergency flair." *Shit! That's all I need, an attack by friendly fire.*

"Going to six hundred feet, ten degrees down bubble, ahead one third, aye." The OOD repeated.

"Anything Sorenson?" Scott asked. Tension in his voice as he tried to maintain his composure. He worried about another attack, this time from the air. *Let's hope he sees the flair before he drops a torpedo.*

"No Sir," Sorenson said, changing the search parameters and scanning the spectrum analyzer.

As he hurried into Control, Scott realized that if the helicopter pilot became trigger-happy, what would follow would be one or two Mk-50 torpedoes. His decision to launch the emergency flair was his attempt to let those trigger-happy "Rotor Heads" know they were attacking a friendly.

"Shit! Torpedo in the water! Torpedo in the water!" Sorenson's high-pitched voice blasted over the 27MC.

Ah, shit! Damn, you to hell you bastard! Scott thought. "Left full rudder, all ahead flank, make your depth four hundred feet, 10 degrees up bubble" he ordered, hoping to move above the weapon's search depth. Scott knew the Mk-50 would descend to an initial depth of six hundred feet before beginning its search.

"Coming to four hundred feet, all ahead flank, ten degrees up bubble, Skipper", the OOD said.

"We're cavitating," Sorenson reported. He grabbed the strap on his seat belt and pulled it tighter against his waist.

As the MK-50 spiraled down to its initial search depth, *Buffalo* vibrated as her speed increased. The *ASDV* docked on her back limited *Buffalo's* speed from thirty down to twenty knots.

"Talk to me, Sorenson," Scott commanded over the open mic.

"Weapon is passive and conducting a circle search astern as it dives deep."

"XO launch second emergency flare," Scott ordered. He heard the faint burst of air from the ejection tube. "Standby to launch a countermeasure!"

"Weapon appears to have reached its search depth," Sorenson announced in a more controlled voice. "Torpedo is active, long pulse, and in circle search."

"Make your depth three hundred feet, five degrees up bubble," Scott barked at the Diving Officer. "XO, let's decrease our depth to get out of the weapon's search cone."

"Do you know at what angle the weapon can look up?" Varney asked.

"No," Scott replied. "But by heading to the surface, I'm hoping to go outside the weapon's search area.

"Weapon has acquired," Sorenson announced. "Weapon is changing depth."

"Looks like three hundred feet was not shallow enough, XO," Scott said, listening to the high pulse rate of the active transmission of the weapon.

Varney looked at Scott. "Should we launch countermeasures?" He asked.

"Not yet, XO. We'll launch the countermeasure once the weapon matches our depth. Sonar, weapon depth?"

"Four hundred feet. Wait! The torpedo just reached three hundred feet," Senior Chief Richardson announced.

"Launch countermeasure," Scott ordered.

The countermeasure housed in an injection tube burst into the water. The explosion from the chemical reaction with seawater caused it to release millions of tiny bubbles creating a massive noise field, which, to an acoustic homing torpedo, sounded like a cavitating propeller, a fat target.

Scott waited anxiously, hoping the noise barrier would trick the torpedo into initiating another search cycle. He wanted to exhaust the weapon's fuel so he could gain some distance. He knew his max speed at twenty knots the torpedo could quickly overtake *Buffalo*. "Ten degrees up angle. Make your depth two hundred feet," he ordered.

"Torpedo searching. Long interval pulses," Sorenson announced.

"Looks like we beat this one, Captain," Varney said.

"Don't be so sure," Scott said. "Until we exhaust its fuel cells it could still kill us."

USS *Winston S. Churchill* –

"Cease, fire! cease, fire!" *Churchill's* Tactical Action Officer (TAO) shouted over the secure phone.

"What the hell is going on?" the CO shouted stepping into CIC.

"Sea Dipper 610 launched a torpedo."

"He did what?" Captain Smith barked.

"Combat Center, hold emergency red flair on the horizon," the bridge lookout reported.

"My God, we're attacking one of my submarines?" the Captain yelled. "Who the hell authorized him to launch a weapon?"

"No one," the TAO replied. "The pilot reported gaining contact and announced weapon in the water the next minute."

"When he returns, I want his ass in my stateroom. Understood? I'm heading back to the bridge," the CO shouted, hurrying through the door and up the ladder.

"Combat Center sighted another emergency red flair," the OOD on the bridge reported.

Captain Smith reached the open bridge in time to see the second flair drop to the sea. He stared angrily at the disruption in the water from the torpedo's detonation. *What the hell am I going to tell Admiral Dussault I sank one of my submarines...?*

Sea Dipper 610 –

"Emergency red flair off our port side," the Airborne Tactical Officer yelled. "No. Make that two red flairs," she shouted, watching the flares arch almost in front of her side window.

"Christ! I've dropped a torpedo on one of ours?" Lieutenant Peterson hurriedly radioed over his internal communications circuit. Unable to dwell on his mistake, afraid of the potential damage, Peterson flew to a new dip location. He knew the torpedo was unstoppable until it detonated or ran out of fuel.

Both the pilot and airborne tactical officer followed the flares floating toward the sea.

Listening to the Mk-50's high-pitched whine, the ASO could only wait in horror as the position indicator tracked the weapon's progress. She knew that a fifty-plus-knot torpedo could outrun any American submarine. She turned down the gain on her headset, terrified to hear the explosion. "Oh, God! What have we done?"

USS Buffalo –

"Talk to me, Sorenson," Scott asked trying not to show how he was struggling to maintain control. His heart throbbed against his chest. "Where's that damn weapon?"

"Torpedo chasing our stern," Sorenson announced.

Knowing *Buffalo* couldn't outrun the weapon, the question was, could Scott slow it down by forcing the weapon to return to a circle search? "Launch another countermeasure," Scott ordered, hearing the active weapon ping become louder as it bore down on *Buffalo*.

The two-hundred-five-pound countermeasure shot twenty feet astern of *Buffalo's* hull. As the submarine evaded, the countermeasure's warhead exploded, releasing a wall of bubbles. The noise, created from millions of tiny bubbles imploding shielded *Buffalo* from the torpedo's acoustic sensors.

Would it work? Scott worried as he heard the torpedo's high-pitched noise over the overhead speaker. He braced himself for impact.

"Weapon reverted to long pulse," Sorenson reported.

Thank God, Scott thought. He listened as the noise from the torpedo increased, and faded as the weapon turned to run its search pattern away from Buffalo.

"How many times can we trick our torpedoes?" the XO asked. "We're running out of options."

Scott nodded. "If the acoustic package in the Mk-50 torpedo is anything like our MK 48 ADCAP torpedo, maybe one or two times at most. The torpedo sensor will keep looking above the generated noise barrier of our countermeasures. If it acquires us again, I'll release another noisemaker to distract it."

"We need time to exhaust the torpedo's fuel cells," Varney replied.

"Weapon is steering back toward *Buffalo*," Sorenson announced. "Dear God please allow me to return home to his wife and unborn child.

Scott looked at the clock. "Weapon run time, XO?"

"Four minutes, Captain," Varney felt the pressure of the impending explosion.

"Standby to release, noisemaker." Scott looked at the clock again. "Now! Now! Now! Release noisemaker!"

"Noisemaker released," Varney shouted. He waited for the explosion. All he could do is create a wall of bubbles to mask his screw.

Scott counted, "One-one hundred, two-one hundred, three-one hundred. Now! Release countermeasure." He waited anxiously fearing the worst. Would the noise generated by the decoy fool the torpedo?

"Weapon reverted to a circle search," Sorenson announced, breathing a sigh of relief.

Thank God, Scott thought. Turning to Varney, he whispered, "Now we wait and pray."

"Forty-five seconds until torpedo shut down," Varney announced, sweat dripping down his neck.

Scott watched intently as the seconds ticked off on the digital clock. Had he fooled the Mk-50?

"Torpedo has reacquired. Closing," Sorenson shouted, the pings accelerating from the weapon. "Oh, God," he exclaimed.

"One thousand yards and closing," Senior Chief Russell announced, standing in front of the Fire Control Console.

"Sound the collision alarm, emergency surface, emergency surface" Scott ordered.

The diving officer hearing the order slammed the forward group's emergency blow valve upward. Nicknamed "the chicken switches," the smaller pipes in the control room screamed as air bled from much larger tubes. High-pressure air was dumped from the air banks into the ballast tanks through four-inch lines. The forty-five hundred-pound air screaming through the four-inch piping whistled in Control, adding to the crew's tension. It was followed three seconds later by the Chief slamming open the after group's valve. The delay in the sequence allowed *Buffalo* to take a slight up angle before blowing the after group.

"Planesmen, maintain a twenty-five-degree up bubble," the Diving Officer ordered.

Grabbing the phone, "Dennis give me all you got," Scott said.

"Aye, Aye Skipper," the engineer said.

Buffalo shook and rumbled, pitched up, and rose slowly at first, then rapidly increased its speed upward. At two hundred feet, the four thousand five-hundred-pound air met little resistance in pushing the seawater from the ballast tanks via the bottom flood ports. Air filled the tanks and expanded, increasing the positive ship buoyancy. *Buffalo* was rising with increasing speed.

Scott looked at the speed indicator. Twenty-two knots, two knots above the twenty normal with the submersible on *Buffalo's* back.

"Passing through one hundred feet," the OOD reported. The digital depth gauge now changed too fast to read the specific numbers.

Scott felt the angle increase. He saw the planesmen pull back on the steering yokes to hold the ordered angle. If we're hit, the closer to the surface, the better the chances for the crew's survival, he thought holding tight to the rail.

Buffalo shot to the surface, her bow rising forty feet out of the water at a twenty-five-degree angle before plunging back into the sea.

Seconds later, the submarine sat on the surface. *No longer restricted by the ASDV on her hull, Buffalo's* speed increased to thirty knots.

Scott's hands were still grasping the stainless-steel railing. He knew the sub was still not out of danger, but he forced himself to appear calm. He switched on the 1MC. "All stations brace for possible impact." The collision alarm blared throughout the ship.

In the wardroom, Janice shouted, "Brace yourselves!"

Everyone with her scurried under the table, pressing against its iron legs, bracing for the detonation.

Scott prayed Janice was all right. He found it surreal that an American torpedo might send *Buffalo* to the bottom of the sea. Was it his fault?

The MK-50 torpedo detonated twenty seconds later. The one hundred-pound warhead exploded two hundred fifty yards astern of *Buffalo* slamming the shock wave against the stern.

Scott felt the submarine rock from the explosion. *How close? How much damage? Was anyone injured...killed raced through his mind.*

The reactor operator heard the alarm and saw one of the reactor's rod's bottom lights on the Control Panel snap on. Ignoring the blood dripping from his forehead, he grabbed the phone, "Conn, Maneuvering, Reactor Scram. I'm rigging the ship for reduced electrical power. Standby to snorkel."

Scott, shaken but grateful he was not being bombarded by damage alarms, grabbed his mic. "Officer of the Deck, prepare to snorkel," He ordered on the 1MC. He fought the weariness of post-crisis fatigue. He could not rest until the ship and crew were out of danger.

Buffalo's black hull sat glistening in the sun like a gigantic Orca, now five hundred yards from where the torpedo exploded. Still holding the periscope railing, Scott tried not to show any sign of the fear he felt seconds ago.

"Captain. Captain," Varney said, trying to get Scott's attention. "Are you okay?"

Scott smiled. "Yes, XO. Just mad as hell at our guys." He turned serious again. "OOD, send the lookouts to the bridge. Engineering, Control, get me a damage report. Sonar, keep looking for that third submarine." He barked out orders as if to prove he was unshaken by their close call. He thought of Janice. How many more of these close calls could they survive?

Chapter 35

USS Winston S. Churchill; Gulf of Oman –

All eyes on *Churchill's* bridge couldn't believe what they saw when *Buffalo* exploded to the surface one thousand yards off the destroyer's starboard side.

Captain looked at *Buffalo* as the submarine increased speed. Suddenly at the astern of the submarine, a huge ball of water erupted twenty feet high.

"Jesus," Captain Smith said as the turbulence from the explosion settled down. Smith was boiling mad. "I'll hang that son of a bitch when he returns to the ship," He said loud enough for the men on the bridge to hear him.

"American submarine," the forward lookout yelled into his sound-powered phones.

Smith pulled the red phone from the bulkhead. "OOD what's the *Buffalo* call sign?" he asked.

"Lima Bravo," the OOD said.

Smith keyed the phone, "Lima Bravo, this is Charlie Whisky, OVER."

Scott heard the call over the secure speaker. He grabbed the phone, "Charlie, Whisky, this is Lima, Bravo. We surrender! OVER."

"Captain, I am sorry for the release of our weapon. One of our pilots became over-excited at the prospect of sinking an Iranian submarine. Do you need assistance?"

"No. Charlie, Whisky, inform the trigger-happy pilot that if I get him hovering near me, I'll shoot a harpoon up his kazoo! OVER," Scott said, smiling at the XO the tension lessened in his shoulders.

"Understood, I will relay your message, OVER," *Churchill's* CO responded.

"Break, I'm not sure the area forward of your position is clear. I am recovering from a reactor scram caused by the torpedo's detonation. I have limited forward headway for the next ten minutes. I would suggest you stand off until I can place the power plant back online. Also, recommend you prohibit crew members from alerting anyone of my presence. We are not here, OVER."

"Lima, Bravo understood and will take corrective action. We will take station two thousand yards off your starboard beam until you are underway, OVER."

"Thanks! Lima Bravo, OUT." Scott hung up the red phone. He waited for the engineer Lcdr. Finder in the reactor space to announce the ship was ready to secure diesel and switch to nuclear power. "We're not done yet," he said to Varney. "I have a feeling there is another Iranian submarine in the areas of the mine barrier. The longer we remain on the surface the more vulnerable we are to attack."

"Then let's get deep and start searching for that third submarine," Varney said.

USS Carl Vinson –

"Admiral just received a flash message from *Churchill's* CO. He reports his LAMPS launched an Mk-50 surface ship torpedo on top of *Buffalo*," Captain Wills relayed from the call received by Captain Newhouse.

"They did what? Give me that damn phone." His hand shook as he shouted into the mouthpiece, "Clarence! What the hell is going on?"

Newhouse replied, "Admiral, Sea Dipper 610 conducted an unauthorized weapon launch on what he thought was an Iranian submarine after the attack on the *Carl Vinson*."

"*Buffalo*. What's her status?" the Admiral asked, furious at the mistake.

"Scott was able to evade the weapon, but the explosion caused a reactor scram." He hesitated. "She is on the surface, snorkeling. Her hull is intact—"

"Goddamned good thing!" Dussault interrupted. "Inform Captain Smith he better get control of his LAMPS pilots. If I receive another report one of his pilots attacks *Buffalo*, I'll court marshal the lot of them. Is that understood?"

"Yes, Sir," Captain Newhouse said.

Dussault slammed the phone down. He turned to Wills, eyes fiery. "If I had to inform Washington one of my assets sank *Buffalo* my career would be over in a split second. Thank God it was Scott at her helm. The sonofabitch has nine lives like a damn cat. I just pray his luck doesn't run out."

K-903: *Strait of Hormuz* –

Captain Giv Alizadeh stood in Control of Submarine K-903. The fire control operators were verifying the equipment settings between the Weapon Console and the Torpedo Room.

"Sonar, Control, detected underwater explosions in our southern sector," Sonar Specialist Jamshidi reported.

Alizadeh walked into Sonar and stood over the technician's chair. "Where?" He asked.

"Captain, I picked up a faint noise south of our position, near the entrance to the Southern Straits."

"Was it an underwater detonation?" the Captain asked. "The last report from Q-100 placed her near this area. She was preparing to launch an attack on the carrier."

"Sir, At this range, I can not be sure. The noise appears to originate south of the Mine Barrier reported by K-903," Jamshidi replied.

Alizadeh straightened. "Okay. Inform me if you detect any other explosions or contacts in the region." Returning to Control, the CO ordered, "OOD, reverse course and increase speed to seven knots." His thoughts were racing. *Had Q-100 launched the first attack on the carrier? I must move closer to the southern choke point and prepare for my role in attacking the Americans. Not one will escape Allah's wrath.*

USS Buffalo –

"All departments report," Scott ordered over the 1MC. He turned to Varney. "Christ XO, that was close."

"Captain, the engineer," the XO handed the phone to Scott.

"Go ahead, Dennis," Scott said, not eager for the bad news.

"The reactor scram was caused when one of the breakers was jarred open by the explosion. We checked the remaining breakers in the control rod cabinet. None appear damaged. They are in good working order. We replaced the one that caused the problem. I recommend we latch rods and commence a fast recovery startup," Fender said.

"'Permission granted," Scott said. "Is the diesel able to support the hotel loads?"

"Yes, Sir," Dennis answered, "but we are limited to ten knots."

"So, there is no apparent damage to the reactor?" Scott asked.

"Other than the one control rod, there is no indication of any damage to any part of the propulsion plant or stern tube."

"Thanks, Dennis."

"Captain," the XO announced. "All departments have reported. The ship is intact. Any closer, though, and we might be sucking water," he added.

"Looks like we came away unscathed. Three more seconds and that Mk-50 would have blown are stern to hell," Scott said.

Lieutenant Commander Dennis Fender stood behind the Engineering Officer of the watch, observing the reactor and the electrical operators. He listened to the Engine Room Upper-Level and Lower-Level reports. "Reactor Operator, how much longer before the reactor is critical?" He asked.

"Ten minutes. I'm waiting for the temperature to move into the green band again," the Reactor Operator replied.

"Captain, Engine Room. We're warming the engines and loading the ship's service generators now; you can secure snorkeling in about one minute," Fender relayed.

"Inform your men, great job, Dennis," Scott replied. "XO, time to locate that third submarine I know is waiting for the fleet to cross the minefield. OOD make your depth two hundred feet, speed five knots, course zero nine zero degrees," he ordered. Scott waited as the plainsman and helmsman worked the handwheels driving the boat to the requested depth, speed, and course. He thought about the crews of the submarines he had sent to the bottom. Now, *he thought I must hunt another adversary and kill him.*

Chapter 36

K-903; Gulf of Oman –

Captain Giv Alizadeh, commanding K-903, snapped the handlebars against the search periscope. "Navigator, distance to the torpedo minefield?" he asked.

"Five thousand yards, Captain."

At sixty-two, he was the oldest Naval Officer in the fleet. He was due to retire in four months.

"Up scope," Alizadeh ordered. "Scope breaking the surface." He started to slowly turn the periscope back and forth across the bow. Nothing XO," as he continued to search the waters flipping the optics from low to high power. "There is no wreckage or smoke," XO," he said. "Down scope."

"It doesn't make sense," he mumbled. "Sonar, are you sure you detected an explosion in this area?"Captain Alizadeh questioned.

"Captain the explosion I detected was very faint. I believe there would be more explosions if a surface ship was hit with a Russian torpedo. I searched several times and I could not detect a secondary explosion. There was none."

"There got to be some wreckage, bodies, floating debris," as he scanned the water ahead of his submarine, "XO."

"How far to the barrier?" Alizadeh asked.

"Four thousand yards, Sir," the Navigator responded.

"Down scope," The Captain ordered. He moved over to the monitor and stared at the picture taken from the periscope camera. "OOD, let's continue to close the barrier."

"What are you thinking Captain?" Commander Dalir Gilani the Captain's

XO asked.

"There is no indication of any wreckage. What if the explosion Sonar detected was not a surface ship or carrier but an American submarine?" Alizadeh replied.

"What if the explosion was the sinking of the *Qaaem*? It's the only explanation," the Navigator interjected.

Gilani was taken aback by what his Navigator was suggesting. "I can't believe Captain Naceri would allow an American submarine to get the upper hand and attack him."

Then explain why he has not checked in over the past eight hours," Alizadeh asked. "OOD range to barrier?"

"Two thousand yards, Captain."

"All Stop! Raise the periscope. Alizadeh stepped up on the pedestal dropped the handlebars and started searching the waters off the bow of his submarine.

Commander Gilani looked at the monitor as Alizadeh moved the scope back and forth across the water.

"Wait, go back to the right," Gilani asked. "Stop! Do you see a discoloration of the water?"

"Yes! It's an oil slick," Alizadeh said.

Gilani's jaws tightened at the thought of the Americans sinking another boat.

"Sonar Control detecting a dipping helicopter to the south," Jamshidi reported.

"XO, stay on this heading until the dipper jumps to a new location. If he continues to open toward the south, we will remain here," Alizadeh ordered. "OOD, make your depth one hundred feet, speed three knots. We will stay well under and behind the floating mines."We will find and sink that American submarine. Set Ultra-Quiet through the ship, XO. Quitely announce Man Battle Stations Torpedo."

"Yes, Sir," the XO answered. "Man Battle Stations," he repeated flipping down the lever on the internal 1MC.

Alizadeh addressed his XO, "We'll continue to wait, and if the opportunity permits, launch a torpedo mine at the first ship that passes through the barrier. I believe by attacking one of their ships the American submarine will expose his location. We'll unleash four torpedoes at that submarine. The Americans' arrogance at not adhering to our sovereign boundaries will cost them many lives."

USS Buffalo: Gulf of Oman –

"Officer of the Deck, rig ship for Ultra-Quiet," Scott ordered. "Sorenson, give me an update." Eager to locate the third submarine, he hoped the Iranian boat would be detected before she attacked.

"Nothing, Skipper. The helicopter's active sonar is masking my sensors," Sorenson said.

"Christ, first he tried to kill us, now he is interfering with our sensors. Let's wait and see if our trigger-happy pilot can flush the fox from the hen house," Scott said still angry at almost losing *Buffalo* to a friendly.

Scott looked at the chart on the dead reckoning table (DRT). He saw the placement of floating and torpedo mines to the north of his location. He picked up a red pencil and a set of dividers. Scott placed rings around the possible submarine locations along the center of the mine barrier. "XO, I want Sonar to concentrate their search across the barrier field," he said pointing to the red circle on the chart. "If he intends to release his weapons then I believe he will remain north of the torpedo barrier. According to Dr. Mahman, his antenna must be within four thousand yards of the torpedo floating antenna."

"I concur Captain. I agree that the center of the Strait is the most likely place," Varney said, studying the minefield's location.

Scott drew four overlapping circles, each representing four hundred fifty yards the submarine would travel at six knots in two minutes. A center search sector of zero-nine zero degrees was then placed on the chart. Scott then drew two lines each forty-five degrees on either side of the center line.

Varney looked at the results after Scott was finished. "You believe the submarine may delay closing *Churchill* and try to avoid getting detected by the dipper's sonar," Varney said.

"I'll wager he'll place his ship north of the torpedo minefield. If he intends to attack the carrier, he'll remain in the center circle. He'll let *Churchill* pass and go for the larger target," Scott replied.

"Won't sitting here make him more susceptible to detection," Varney said.

"What other choice does he have? We know that *Vinson* will position his destroyers on the port and starboard side of the carrier. He'll wait for *Churchill* to pass over him before he releases the torpedo mine," Scott surmised. "What were you thinking XO?"

"Placing *Buffalo* here, pointing to the easternmost circle?" Varney said unless sonar detects his location. I believe—"

"Captain," Sorenson interrupted, "Except for *Churchill's* active sonar, it appears we own the ocean."

"Thanks, Sorenson," Scott said. I wish that was the case, he thought.

"You were saying, Tom?" Scott asked.

"Taking up station in the outer circle will reduce the possibility of *Buffalo* being in the line of fire when he attacks the carrier.

Scott studied Varney's suggestion. Using the dividers, Scott measured the distance from the center circle to the one on the eastern side. "Okay. Let's contact *Churchill's* CO," Scott said. He pulled down the red phone and pressed the transmit button. "Charlie, Whisky, this is Lima, Bravo, OVER," Scott said into the phone, about to alert *Churchill* of the threat of another submarine in the area.

"This is Charlie, Whisky. OVER."

"Captain, I am concerned there may be a *Kilo* or *Qaaem* in the area. I will close the minefield on the eastern side of the entrance to the Straits. I intend to remain in sector Charlie Fox Trot until the Battlegroup passes. I request you keep that trigger-happy pilot out of my search area. Also, recommend you move toward the western end of the barrier and conduct an active search toward the east. OVER."

"Copy all, Charlie, Whisky. What are your intentions? OVER."

"I want you to go active, high power on your sonar. I believe I can detect his location using biostatics," Scott said. "Lima Bravo. OUT."

"Biostatics Captain?" Varney asked. He had heard the term but knew nothing of what Scott intended.

Scott picked up a grease pencil and drew a triangle on the chart. "Tom, we'll take up station here." He marked the point with a small circle. "*Churchill* will reach this point within an hour. He marked another point on the paper denoting *Churchill's* position and naming the point 'Projector'. Scott then connected the two dots. "To the left of our position, we have a projector *Churchill's* active sonar. Over here," pointing to *Buffalo's* location, "a receiver." meaning *Buffalo's* hydrophones. He placed a point near the mine barrier line and named it the *Qaaem*. "If the *Qaaem* intends to launch torpedo mines, she will move closer to the middle of the barrier." Scott then drew an elliptic circle around the three points. *Buffalo, Qaaem,* and *Churchill.*

"What you see is referred to as a Bistatic Dead Zone. The active pulse from the projector, *Churchill's* sonar, will be reflected off the target. With luck, Sorenson should be able to find the submarine's location. It's all we have unless we go active and search the area," Scott concluded.

"Let's hope it works, Captain," Tom replied.

"Sonar, have you cleared the area east of all contacts?" Scott asked.

"Captain, the area is void of all surface and sub-surface contacts," Sorenson replied.

"Okay, now we wait for the *Churchill* active sonar to light up the target," Scott said, hoping he had guessed right.

Chapter 37

USS Buffalo; Southern Strait of Hormuz –

Scott and the XO were sitting in the wardroom, having lunch. They were reviewing their approach to detecting the Iranian submarine when Drs. Fred Stone and Glen Thomas entered.

"Captain, did I hear you mention Bistatics?" Dr. Stone inquired.

"Yes, you did, Fred," Scott replied. "I am going to try and detect the location of the third submarine using Bistatics."

"Bistatics is right down your alley, is it not, Glen?" Fred asked.

"If you are knowledgeable about using Bistatics in counter detection, your help would be appreciated, in confirming our approach to our problem," Scott said.

After listening to the Captain's plan and studying the locations of *Churchill*, *Buffalo*, and the intended target, Thomas smiled. "I think this could work. In your assumptions, have you considered the return signal's loss due to spreading, absorption, and scattering by the ocean?" Thomas asked.

Scott looked at Varney, then back at the engineer.

"You've answered my question. I suggest you get Dr. Lace and Lt. Morton in on this conversation," Thomas said.

The XO got up and left the room, returning with both women.

Dr. Stone briefed the two women on the Captain's intention of using *Buffalo's* hull array as a receiver.

"You want to take a stab at this problem, Patricia?" Janice asked.

Morton nodded. "Your assumption, Captain, does not consider the major problem you will encounter, the target scattering pattern." She drew a target

188

representation showing the signal pattern from the target to the receiver, *Buffalo*, and projector *Churchill*. "Targets do not reflect sound in all directions. The direction of maximum echo Sorenson will hear also depends on target shape."

"We studied these waters for years," Janice interjected. "If I understand, your problem is where to aim your weapons. Is this correct?" *Not another fight, Joe, she thought, eager to be of help.*

"Correct," Scott responded hoping the two women would solve his problem.

"Then I would suggest once you determine the target's approximate location, launch a pattern of four torpedoes," Janice said.

"My primary concern is the Iranian submarine. The Battle Group surface ships must take their lumps until there is no longer a threat," Scott said.

"When the time comes, I will sit with Sorenson to help him identify the target submarine," Lt. Morton offered.

"Thanks for all your help," Scott said.

Fred and Glen left the wardroom.

Janice and Morton followed.

When is this 'cat-and-mouse' game going to be over? Janice thought. Following Patrica up the ladder. *How long before more men need to die?*

Joe and Tom sat in silence. Both were subdued by the thought of destroying another adversary and the loss of lives.

"Tom I know what you thinking. I feel the same way, but I will not let an Iranian submarine attack go unanswered. If it means the death of another crew, so be it," Scott said.

"I agree Joe," Varney said. "I don't like it but the Iranian Navy seems hell-bent on sinking the carrier."

K-903: Southern Strait of Hormuz –

Captain Giv Alizadeh, stood in Control, reading the current message he received from Rear Admiral Al Jujair. The news was not what he expected.

"Is there a problem?" His XO Lieutenant Commander Farbod Gilani asked.

"That oil slick confirms my suspicion. The explosion that we detected confirms Q-100 was sunk," Alizadeh said his lips tightened and curled upwards. "XO it is up to us to sink the carrier. We must hold the line."

"One of our submarines, Q-100, did not report in at her assigned time. W/T Seed reported the sinking of K-901 when an explosion occurred while loading torpedoes. The fire is out, but the tanker must return to the yards to conduct repairs." He frowned. "For now, we lost the element of surprise against the Americans." He pointed to the chart. "Let us move into the middle of the torpedo minefield, just north of the line. Once we are within range, test the communication antenna to determine if we hold continuity with the torpedo mine distribution boxes."

"Control, I received a report from our fishing fleet. The Battlegroup slowed and delayed entering the Straits. A guided missile destroyer Churchill has moved ahead of the carrier. There is also an increase in aircraft and helicopters."

"XO get my officers in the wardroom now," Alizadeh demanded.

Alizadeh, after leaving his stateroom, entered the crowded and stuffy wardroom. Some officers sat others stood. He moved to the end of the table and addressed his men.

"Gentlemen, I want all departments at battle stations torpedo in two hours. I just received a message that confirms Q-100 was attacked and sunk. There were no survivors. I have a feeling the American submarine responsible is sitting waiting for me to make a mistake. That won't happen, Understood?"

The officers nodded. Several voiced their anger at the Americans.

Alizadeh continued. "At present, we are setting up to attack the American carrier. We will get our revenge for sinking a fellow submarine."

"Death to the American," they shouted.

Engineer, how are our batteries?"

"Excellent! Our storage capacity allows us to remain submerged for at least twenty-five hours. Of course, assuming you can maintain seven knots or less."

"Then we are ready," Get to your stations and prepare *Qaaem* for battle," Alizadeh said, eager to lead his crew to victory.

USS *Buffalo* –

"Battle stations are manned and ready, Captain," the XO announced, standing behind the Fire Control Tracking Party.

"OOD," Scott called. "Bring us down to steerage way, and don't cavitate." The steerage way was slow, a knot or two depending on what was needed to maintain headway against the ocean current. "Going to Sonar, XO," Scott said, moving away from the chart table and the game board he had been studying.

Varney looked down at the players and their projected locations. *Churchill* was steaming along the coast of Oman, designated Sector George Papa. The USS *Fitzgerald* was searching along the coast of Iran, designated Sector Delta Oscar. Two Destroyers, the *Decatur* and *Oscar Austin*, were assigned to search the inner circle ahead of the Carrier. All but Churchill's sonars were passive.

Scott hurried into Sonar. He spotted Lt. Patrica Morton sitting alongside Sorenson, studying the monitor.

"Sir, all are quiet, except for Churchill's sonar," Sorenson announced.

"Let's hope it stays that way. Good hunting," Scott said. "He's out there just waiting for the carrier to cross the barrier." As he left sonar, he thought, Now we wait for the fox to show himself.

K-903 –

Captain Giv Alizadeh was losing patience. The radioman was explaining why they could not connect to the torpedo antennas. "The problem rests with our equipment, Captain. I just completed several continuity tests and found the transmitter will not link with the antenna."

"Can you fix the problem?" The XO asked overhearing the radioman.

"I have electricians working on finding the trouble," the Radioman said.

After Alizadeh listened to the explanation, he motioned his XO to follow him out of Control. They entered his stateroom. "XO, we must use our torpedoes to stop the Americans."

Gilani looked into the eyes of his CO and knew he was dead serious. "How many weapons do you intend to shoot?" He asked.

"We will remain north of the line and fire two of our torpedoes. One for each of the forward screen ships. This will appear as if they were released from the sea bottom and not from a submarine. With the confusion of our attack, we will move in for the attack on the carrier. I believe the Americans will be too busy assisting the burning destroyers and searching for survivors."

It will fool them into thinking their ships triggered the detonation." He smiled. "Load all tubes and open the outer doors. We will attack the American ships as they enter the barrier."

Chapter 38

Scott and Varney were in Control, waiting for Sorenson and Lt. Morton to provide their new target's location. The navigator was recording the position of the two Arleigh Burke Class destroyers on the DRT. They waited for the first of two destroyers to approach the torpedo mine barrier. Both men were beginning to wonder if there was another submarine to the north.

"It's going on four hours. The first two destroyers are less than three thousand yards from the minefield. If it's going to happen it must be soon," Varney said.

Sorenson was staring at the three-dimensional printouts representing distinct search sectors in the ocean. The printouts, or 'lava grams,' recorded background noise detected on *Buffalo's* hydrophones. After three hours on the headphones, he said. "My ears hurt removing the headset and rubbing both ears.

Lt. Patricia Morton sitting in front of the second stack cocked her head. "Sorenson, did you hear that?

"What?" Sorenson said, putting his headphones back on.

"Look at the top of your Lava Gram. Wait there's another thud," Patrica said.

Sorenson spoke into his mic, "Conn, Sonar, possible transit detected."

"Make that three," Lt. Morton said, looking at the third black smudge starting to imprint at the top of her lava gram. "What's causing that noise?"

"Torpedo doors. They're opening." Sorenson looked at Morton. "The Captain was right; we are in for a fight."

"Control, Sonar detected three torpedo doors opening," Sorenson announced.

"It won't be long now, so keep your eyes glued to the screen," Senior Chief Richardson added standing behind Sorenson and Morton.

Scott entered sonar. "How many doors did you hear?" He asked starting to feel the tension in his back.

Sorenson replied, "Three, Sir. I classified this target as a *Kilo.*"

"It got to be K-903. That's the only submarine left in the Iranian fleet," Scott said.

"Make it four," Lt. Morton said, pointing to another black smudge on her screen.

"Keep on him, you two. Good work," Scott said and left.

Morton stared at the spectrum analyzer. Would the submarine launch an attack at *Buffalo?* Can't believe I begged to be attached to a submarine. I never thought I would be in the middle of a fight.

Scott hurried to Control. "We've got another fight, XO," Scott said in a low voice walking over to the DRT. "She is right here," drawing a circle around the target's reported position.

"The target is sitting two thousand yards behind the minefield." the XO said picking up a set of dividers. He measured the distance between the target and Buffalo. "She is eight thousand yards from our location. Easy reach by our torpedoes."

"She is waiting for the Battle Group," Scott replied.

"My bet is she will shoot at one or both outer screen ships," Varney said.

Scott studied the display. "I think K-903 will not move through the minefield," he said. "First, Iran does not want to be held responsible for an attack on American warships. Second, there is a greater possibility of her being detected by the dippers or active sonar from the destroyers in that location. Third, if the CO of K-903 waits for the carrier and launches one or two torpedoes, Washington will announce to the world that Iran was responsible for the attacks. Bad publicity and an act of war. I don't think Iran has the stomach for war. Not yet." He smiled. "They need to make it look like an accident."

"That makes sense," Varney replied. thinking about Beth and the kids.

Scott made up his mind. "Tom, inform *Carl Vinson* that we are tracking another *Kilo*. Tell them we believe she will launch her torpedoes at the carrier when the outer ships enter the minefield." Scott noticed Varney's expression change.

"Are you thinking of a better approach XO?" Scott asked.

"Yes," Varney replied, "The Admiral might try and flush him out or deter an attack by sending the dippers in to search the area. But, of course, all bets are off if he does, and some trigger-happy pilot will again mistake us for a *Kilo*."

"Then countermand my order. We will hold tight and launch our Mk-48 ADCAPs weapons in response to the *Kilo's* torpedo launch," Scott said. "The fleet will have to fend off an attack from the *Kilo*. My priority is that Iranian submarine."

🔹

Kilo, K-903, Torpedo Barrier—-

Captain Alizadeh peered through the search periscope. The sun was starting to rise from the horizon. He noticed the sea was calm and sky clear. "Allah be Praised," he said. "Down scope."

"XO we have two American destroyers heading toward his location viewing the monitor. We will launch two torpedoes and sink them both. "Up scope," he ordered. "The two destroyers turned inward, presenting a bow aspect," he said aloud. "Down scope."

Alizadeh went over to the chart table and looked at the bearing dots recorded on the chart. "Galani the screen ships are conducting a zig pattern as they approach the barrier. We will launch our attack in thirty minutes when they again turn toward us, XO."

"Control, both destroyers have reduced their speed. The carrier is reversing course," the Fire Control Coordinator reported.

"What? The carrier is turning." Alizadeh said, a bitter taste in his mouth "Up scope." Flipping down the handlebars, he peered at the two forward ships. "Range to the carrier," the CO demanded, his eyebrows lowered gripping the handlebars tighter.

"Five thousand yards and opening," The XO said reading the Fire Control range dial.

"XO we'll shift our targets to the two destroyers," Alizakeh said. "Range?"

"Ten thousand yards and closing," Commander Gilani said.

"Down scope." Alizakeh looked disheartened.

His XO was waiting for orders from the Weapons Console. "They will not escape," he said looking at his CO.

"We'll launch our weapons when they reach eight thousand yards," Alizakeh said.

Gilani nodded. "We're left with no other options but to attack the two forward ships." Anger was almost palpable in his voice at the thought of not having the glory of sinking the American carrier.

"XO, prepare to launch torpedoes," Alizakeh ordered.

"Torpedo room load tubes one through four," The XO called down to the torpedo room.

"Tubes have been loaded," XO Master Chief announced. "All flooded and equalized. Waiting for your orders to launch weapons."

"Weapons ready," the XO announced mechanically. He cared nothing about sinking two destroyers and killing its crew.

Alizadeh counted the seconds, waiting anxiously for the destroyers to close the distance. "Range to the two targets?" he asked.

"Five thousand yards," the XO announced.

The Captain waited. "No errors," he mumbled. He heard the active transmissions of the American destroyer grow louder. He saw the Control Room attack personnel glancing overhead. He knew anticipation was high as they waited for his order to launch their deadly weapons. Sweat beaded on his forehead. "Match bearings. Shoot tubes one and four," he ordered.

USS Buffalo –

"Captain, the forward screen ships are two thousand yards from the minefield," the OOD reported to Scott.

"XO, Firing Point Procedures," Scott ordered. "It won't be long now Tom."

"Weapons ready," the XO responded.

Scott felt the tension building as he surveyed the officers and men at their Battle Stations. He saw Varney waiting by the Weapon Console for the order to launch.

"Weapon in the water! Weapon in the water!" Sorensen shouted over the open mike.

"Shoot number one," Scott ordered. He tapped his thumb and forefinger against each other, counting the seconds.

The air-driven pneumatic/hydraulic ram blasted the weapon one from the tube with a burst of water.

"Shoot two." Scott waited. "Shoot three."

"All weapons running hot and normal. Hold continuity with each torpedo. Commanding active search in five, four, three, two, one. Torpedoes acoustic warhead activated," the XO reported, pressing the command button. He read each weapons parameter transmitted back to the Weapons Control Panel. "The first and second torpedo has locked on the target and racing in for the kill," Varney reported. He held his breath.

Chapter 39

K-903, Southern Strait of Hormuz—

"Weapons in the water! Weapons in the water!" Sonar Technician Jamshidi screamed over the internal speakers.

Alizadeh panicked. "Those are our weapons," he yelled. "NO! NO! Can't be American torpedoes. Those are our weapons," he shouted again.

"American Mk-48 torpedoes," Jamshidi repeated in a more controlled voice.

"Right hard rudder, all Ahead, flank," Alizadeh screamed. "But how did the American Captain find us XO?" he demanded losing control.

But how was the question that would remain unanswered for his short life?

Gilani stood next to the Weapon Console looking and listening to his Commanding Officer. He could not believe how fast his Captain went from a rock-solid leader to one who had lost control. He saw the look of fear on his face.

"Match bearings and shoot tubes two and three," Alizadeh ordered his lips tightened. "Shoot two," pressing the button. "Shoot three Allahu Akbar (God is Greater)!"

The sound of the active pinging of the American torpedoes filled Control as they drew closer.

The men looked at the CO. The fear they saw was reflected on his face.

Alizadeh's closed his eyes, his lips silently repeating prayers.

Sonar Technician Jamshidi was strapped in his seat, fear mounting as he listened to the American torpedoes bearing down on him. "Weapons have switched from slow speed to fast. Weapons have locked on us," Jamshidi hurriedly said." He sensed he was going to die. "Weapons switch from long to rapid pulses." He bowed his head in prayer.

"XO, launch countermeasure," Alizadeh shouted gripping the railing surrounding the two periscopes.

Standing next to the Weapon Console, the XO pressed the launch button.

The submarine quivered from the explosion of the countermeasure jettisoned from the after-ejection tube.

The second explosion and corresponding snapping air bubbles produced a massive wall of air blocking the Mk-48 weapon sensor.

"Sonar report," Alizadeh demanded still gripping the railing.

"Can't see or hear. Sensors masked by the exploding air bubbles. Wait! Torpedoes conducting a circle search," Jamshidi said. His voice cracked from the hysteria he was feeling.

"Weapons locked on," Jamshidi screamed, starting to cry.

Alizadeh looked at the speaker overhead. He knew there was nothing he could do to stop the death of him and his crew.

The first Mk-48 ADCAP torpedo found its mark. As programmed the weapon's two hundred-pound payload exploded directly under the hull of the *Kilo*. The explosion caused the submarine to lift ten feet breaking her back. She was split into. Tons of water burst into Control, immediately killing the crew. Communication wires between the four Russian torpedoes and the submarine's weapon console were severed. No longer controlled by the Weapon Operator, the four Russian torpedoes were left to respond to the information received through their acoustic warheads.

USS Buffalo –

"Captain lost continuity on all weapons," the XO reported watching the digital readouts from the wire stop updating "Cutting the connecting wires on tubes one, two, and three."

"Talk to me, Sorensen," Scott demanded.

"Too much background noise is interfering with my hearing. Wait! Hold weapons running, two toward our surface units, and — shit! We're under attack!" His voice raised higher than normal. "Two Russian torpedoes heading our way," Sorenson said.

Scott reacted quickly. "All ahead flank, left full rudder, prepare to launch countermeasures," He thought, With only three hundred feet of water under me, diving to evade is not an option. This must work.

"Weapons in active search," Sorenson announced.

Scott and the XO stood under the speaker, listening to the torpedoes' high-pitched whine. They knew what would happen if they could not evade the destructive power of the two hundred kg explosive warhead. They and their crew would follow the sinking *Kilo* to the bottom. "Run time on the Russian torpedo, XO?" Scott asked.

"Ten minutes. Seven remain if my calculations are correct." Varney replied looking down at his stopwatch.

"Explosion astern of us," Sorenson reported. "Detected no secondary explosion."

"Let's hope the torpedo homes in on one of the destroyer's countermeasures, XO," Scott said, listening to the advancing torpedoes.

"First torpedo has locked on!" Sorenson yelled over the speaker.

"Standby to launch Countermeasures. Prepare to launch the Noisemaker," Scott ordered. "Torpedo range?"

"Two thousand yards and closing," Senior Chief Richardson responded, standing between the two sonar operators.

Scott kept his eyes on the clock. Two minutes and thirty seconds before detonation. Trying to evade the torpedoes rushing to kill him, each active ping pounded in his brain like a hammer. "Launch the countermeasure," he ordered. He tapped his thumb against his forefinger, waiting to see if the torpedoes were influenced by the shield of snapping bubbles.

"Weapons have reverted to a circle-search," Senior Chief Richardson said.

"Yes!, Scott shouted. "Steady as you go. Let's use the sound barrier to cover our screw noise, XO."

"Weapons still searching," Sorenson reported in a more relaxed voice.

Scott looked at Tom and breathed a sigh of relief. "Time remaining, XO?"

"Three minutes," Varney replied. "We're still not out of the woods."

Sorenson's voice interrupted, "One weapon has reacquired. The second is still searching," he announced, alarmed by the increasing pings from the fast fifty-knot torpedo.

"Fifteen hundred yards and closing, "Varney announced.

"Standby to launch a Countermeasure," Scott ordered. He counted off the seconds. Launching the countermeasure too soon would not decoy the torpedo. Too late? The weapon would shoot through the barrier of bubbles. He knew it had to be perfect.

"One thousand yards and closing," Varney announced.

"Launch Countermeasure!" Scott ordered, his insides were churning. His heart jumped in his chest. "Now!" He could do nothing more but. Wait. Wait. Wait.

"Weapons shut down!" Sorenson shouted breathing a sigh of relief.

"What? How is that possible?" Scott asked still not believing what happened.

"Maybe I miscalculated the time remaining for the weapons to run out of fuel," the XO responded.

There were audible sighs of relief from the men standing at their stations.

"All right men. Quiet Let's not let our guard down. There could be another submarine lining up to attack *Buffalo*," Scott said.

Scott was not ready to celebrate. "Sorenson, what do you hear?" He asked, hoping the sea was clear. He did not relish another encounter.

Sorenson replied, "Nothing. There is a lot of background noise from the torpedo's detonation."

Scott ordered, "Keep searching. There could be another submarine lurking in the area."

Varney approached. "Christ that was damn close Joe. Do you think We're in the clear?"

"Let's hope so," Scott replied. "We'll remain in this area. I don't want the fleet to enter the barrier until we search this sector for the next few hours."

After an exhaustive search confirmed *Buffalo* was alone, Scott ordered a final baffle clear, followed up by coming to periscope depth. He reached for the red phone above his head. "Charlie, Whisky, this is Lima, Bravo. OVER," Scott said.

Only static came through the speaker.

Scott looked at Varney. He wondered if the explosion had been an attack against *Churchill.* He waited tensely for the response.

"Lima, Bravo, this is Charlie, Whisky. OVER."

"Charlie, Whisky, we detected an explosion. Were any of the surface ships hit? OVER."

"Negative. *Fitzgerald* took a hit on their Nixie. OVER."

"Charlie, Whisky, you are clear of submarine threats in this area of torpedo mines being launched by an Iranian submarine. Break! When will your attached submarine join you ?"

"She is due tomorrow. OVER."

"Good news. I am transferring all information related to the area to you now. Intend to stand down and wait for further orders from Washington. OVER."

"Thanks, Charlie, Whisky. You did a great job. OUT."

Scott breathed a sigh of relief. The anxiety he had felt moments ago was subsiding.

Chapter 40

The Office of the President; Washington, DC –

"Morning, Mr. President," the Secretary of the Navy said, sporting a rare grin.

"You have good news? I can use some right now," Washburn said, looking up from the paper he was reading.

The President's Chief of Staff Ian Williams stood in front of the President, waiting for his signature on another document.

"Mr. President," Secretary Richards said, moving to the front of his desk and handing Washburn a note.

Washburn read the note and switched off the recorder. "Let's hear this," he said.

"Sir, *Buffalo* reported sinking an Iranian *Kilo* after it launched an attack on two of our surface ships."

"Say that again," The President looked shocked.

"Scott sank an Iranian *Kilo*," Richards repeated.

"Christ that makes three submarines Scott has sent to the bottom," The President said. "Is the fleet safe?"

"*Buffalo* and the fleet had no casualties. Captain Scott reports no enemy submarines are patrolling the waters south or north of the barrier," Richards responded.

"My God, that's the Iranian's second attempt to sink one of our ships," The President exploded. "What about the torpedo mines Scott reported. Any possibility the mines could be launched at the Battlegroup?"

"No, Sir. Reports from *Carl Vinson* indicate there are no Iranian surface ships or aircraft within twenty thousand yards of the barrier that could activate the mines. By sinking all three Iranian submarines he has neutralized the torpedo mines for now. There are still floating mines the Battle Group must be aware of as they head into the Straits of Hormoz."

"Is there a submarine attached to the Battlegroup?" Washburn asked.

"The USS *Columbia*, SSN-771, has been ordered to support the Carrier Strike Group. She will join the Battlegroup tomorrow," Richards answered.

"Any reason why *Buffalo* should remain in the Gulf?" Washburn asked. "Scott and his crew must be exhausted."

"No, Sir. I was going to recommend we order her to return to Guam," Richards replied.

"Good. Commander Scott has done an excellent job carrying out his orders. Bring him home and schedule upkeep. Contact Northrop Grumman to perform maintenance on the *ASDV*. I want Commander Scott and *Buffalo* ready to re-deploy in three months or sooner if needed."

"Yes, Sir. I will order Rear Admiral Armstrong to meet the ship and brief the crew on the need to keep their latest operations under their hats," Richards said.

"Just get *Buffalo* home safely," The President said. "His audacity to take bold risks saved our Battlegroup."

"Yes, Sir," Richard replied smiling as he left the Oval office.

***USS Buffalo: Gulf of Oman* –**

"Captain," IST1 Weathers said, "Received a message from Commodore Whitfield."

Scott took the message board and leaned against the bulkhead.

R 082100ZNOV16

FM: COMSUBRON FIFTEEN

TO: CO USS Buffalo

BT

SECRET

SUBJ/Operation TipToe//

GENTEXT/RMKS/1. USS Buffalo is hereby ordered to return to Guam at the best possible speed. Upon arrival, you are to report to Rear Admiral Armstrong.

BT

NNNN

SECRET

"Is that it, Weathers?" Scott asked.

"That's all, Captain," Weathers said a broad smile on his face.

Scott left the radio and walked into Control. "Tom, we've been ordered to return to Guam."

"Why?" Tom asked.

"None given. When the operation is complete, Washington orders you home. Tom, the crew is ready, don't you think?"

"I know I am," Tom replied. "This has been a hell of a deployment."

Scott walked over to the 1MC and flipped down the switch connecting the intercom throughout the ship. "Attention, all hands. I just received a message ordering *Buffalo* to return home to Guam at the best possible speed. I am asking the engineer to pour it on." He added, "Everyone, well done." He turned to Varney. "Tom, you did a great job."

"Thank you, Sir," Varney replied smiling.

Scott said to the OOD, "Lieutenant, make your depth three hundred feet, ahead flank. Navigator, chart us the fastest course for Guam."

"Yes, Sir. Three hundred feet, all ahead flank," Obermeier replied.

Scott turned to Varney and motioned him to follow. Entering the wardroom, he saw Janice and Morton drinking coffee. Morton smiled. "Congratulations on two accounts," she said.

"Janice, does she know of our plans?" Scott asked.

"She agreed to be one of my bridesmaids," Janice replied, a broad smile on her face.

Scott smiled and looked at his second in command. "Let's keep this under our hats for now. It will be hard enough to explain our nuptials to the Admiral."

Janice laughed. "He'll be thrilled his 'bad boy' is settling down."

Scott laughed but quickly became serious. "Lieutenant Morton, have you decided to take the Navy's offer that we discussed?"

Morton's smile vanished. "Captain, I think I would be doing my country a disservice if I remained aboard *Buffalo*. After what I experienced over the past several months, I found the decision difficult. I concluded that I need to leave the Navy and continue my education," she replied.

"Understood," Scott said. "The two of you must complete your report before returning to Guam. I wish you the best of success, Patricia."

Janice smiled. "Pat, after Joe told me what he offered you, I contacted the University and submitted a draft of your thesis proposal to their review board."

"How did you know what my proposal was?"

"I've been looking for a graduate student who thinks as I do. If you remember, during our research and analysis, I asked you about your interest in continuing to study shallow-water environments. After hearing that my future husband is to remain aboard *Buffalo*, I realized there would be little chance of me sailing with him for the remainder of my sabbatical. You can become my 'lab rat' and, at the same time, work on your doctorate. Of course, I'd love to be your advisor as well as your friend," Janice said. "What do you say? We make a great team."

"Captain, has she always been this pushy?" Morton asked, laughing.

"You'll find out if you accept her offer," Scott replied, looking a Janice.

Morton frowned and then smiled. "I'll have the best of two worlds. If accepted, I get to continue as a member of this crew and work on my doctorate at the same time. Any chance of requesting NUWC to send a UUV to assist in my research?"

Now, who's pushy?" Scott laughed. "But funny, you should ask. I received a response to my request to DARPA and they will provide a next-generation UUV for further testing in the Gulf. The New Hunter will arrive before our deployment."

"Will Drs. Stone and Thomas be assigned to *Buffalo* again?" Morton asked.

Scott shook his head. "Unfortunately, no. They will be returning to NUWC, and two engineers will replace them, so they can work on their reports."

Janice placed her hand on top of Scott's. "You will inform the Admiral that before you are sent off again on your next mission, you have a more dangerous one. We are going on our honeymoon." She eyed him sternly.

"You know I will," Scott replied, smiling. *God, I can't wait to get you alone,* he thought.

Janice saw Scott's eyes move from her eyes to her body. *Ha! I have seen your sexual longing grow over the past several months. I intend to take full advantage when I get you alone, Captain.*

Scott did not want to be distracted. Not yet. He turned to Morton. "Commander Walsh informed me he wants to establish a SEAL team training site in Guam," he said with a smile. "I understand his request was approved and he will be stationed there for at least a year."

"Yes, Sir," Morton said, hiding her excitement.

"Three months should be more than enough time for you two to get to know each other better," Janice said, smiling.

Patricia nodded. " I'm hoping for a lifetime.

"I won't warn Walsh about the trap you two are setting," Scott laughed. "I've got work to do still." He thought of kissing Janice, but there would be lots of time for that soon. He left the wardroom, feeling better than he had for a long time.

Chapter 41

Guam - The Final Chapter

Scott was in his stateroom speaking with Tom Varney when they heard a tap on the door.

"Enter," Scott said.

"Morning Tom," Janice said as Tom got up to leave. "Please stay. I'll only be a minute."

"Joe, I'll meet you at our quarters after you finish with Admiral Clarke and Commodore Whitfield," Janice said smiling.

"I'll join you once the review board is finished," Scott said.

The anticipation of their first night together off the ship was all she could think about as she climbed into the car that would take her to the Officer Housing.

Scott and Tom continued to proof their slides when the Duty Watch Officer phoned, "Sir, Admiral Clarke, U. S. Fifth Fleet, Admiral Armstrong Commander Submarine Group Seven, and Commodoer Whitfield, Squadron Fifteen, is arriving."

"You ready for this Tom?" Scott asked.

"Yes, but are you?" Varney replied.

"We'll soon find out if Washington intends to court martial me for disobeying orders," Scott said.

Scott and Varney headed for the forward escape hatch to greet the senior officers.

"Great to see you, Captain," Admiral Clarke said as he extended his hand. "I understand you both had an exciting deployment."

"Challenging," Scott replied.

"Admiral Armstrong was next to descend the escape trunk followed by Commodoer Whitfield.

"Good to see you again, Admiral Armstrong," Scott said shaking his hand.

"Commodore," Scott acknowledged Whitfield as he stepped off the ladder.

"Can't wait to hear you debrief," the Commodore said.

"I hope it is what you expect," Scott replied.

Let's hope I don't lose my commend, Scott thought as he led the officers to the wardroom.

Scott waited for everyone to get settled before he handed out the briefing highlights.

Vice Admiral Clarke called the meeting to order. "Let's get started," He said. I can't wait after reading his reports, he thought.

For two hours, Scott and his XO ran through the details of *Buffalo's* deployment. He began with the destruction of the Iranian weapon facility, "Scott told them Dr. Mehman was instrumental in providing the necessary information to Commander Walsh. Walsh and his SEALs did an outstanding job." He added, "I recommend commendations for the entire team."

Clarke made a note and continued, "I understand Washington ordered you to remain in the Persian Gulf." He aimed his eyes at Scott. "Why did you disobey your orders and follow an Iranian submarine into the Gulf of Oman?"

Scott folded his hands on the table. "Sir, after picking up an underwater communication between K-901 and Admiral Jujair mentioning *Carl Vinson*, I suspected some sort of trap. As you know, our communications were down, so I felt the best option, without being able to warn the *Vinson,* was for us to follow the submarine." He glanced at Varney and continued, "I believed the Iranians intended to mine the Southern Straits with torpedo mines and release them as our ships entered the area. This would allow them to blame any casualties on the accidental detonation as our Naval units crossed the minefield."

"What about the tanker," Armstrong asked. "Why did you consider it a threat?"

Scott bit his lip. "That was a shocker. The discovery of the supertanker being used as a support ship, and possible concealment, for Iranian submarines was something I did not expect. When we saw two submarines within its hull, it confirmed my suppositions that the battle group was in danger."

"Do you think sinking K-901 and the other diesel boats put a stop to their plans?" Commodore Whitfield asked.

"Not completely. Their torpedo mines are still sitting at the bottom of the Strait. We sank the submarines that could trigger the torpedo mines to launch from the ocean floor. That delayed them but the Iranians could send one of their surface ships to launch the torpedoes. Care must be taken by the Battle Group when they transit through the area."

"Gentlemen," Admiral Clarke announced. "Are there any more questions you would like to ask Commander Scott?"

"The officers around the table shook their heads.

Admiral Clarke stood followed by the men around the table. He extended his hand to Scott. "I agree with Admiral Armstrong, you were the right man for the job. Good luck on your next deployment."

"Thank you, Sir," Scott said, shaking the Admiral's hand. "I have a great XO and crew."

"Congratulations, Commander Scott, Armstrong said. We are all in agreement on a job well done."

"Here! Here," the officers joined in.

The tension in Scott's back subsided as he started to relax.

Varney was relieved.

Armstrong smiled, "I also want to congratulate you XO, and the crew, on a job well done. Unless Commodore Whitfield has additional tasking I recommend *Buffalo* stand down and grant liberty as you deem fit. You have three months before Washington issues orders to return to the Gulf."

"I agree Admiral. XO you have one month to allow the crew to stand down. Get your men on the beach," Commodore Whitfield said smiling. "Great job. Between the two of us, the Captain and I will recommend you for your command. Your next move will be to the Prospective Commanding Officer School (PCO)."

"Thank you, Sir," Shaking the Commodore Whitfield's hand.

"Captain I understand there is a wedding planned?" Admiral Clarke asked as he was leaving.

Scott nodded. "Yes, Sir. Dr. Lace and I are to be married on Wednesday. I'd like to request a two-week leave."

"Commodore, do you have any reason Captain Scott can't be granted leave?" Clarke asked.

"No, Sir," Whitfield replied.

"Thank you, Sir," Scott said.

"Then why are you still here? You're dismissed," Clarke said and laughed. "Give our best to Dr. Lace," as the officers left the room.

Scott and Varney remained standing as their superiors again shook their hands, saluted, and left.

Varney smiled. "I was worried for a few seconds back there."

"I wasn't," Scott lied. "Hell, Tom, I was too. But I knew we did the best we could do given very difficult circumstances. Thank you for your support and council."

Varney nodded. "See you at the wedding, Sir."

"Thanks, Tom."

Scott left the wardroom, picked up his bag, and walked down the gangway to the waiting car. A first-class Petty Officer stood next to the open door. He saluted. Scott returned his salute.

"May I take your bag, Sir?" the sailor asked.

"No thank you." He tossed his overnight bag in the back seat and slid in. The Petty Officer shut the door.

All he could think about was Janice. They had dreamed about this day for months. Now that it was here, he couldn't get to her fast enough.

The driver got behind the wheel.

"Scott said, please take me..."

"Sir," the driver interrupted, "I have been ordered to take you to the Married Officers Quarters. Sit back and enjoy the ride. We should arrive in twenty minutes."

Scott relaxed in the leather seat. He mused about how he cajoled Janice back into his life. He had asked Washington to award the University of Hawaii a one-million-dollar grant. He remembered how furious she was when she realized she was going to the Persian Gulf aboard the USS *Buffalo* as his science advisor. As he reflected on their months locked in a submarine, he realized that working with the woman he loved had proven to be more difficult than he anticipated. But it was all worth it. God, can't this driver go faster, he thought. "How much farther?" Scott asked.

"Another mile Sir." The driver said glancing in the rearview mirror.

Scott felt his heart beat faster as he thought of holding Janice in his arms.

"You're here, Sir," the driver said, pulling next to the curb.

The driver started to get out of the car.

"Thanks," Scott said, grabbing his leather bag. He jumped out of the car and hurried to the front door. He hesitated, knowing Janice was on the other side. Was she as anxious as he was? His hand shook as he reached for the handle and pressed down on the catch. He pushed open the door. Standing not ten feet in front of him was Janice. She smiled. He saw her wet her lips.

He froze inhaling the sweet fragrance of her perfume. Joe recognized the smell, Chanel No. 5. He had given Patrica the perfume to slip into her bag before Janice left the boat.

Janice did not move. He saw she was dressed in a Nile Mist Drop Shoulder Sheer Robe.

Joe recognized the robe. He had given her it for her birthday two years ago. She must have known they would be together.

He dropped his bag and pushed the door shut with his foot. He stood looking her up and down. The sheerness of her robe left nothing to his imagination. Her breasts were round and firm as he remembered them. Her erect nipples pressed against the fabric.

Smiling he walked up to her stopping just inches from her body. He looked into her beautiful blue eyes. Scott moved a strand of blond hair behind her left ear and began to kiss her neck. "I am deeply in love with you," he whispered continuing to nibble around her ear.

She moaned as his lips brushed against her shin.

He felt the blood surge in her neck as her heart beat harder in anticipation of their lovemaking.

Janice leaned her head toward his and wrapped her arms around his neck.

Scott pressed his body against her. Lifting her chin, he stared into her eyes. Neither spoke a word.

She placed her arms around Joe's back and rested her head against his shoulder.

"Oh, Joe, I waited for you to hold me so many times," looking up into his eyes. She moved her hands from his back to his neck. She rose on her toes. Her mouth was just inches from his. He felt her warm breath caress his face.

Scott pulled her tighter against his body. His first kiss pressed lightly against her lips. His next became harder and more demanding as his hunger to have her increased. Neither wanted to break away. Finally, he pulled back and looked into her eyes.

"I—"

"Shush," Joe said, placing his finger on her lips. "Don't talk."

They embraced again, neither saying a word as they held each other. Janice felt breathless and her knees buckled. He kissed her again, his tongue moving between her lips. She tried to hold on when he drew back again and said, "I got the two-week leave I requested. What on Earth are we going to do to fill the time?" Without waiting for an answer, he pulled the shoulder straps down and let the robe fall to the floor. Joe stepped back and looked at her nakedness.

"I believe," she moaned, as he stepped close and kissed her neck. "I have a pretty good idea." She placed her hands on his chest and pushed away. She smiled seductively as she tossed his hat on the chair and started to unbutton his shirt.

"I see you have a plan," Joe said, staring down at the hardness of her erect nipples.

"Yes, a pretty good one," Janice said running her fingernails lightly up and down his chest. Lifting her head, she kissed his neck while searching for his belt.

Joe's heart beat faster. Enough of the foreplay, he thought, picking her up and carrying her to the bedroom. "Six months was a long time to wait," he said, pulling off his clothes. Climbing into the bed, he kissed her long and hard. His voice was raspy as he said, "Janice, I love you."

Janice looked up into his eyes and smiled. "Joe Scott, I've loved you for a long time. You just never realize." She kissed him tenderly on the lips. "Oh Joe, let's not waste any of the time we have together," she said and climbed over him.

"Is this how you plan to take charge?" He asked feeling her straddling him.

Janice bent down and kissed him again, "Yes, Captain," she whispered and started to move rhythmically like the sea they both loved.

THE END

Characters

President's Security Council/Advisers

Mr. John Washburn, President of the United States – Commander in Chief U.S. Armed Forces

Mr. Jack Kindly, Vice President

Mr. Ian Williams, President's Chief of Staff

Mr. Chuck Aspin, Secretary of Defense

Mrs. Margaret Rice, Secretary of State

Mrs. Sally Wheatfield, Deputy National Security

Mr. Raymond Richards, Secretary of the Navy

Dr. Chris Habshaw, Defense Advanced Research Project Agency

Dr. Jack Ure, Director of the Central Intelligence Agency

General Richard Shaw, Chairman of the Joint Chiefs of Staff

General Sam McAllen, Ret. Director of National Intelligence

Mr. James Smithfield, Deputy Legal Advisor

Mrs. Beverly Yancy, President Secretary

U.S. Navy Senior Command

Admiral Samuel Westfield, Commander Naval Special Warfare Command

Rear Admiral Tom Armstrong, Commander Submarine Group Seven

Vice Admiral Charles W. Clarke, U.S. Fifth Fleet, Manama, Bahrain

Captain Whitfield, Commander Submarine Squadron 15 Apar Harbor Guam

National Geospatial-Intelligence Agency

Colonel Bill Johnson

Lieutenant Colonel Sandy Smith

Technical Sergeant Wallace

USS *Carl Vinson* **CVN-70**

Rear Admiral Stan Clint Dussault, Commander Carrier Strike Group One

Captain Jim Wills, Rear Admiral Stan Dussault's Chief-of-Staff

Captain Clarence Newhouse, *Carl Vinson* Commanding Officer

Captain Chuck Reed, Strike Warfare Commander

Commander Gary Langdon, Air Wing Commander

Commander Robert Connors, Command and Control and Electronic Warfare

Captain Gene Riddel, Sea Combat Commander

Commander Sam Miller, Surface Warfare

Commander Warren Prorock, Undersea Warfare

USS *Buffalo* **SSN-712**

Commander Joseph Leo Scott, Commanding Officer

Lieutenant Commander Thomas Varney, Executive Officer

Lieutenant Commander Dennis Fender, Engineering Officer

Lieutenant Jeff Obermeier, Navigator

Lieutenant Steve Wilkinson, Weapons Officer

Lieutenant Patricia Morton, COMSUBGRU 7 staff, TDY to USS *Buffalo*

Lieutenant Gerry Powers, Damage Control Assistant (Auxiliary Division Officer)

Lieutenant Junior Grade, Terry Washington, Supply Officer

Master Chief Sonar Technician Submarines, (STSCM) Jack Norris

Master Chief Machinist Mate (Auxiliary) Doug Cook, Chief of the Boat

Senior Chief Fire Control Technician, Jack Russell

Senior Chief Sonar Technician Submarines (STSCS) Paul Richardson

Sonar Technician Submarines (STS) First Class Lefty Sorenson

Chief Machinists Mate (Weapons), Juststone

Electronic Technician (Navigation) First Class Jeffery Kinley

Information System Technician First Class Carl Weathers

Sonar Technician First Class William Clouse

Culinary Specialist Second Class, Chad Brady

Dr. Fred Stone, NUWC Mechanical Engineer

Dr. Glen Thomas, NUWC Electrical Engineer

Dr. Janice Lace, Professor Oceanographic Department University of Hawaii

Dr. Aslan Mehman, Iranian Nuclear Physicists

USS *Winston S. Churchill* DDG-81

Commanding Officer, Captain Rusty Smith

Lieutenant Tom Ralph, Tactical Action Officer

Lieutenant Lester Philips, Launch Safety Officer

Sonar Technician Submarines First Class, C. Rydell

Helicopter Anti-Submarine Squadron Light (HLS) 42 Detachment 7

Lieutenant Will Peterson, Pilot

Lieutenant Junior Grade Brendan Tan, CO-Pilot

USS *Oscar Austin* DDG-79

Commanding Officer, Captain Lenard Willard

Lieutenant Peter Blair, Tactical Action Officer

U.S. Navy SEALs

Commander Mike Walsh, SEAL Team Leader, and Mission Leader

Machinist Mate First Class Willy Hamerman

Boatswain Mate First Class Bob Rose

Boatswain Mate Second Class Mark Stanley

Information System Technician Second Class Bruce Freeman

Hospital Corpsman Third Class Chad Barns

Iranian Diesel Submarine K-901

Commander Atash Karini, Commanding Officer

Lieutenant Commander Mohsen Pejman, Executive Officer

Lieutenant Commander Jav Hoseini, Engineering Officer

Lieutenant Nouri Norouzi, Officer of the Deck

Sonar Technician Specialist, ShahrAm Pahlavi

Iranian Diesel Submarine K-903

Captain Giv Alizadeh, Commanding Officer

Lieutenant Commander Dalir Gilani, Executive Officer

Sonar Technician Specialist, Jamshidi K-901

Bandar 'Abbas Naval Station Iran

Admiral Al Jujair, Islamic Revolutionary Guards Corps Naval Commander

Vice Admiral Salehi, Commander of Islamic Submarine Forces

Admiral Mokri, Commander of Islamic Surface Forces

Commodore Garshasp Pahlavi, Islamic Submarine Squadron 10

Mahbod Khadem, Ministry of Intelligence and National Security of the Islamic Republic of Iran

Captain Tousi, Admiral Al Jujair Chief of Staff

Captain Husseini Firouz, Base Security

Iranian *Qaaem* Diesel Submarine Q-100

Commander Ardeshir Naceri, Commanding Officer

Lieutenant Commander Yousefi, Executive Officer

Lieutenant Farrokh Habibi, Officer of the Deck

Sonar Technician Submarines, Giv Parsi

Iranian *Qaaem* Diesel Submarine Q-104

Commander MortezA Mokri, Commanding Officer

Lieutenant Commander Nouri Azizi, Executive Officer

Sonar Technician Submarines 2nd Class, Rashid Namazi

W/T Seed

Captain Dalir Sassani, Ship's Master

Acronyms

Advanced Capability Torpedo ADCAP

Advanced SEAL Delivery Vehicle ASDV

Air-independent Propulsion AIP

Airborne Surveillance and Control Operator ASCO

Anti-Submarine Warfare ASW

Atlantic Undersea Test and Evaluation Center AUTEC

Auxiliary Machinery Room AMR

Anti-Submarine Rocket Vertical Launch ASROC

Bachelor Officers Quarters BOQ

Basic Underwater Demolition BUD

Boatswain Mate BM

Cathode-Ray Tube CRT

Casualty Report CASREP

Central Intelligence Agency CIA

Combat Air Patrol CAP

Combat Information Center CIC

Combat Direction Center CDC

Chief Fire Control Technician FTC

Chief of the Boat COB

Chief-of-the-Watch COW

Chief Sonar Technician Sonar STSCCable News Network CNN

Combat Control System CCS

Commanding Officer CO

Commander Submarine Atlantic COMSUBLANT

Commander Submarine Pacific COMSUBPAC

Commander Submarine Squadron COMSUBRON

Commander, U S Naval Forces Central Command NAVCENT

Communication COMMS

Control CON

Close-in Weapon System CIWS

Closest Point of Approach CPA

Destroyer Guided Missile DDG

Dead Reckoning Table DRT

Defense Advanced Research Project Agency DARPA

Department of Defense DOD

Directional Command Activated Sonobuoy DICAS

Directional Frequency Analysis and Recording DIFAR

Duty Officer of the Watch DOOW

Electronic Countermeasures ECM

Electronic Intelligence ELINT

Electronic Support Measures ESM

Engineroom Upper-Level ERUL

Engineroom Lower-Level ERLL

Executive Officer XO

Engineer ENG

Estimate Time of Arrival ETA

Navigation Electronics Technician Senior ETVSC

Fire Control Technician Senior Chief FTCS

Fitness Reports FITREPS

Flat Line Towed Array FLTA

Forward-Looking Infrared FLIR

General Quarters (Surface) GQ

Hospital Corpsmen HMI

Identification Card ID

Identification Friend or Foe IFF

Israel Defense Force IDF

Information Technician IT

Integrated ASW Combat System AN/BSY-1

Islamic Revolutionary Guards Corps Navy IRGCN

Light Detection and Ranging LIDAR

Light Emitting Diode LED

Lieutenant LT

Lieutenant Commander LCDR

Light Airborne Multi-Purpose System LAMPS

General Announcing System (Navy) 1MC

Machinery Space Upper-Level AMSUL

Machinery Space Lower-Level AMSLL

Magnetic Anomaly Detector MAD

Chief Machinist's Mate Weapons CMMW

Manual Adaptive TMA Evaluation MATE

Massachusetts Institute of Technology MIT

Master of Science MS

Master Chief MC

Master Chief Machinist Mate MMCM

North Atlantic Treaty Organization NATO

Navigator NAV

Navigation by Satellite NAVSAT

Naval Undersea Warfare Center NUWC

Towed Torpedo Decoy NIXIE

Nuclear-powered Aircraft Carrier CVN

Officer Candidate School OCS

Officer of the Deck OOD

Operations OP

Operations Order OPORDER

Operations Specialist Master Chief OSCM

Periscope Depth PD

Perspective Commanding Officers PCO

Doctor of Philosophy PhD

Print Screen PrtScn

Primary Tactical Circuit PRITAC

Ranging Exercise RANGEX

Rigid Inflatable Boat RHIB

Sea Air Land SEAL

Secretary Navy SECNAV

Self-Contained Breathing Apparatus SCBA

Self-Contained Underwater Breathing Apparatus. SCUBA

Ship Service Motor Generators SSMG

Signal-to-Noise Ratio SNR

Secret Internet SIPERNET

Sink Exercise SINKEX

Sonar Technician Specialist Senior Chief STSCS

Speed of Advance SOA

Submarine Expendable Bathythermograph SSBT

Submarine Note SUBNOTE

Submarine Atlantic SUBLANT

Submarine Pacific SUBPAC

Submarine Radio Direction Finding AN/BRD-7

Submarine Squadron SUBRON

Subscriber Identity Module SIM

Synchronous Dynamic Random-Access Memory SDRAM

Target Motion Analysis TMA

Thin Line Towed Array TLTA

Torpedoman TM

Training Readiness Exam TRE

Ultra-High Frequency UHF

Ultra Large Crude Tanker UCLL

United Nations UN

United States U.S.

United States Marine Corps USMC

Unmanned Underwater Vehicle UUV

Weapons of Mass Destruction WMD

Glossary

1MC Main ship-wide announcing circuit on U.S. submarines.

ADCAP Advanced Capability. The newest version of the Mark 48 torpedo onboard U.S. submarines.

AN/WLR-12 Acoustic Intercept Receiver found on U.S. Navy submarines.

Angles and dangles A series of maneuvers that a submarine crew exercises to prove their readiness for sea.

ASDV Advanced SEAL delivery vehicle. Built to address the need for stealthy long-range insertion of special operations forces on covert or clandestine missions.

VLS ASROC Vertical Launch Anti-Submarine rocket carries a Mark 54 homing torpedo.

ASW Antisubmarine Warfare.

AUTEC Atlantic Undersea Test and Evaluation Center, Andros Island. An acoustic test range located off Andros Island in the Bahamas.

Bridge Small observation area on top of the fairwater. The OOD stands his watch there when the submarine is on the surface.

Cavitation The formation and collapse of tiny vapor bubbles on the trailing surface of a propeller.

CENTCOM U.S. CENTral COMmand.

CIWS Close-in Weapons System. Fast reaction, a rapid-fire 20-millimeter gun system capable of firing 3,000 or 4,500 rounds per minute.

CO Commanding Officer. The title is given to an officer in command of a ship. Often called 'Captain.' or 'Skipper.'

COB Chief of the Boat. A senior enlisted man in the crews of the submarines, usually a senior, our master chief petty officer. Interfaces with the XO on issues that affect the enlisted personnel.

Control room. All primary submarine functions are controlled from this location.

CPA Closest Point of Approach. An estimated **point** in which the distance between two objects, of which at least one is in motion, will reach its minimum value.

DRT Dead Reckoning Table. In navigation, dead reckoning is calculating one's current position by using a previously determined position or fix and advancing that position based on known or estimated speeds over elapsed time and course.

EAB Emergency Air Breathing System. A low-pressure air system, crew members can plug into and obtain breathable air during emergencies, such as a fire, when the ship's atmosphere has toxic gases.

Emergency Blow High-pressure air is forced into the submarines' main ballast tanks. An emergency blow creates positive buoyancy.

EOOW Engineering Officer of the Watch. Watch officer monitoring and manipulating the submarine reactor and propulsion system.

Family Grams Short [forty to fifty words] messages that U.S. Navy submarines can receive from family members about once a month while on patrol.

FLIR Forward-Looking Infrared. Also known as thermal imaging.

ESM Electronic Support Measures. A passive receiver system designed to detect radar emissions from aircraft and surface ships.

Gertrude (AN/WQC-2) Old WW II phrase used to describe any equipment whose function is underwater communications.

GPS Global Positioning System. A constellation of Navstar satellites that can vary accuracy verifies the submarine's location.

Harpoon [UGM – 84] U.S. Navy anti-ship missile, fired from an SSN's torpedo tube.

K-901 SS latest Russian diesel-electric submarine. K-901 is a medium-range coastal defense submarine that is being offered on the export market. Using state-of-the-art Russian sensors and torpedoes, the K-901-class compares favorably against older Western designs. Russia has 20 K-901s in its naval order of battle, and approximately 14 have been sold to various countries.

INS Tannin. First Dolphin Batch II class German-made SSK sold to the Israeli navy.

IRGCON Islamic Revolutionary Guards Corps Navy.

LOFAR Low-frequency analyzing and recording. A term used to describe the process by which narrowband 'totals' are displayed on a modern sonar system.

MAD - Magnetic Anomaly Detector is streamed from a wire behind the fuselage. It is used to identify disruptions in the earth's magnetic field caused when a large body of metal passes under the sensor.

Maneuvering The reactor and propulsion control area are located in the engine room. The EOOW stands his watch here.

MK V1 PB1 Patrol Boat At 85 feet in length, the MKVI-PB1 was one of two of the Navy's brand-new Mark VI class patrol boats. Commanded by a senior enlisted and a hand-selected crew, these new littoral patrol crafts were supreme in their element. Designed for inshore shallow water patrols and operations with only a 4-foot draft, it could reach speeds of 45 knots from the 5,200-horsepower diesel and pump-jet propulsion. They were also heavily armed, with four operated 50 caliber machine guns, and 25 mm remote-controlled Bushmaster chain guns, their star offensive weapons.

NIXIE Towed Array Decoy. **Towed** torpedo decoys used on US and allied warships.

NUWC Naval Undersea Warfare Center. The Naval Undersea Warfare Center (**NUWC**) is the United States Navy's full-spectrum research, development, test, and evaluation, engineering, and fleet support center.

SCBA Self-containing Breathing Apparatus. A portable system that chemically generates oxygen for between 2 to 4 hours. Used by damage control teams to fight fires.

OOD Officer of the Deck. U.S. Navy officer in charge of directing a ship's movement and ensuring that essential actions are conducted. The primary responsibility is to keep the ship out of dangerous situations and to keep the captain informed.

OPNAV Office of the Chief of NAVal OPerations.

ORSE Operational Reactor Safeguards Examination.

Otto Fuel The monopropellant (oxidizer and fuel combined) used in Mark 48 and Spearfish torpedoes.

Oxygen Generator & Carbon Dioxide Scrubbers https://cosmosmagazine.co m/technology/oxygen-generators-and-carbon-dioxide-scrubbers-explain ed

Radar RAdio Detection and Ranging.

S6G is the designation of the pressurized water reactor installed in 688 – class SSN.

SCRAM is an acronym for an unplanned reactor shutdown, derived from "Safety Control Reactor Axe Man," the name given to the man at the University of Chicago, where the first nuclear core was tested, who was responsible for cutting the rope holding the control rods should something go wrong. The method of inserting control rods has changed considerably, but the term has been retained with a rapid insertion of control rods the reactor will be made subcritical and will no longer support a sustained nuclear fission reaction.

SEAL SEa–Air–Land. U.S. Navy special forces/commando units.

Signal ejector A small (usually three-inch) torpedo tube-like system for launching flares, noisemakers, and torpedo decoys.

SINS Ships Internal Navigation System. A set of gyroscopes that monitor and project a submarine's position once determined from a periscope satellite fix.

Snapshot Term used to describe the procedure for launching a torpedo in an emergency. In a snapshot, the submarine crew doesn't have time to conduct TMA but simply shoots a torpedo down the bearing of an incoming weapon or close contact. The rapid reaction is the basis for the snapshot mode.

SNR Signal−to−Noise Ratio. A measure used in science and engineering that compares the level of the desired signal to the level of background noise.

SOSUS SOund SUrveillance System. A series of fixed passive sonar raised used by NATO to provide early warning of deployments into the open ocean of former Soviet submarines.

SSXBT Submarine Expendable Bathythermograph. A small torpedo-shaped device that holds a temperature sensor and a transducer to detect changes in water temperature versus depth.

SUBGRU SUBmarine GRoUP

SUBRON U.S. SUBmarine SquadRON

TB − 23 First U.S. Navy "thin line" array found on SSNs and is equipped with AN/BSY − 1 and AN/BQQ − 5E. This array is about four times longer than the TB−16 series and is stored entirely on a reel located in the aft ballast tank area.

TMA Target Motion Analysis. The process by which computers or man determines a target course, speed, and range so that the torpedo or missile can be fired accurately.

UHF Ultra-High Frequency. Designation for radio frequencies in the range between 300 megahertz (MHz) and 3 gigahertz (GHz).

Waterfall Display phrase used to describe the appearance that a modern passive sonar display makes while showing bearing versus time information. A contact will look like a bright line on a CRT against a speckled background of other noise sources.

XO Executive Officer. U.S. Navy term for the second in command of a ship.

Note: Several Glossary definitions were taken from Tom Clancy's Military Reference Submarine: A guided tour inside a nuclear warship.

www.ingramcontent.com/pod-product-compliance
Lightning Source LLC
Chambersburg PA
CBHW071602180626
46819CB00002B/104